CW00796848

Rousseau's Ghost

Rousseau's Ghost

A Novel

Terence Ball

State University of New York Press

Published by
State University of New York Press, Albany

Printed in the United States of America

For information, address the State University of New York Press, State University Plaza, Albany, N.Y. 12246

Production by Diane Ganeles
Marketing by Dana Yanulavich

Library of Congress Cataloging-in-Publication Data

Ball, Terence.
Rousseau's ghost : a novel / Terence Ball.
p. cm.
ISBN 0-7914-3933-X (alk. paper).
PS3552.A45544R68 1999
813′.54—dc21

97-47561
CIP

10 9 8 7 6 5 4 3 2 1

To the memory of
David Ball
1946–1996
brother, friend, critic

9:1.9′ 12:9.18′ 12:5.18′ 5.13.6.1.13.18′
1.20.21′ 5:13.6.1.13.18′ 19.17.14.20.20.5.18

—Jean-Jacques Rousseau's encoded
confession of his darkest secret
(diary entry dated 20 April 1751:
Correspondance complète, vol. II, p. 137)

◄ 1 ►

19 Rue Clauzel
Paris

Urgent you meet me here—stop—Must talk —stop—Need advice—stop—Trust only you—stop

Ted

How like Ted, I thought. In the age of e-mail and faxes and telephones, he sends a telegram. Yet something seemed very wrong, completely out of character. Professor Theodore John Milton Porter, the Ezra Stiles Drummond Professor of Political Theory at Princeton, was ordinarily unflappable. But now he was flapped. He sounded scared, suspicious, desperate.

I had to go. Ted needed me more than my partners at the New York offices of Anderson Davis Stein and O'Brien or the clients who sought my advice about the legal intricacies of intellectual property rights in the information age. Could that be the kind of advice Ted wanted? Surely not. Unlike my clients, who seek copyright protection for everything, Ted was a scholar who happily shared his ideas with anyone who would listen to his lectures or read his books and articles—none of which was written with anything as advanced as a ballpoint pen, much less a computer. He wrote everything in an elegant longhand, with a fountain pen—an antique Waterman inherited from his grandfather.

"Works fine," he'd say. "Small. Lightweight. Take it anywhere. And quiet. None of the infernal tap-tap-tapping that those lap dogs make."

"Lap-tops," I corrected. "Lap-top computers."

"Whatever," he'd say, breaking out his impish grin and his best single-malt Scotch. I didn't share Ted's almost visceral aversion to modern technology generally, and his loathing of computers in particular; but about single-malts we agreed wholeheartedly. Served at room temperature and with a splash of spring water, each small sip would open up taste buds you didn't even know you had. Highland malts, Lowland malts, Islay malts—each region produced its own inimitable varieties, each of which had utterly unique characteristics. We waxed ecstatic about the smoky peaty pungency of Laphroaig, the sharp tang and subtle aftertaste of Glenfiddich, the . . .

"You're on the Concorde to Paris. 1:00 p.m. from JFK. Better hurry, Jack." My Scottish reveries were interrupted by Grace, my secretary, legal assistant, and sometime lover. A Chinese-American Catholic in an unhappy marriage, Grace Wu would not consider divorce, and I had long ago given up trying to talk her into it. Strong-willed and devout, she had her way. I had to take her on her terms, or not at all. I took her. And she took me, organizing my office and my life. That was our "arrangement," as she called it, and it worked well enough. All my friends knew about it, though none but Ted thought it a good idea.

"Whatever is, is," he would say. "Whatever works, works. Your life wouldn't work for me, but it doesn't have to. It only has to work for you."

Next to Grace, I loved Ted best. He was my oldest and closest friend. We had first met as Rhodes Scholars at Oxford in 1968. Bright, articulate, assured, Ted was everything I was not. He talked comfortably with the dons, almost as an equal, and—what I envied even more—women found him attractive and amusing. Although my junior by nearly a year, Ted seemed somehow older and more mature than most of our crowd. He appeared to have stepped out of an earlier age. The language of our day seemed inadequate to describe him, and only old words would do. Noble. Honorable. Valiant. Gallant. Dashing. He wore Harris tweeds and riding boots, sometimes carried a cane, occasionally drank to excess but never showed it, and spoke flawless French. "I can converse in three languages and curse in seventeen," he said. And he could.

"Say 'shit' in Swahili," a skeptic once challenged.

"Kinyesi," he said.

As friends we were a distinctly odd pair. Physically, for starters. Ted was just under six feet, I nearly half a foot taller. His frame was compact and muscular, mine skinny and rangy. His hair was light brown and curly, mine jet black and straight. Ted's game was tennis, mine basketball. He was graceful on the tennis court and off, and a good dancer. I was clumsy everywhere except on the basketball court, where my height was an advantage instead of a hindrance, and an execrable dancer. Ted's athletic abilities were well-nigh legendary. He was, among other things, an avid rock-climber and skillful sailor and sea-kayaker. Although I'm afraid of heights and of water that's more than waist-deep, Ted tried, with mixed success, to teach me to climb and kayak, and, with no success at all, to sail and play tennis. And I tried, with markedly more success, to impart to him some of my passion for college basketball and classic cars.

Our backgrounds were even more different. Ted came from an old New England family that had produced a long line of distinguished clergymen, scholars, artists, and writers. My family tree, which was Welsh, Scots, German, and Cherokee, was otherwise largely untraceable more than two or three generations back. It included, on my mother's side, the Wagners, stolid farmers from Germany, and, on my father's, my Cherokee grandmother Della Bird and her husband, a Welsh-born oil wildcatter named Davies (the e was later dropped) who made a fortune, went bankrupt, killed his crooked partner, and died in prison before I was born. Ted went to Andover and Dartmouth, I to Durant High School and Oklahoma State.

My Oklahoma upbringing had not prepared me for anyone like Ted. That he and I should have become fast friends has always amazed and pleased me. He laughed at my jokes but never at my accent, and he always brought out the best in me. Ted taught me not to be afraid. But now, somehow, for some reason, he was afraid. Of what? And he was counting on me. For what?

I felt a nudge.

"Mr. Davis?," my driver asked. "We're here. JFK. Like you wanted. I'll get your bags for the VIP check-in."

An hour later I was on my way to Paris on Air France 001. It was my first time on the Concorde, that high-tech cross between bird and arrow. The cabin was smaller and narrower than I'd expected. The entire plane was first-class, in both senses of the term. Five French flight attendants for thirty-odd passengers, I noticed, as we taxied bumpily down the runway before turning sharply right. Beginning with a whine that turned into a full-throated roar, the four powerful Rolls-Royce engines revved ever higher. Then, with a loud bang and whoosh that made me jump, the afterburners were ignited, making the entire plane shake and shudder with anticipation. Suddenly, without warning, brakes off and afterburners on, the Concorde shot down the runway like an arrow from a hickory bow. My back pressed hard into the soft leather seat, my stomach felt somewhere behind me, trying—unsuccessfully—to catch up. Once off the ground we seemed to go straight up, as if seeking the shortest route to the stratosphere. Which, I suppose, we were. Then, suddenly, sickeningly, silence. Or relative silence. The afterburners had cut out. I looked in terror across the aisle at an elderly man calmly reading *Paris Match*. He looked back, over the top of his reading glasses.

"De rien," he said reassuringly. "C'est normale."

"Bien sûr," I said in my bad French, and feeling both foolish and relieved. "Merci, monsieur." Putting my right hand into my pants pocket I felt around for my lucky arrowhead. I knew it wasn't there, but the reaction was instinctive. Just as an amputee can still feel sensations in his long-missing limb, so could I still feel the presence and the power of my talisman. It had been part of the medicine pouch that my Grandma Della had made for my tenth birthday. The small buckskin bag with a leather-thong drawstring contained an acorn, a tiny pine cone, a kernel of corn, the tail feather of a hawk, the tooth of a fox, and a small stash of tobacco. Each, Grandma Della told me, had a meaning. And because repetition and retelling was her forte, she told me again and again the meaning of my medicine pouch's contents, until I knew them by heart. The acorn and pine cone came from the forest and stood for wild nature; they also showed that big things come from small beginnings. The corn stood for the fertility of the earth and its human cultivation; like the acorn and pine cone, it was a seed that could reproduce itself, and so represents continuity from one season and generation to the next. The hawk's tail feather stood for the swift flight of birds and the fox's tooth for canine cleverness and stealth. The hawk and the fox were predators; they, like their prey, had their rightful place in the order of nature. The tobacco stood for fraternity within the tribe and the prospect of peace between enemies. To these natural objects was added something else—something taken from nature and utterly transformed by man: a shiny black obsidian arrowhead with two sharply sculpted edges and an even sharper point. This rough-edged isosceles triangle was a Stone Age work of art, a high-tech weapon for its time, with a purpose both deadly and practical—the killing of game or of men, it was equally adept at both. The arrowhead represented human power and our responsibility to use it wisely. This mute shiny stone, slowly and painstakingly chipped and shaped and sharpened by some long-dead ancestor, exemplified the dual character of human creations; human technology is two-edged. Good and bad together. Yin and Yang. The forces of destruction and construction combined. As a boy I would look into its cracked crystalline planes and see my face reflected back to me in its crisscrossing surfaces. A face no longer young or innocent, but old and dark and distorted. A visage so frightening that I couldn't bear to look at it for more than a second or two before slipping the arrowhead back into the blackness of the buckskin bag.

My medicine pouch was the stuff of endless jibes and jokes from the girls who wore charm bracelets and the boys who carried lucky rabbits' feet on key chains. They thought nothing of crossing their fingers or (for the few Catholics) making the sign of the cross before exams and other ordeals. Fearing their taunts, I soon learned to conceal my medicine under my clothes and close to my body, where I could feel it but no one could see it. It was only much later that I finally came to understand that my medicine pouch was utterly unlike lucky charms and rabbits' feet. "Medicine" isn't about luck at all; it's about health—mental, physical, spiritual. The contents of my medicine pouch were really only *reminders*—reminders of my connection to nature, to animals and ecosystems, to my ancestors and descendants. Health is about remembering your connectedness to the whole of creation. Which now strikes me, not as magic or superstition but as simple common sense.

I long ago lost the leather pouch and all its contents—except for the arrowhead, which I had often misplaced but somehow never lost. And when I did misplace it, it seemed to find me, rather than the other way around. I carried it with me until nine years ago. Then, as Ted's marriage went from bad to worse, I thought he needed good medicine more than I did. So on his fortieth birthday I gave him the arrowhead. He seemed strangely moved. I hoped its power, or whatever it had, was helping him now. Especially now.

My ancestral reveries were interrupted by the chief stewardess who announced over the intercom that *les instruments électroniques* could now be used. I opened my IBM ThinkPad and stared at the screen as I called up files that needed my attention. I tried to be attentive. But, truth to tell, I was bored. Bored by it all. The petulant, the petty, the self-important gall and greed of my clients made me wonder why I worked for these people. Why I represented them, or rather, their "interests." The answer was of course obvious: I was as greedy as they. We were all moved by one thing—money, or the lure thereof. I was well-paid—perhaps obscenely so—for seeing that their every utterance or idea received legal recognition as a saleable commodity called "information" to which they owned the copyright. My old friend Ted had chided me, persistently and none too gently, about the larger and longer-term implications of my work. "The neologism 'intellectual property'," he said, "is an obscene oxymoron." My clients, he added, sought nothing less than to impede ideas and the free flow of communication. With restrictions on communication come limitations on community, with adverse consequences for democracy—and for scholarship. Against his views I advanced the usual counter-arguments: that we were entering a new age—an "information age"—with new problems and new prospects; that without the possibility of legally "owning" information there would be little incentive for "developing" it; and so on. I had grown weary of the debate, doubtless because I no longer believed my own arguments. Or rather, arguments I had borrowed from *The Wall Street Journal* and the trade magazines to which I subscribed in hopes of keeping up with my own narrowly circumscribed but fast-changing field and with the "information explosion" that was now deafening us all.

Unable—or perhaps unwilling—to concentrate, I looked around the long narrow tube of a cabin. The digital readout panel at the front showed the Concorde's vital statistics. Altitude 12,200 meters and climbing. Airspeed Mach 1.6 and increasing. External temperature -42 degrees Celsius and dropping. I turned again to my lap-top, and thought I'd amuse myself by calling up the calculator function. I looked again at the readout panel at the front of the cabin. We were beginning to level off. Our airspeed was now approaching Mach 2—twice the speed of sound. Calling up the PC's weights and measures menu, I found that the speed of sound is 660 miles per hour. Tapping the number keys I did a quick calculation: 2 × 660 = 1,320 m.p.h.—way more than twice the speed of a 747. I tapped again. Altitude 35,000 meters × 1.6 = 56,000 feet, divided by 5,280 = 10.6 miles above the Atlantic—half again as high as a 747. Outside temperature -58 Celsius. I looked up the formula for converting degrees Celsius into Fahrenheit, and calculated. 1.6 × −58 + 32 equals 125 degrees below zero, Farenheit. Egad, I thought, that can't be right, can it? Thin air colder than dry ice?

Finding these facts more frightening than amusing, I quickly logged out, closed the cover of my lap-top, and tried to sleep. Without much success. The Concorde is stripped for speed, and the noisiest commercial airplane I've ever flown in. But somehow I managed to doze by fits and starts. Old memories, old terrors, the faces of former lovers crept across a darkened screen. Ted appeared with a quizzical look on his face, and vanished as abruptly as he had come. Grace looked longingly and lovingly at me, and then disappeared. Then I was a boy, playing on the old railroad boxcar on my grandparents' farm in southeastern Oklahoma. It sat alone in the middle of a field, used to store feed for the cattle and an old horse named Dan and a mule called Queen. I was by turns riding Dan, then Queen, and then sitting atop the boxcar looking toward the red clay hills to the west where the sunset gathered.

I was rudely awakened by the painful popping in my ears and a loud thump under my seat. The landing gear was down. I closed my mouth, pinched my nose, and blew gently but persistently. My ears popped again, and then again. I tightened my seat belt and looked outside. I could see only speeding streeks of rain. No sign of Paris. No lights, no Eiffel Tower. Only blackness. This was going to be an all-instrument landing at one of Europe's busiest airports. I pulled my seat belt even tighter and felt in my pocket for the missing arrowhead.

There was a sharp bump, followed by a blast, as the large Rolls-Royce engines reversed to slow the Concorde's fast forward motion. Within seconds this strange stork-like plane was taxiing like a conventional aircraft.

"Messieurs et mesdames," a woman's voice said. "Nous arrivons à Paris Charles De Gaulle. L'heure locale est vingt et une heures et demie."

My French was always bad, but never more so than in France. The translation followed, telling me what I already knew. Local time 2130 hours. I reset my watch to 9:30. Brisk and purposeful businessmen and women bustled about the cabin, preparing for late dinner meetings with their French counterparts. I tried to look brisk and purposeful, but to no good effect. I wasn't sure what my purpose was, or why I was in Paris. I felt cold and apprehensive.

Lashing rain rendered the City of Lights a dim yellow blur as my taxi approached Paris from the northeast. As we drew closer I could just see, for the second or so that the wiper blades slapped water away from the windshield, the top of the illuminated Eiffel Tower, with bright red aviation beacons flashing at its apex. When we arrived at Ted's apartment block on the Rue Clauzel, I haggled halfheartedly with the driver about his exorbitant fare, and then ran through the rain to number 19 and rang the bell to summon the concierge.

I waited. And waited. The wind blew and the rain soaked my trouser legs and shoes. My socks felt damp. I rang the bell again. Then, through an intercom speaker I heard a hoarse raspy voice. It seemed to come from a considerable distance, as though from inside a cavern.

"D'accord, d'accord. Un moment." The genderless voice muttered something else that sounded like a curse covered by a cough caused by countless cigarettes. A long lifetime of nicotine and tar and God knows what else. A blurred face appeared behind the rain-streaked glass door, which then opened.

"Oui?," asked a squat wrinkled woman of advanced years but of indeterminate age. Clad in a ratty old pink bathrobe and black slippers, the small woman loomed in the doorway, blocking any advance into her building. The remains of a cigarette dangled from fat chapped lips. "Oui?," she said again. For someone so small—barely five feet, I guessed—she had the voice of a much larger woman. But what she lacked in height she more than made up for in girth.

"Professor Porter?," I asked in my most polite tone to cover the irritation I was beginning to feel.

The small fat woman stared up at me. Maybe she didn't understand.

"Le professeur Port-air," I said in my execrable French. "Où est-il? Il est mon ami."

Her appearance changed abruptly. She looked less hostile, more human.

"Ah, oui. Le professeur Porter," she said, almost apologetically, stepping aside and motioning me toward the stairway. "Au troisième étage, tout en haut de l'escalier, numéro quarante-deux," she said, shaking her head.

"Merci, madame," I said as I started to climb the stairs to the third floor.

"Je regrette, monsieur, je regrette," she called up after me.

Sorry? About what?, I wondered. Sorry that she doesn't speak English—or that my French is so awful? Maybe she's apologizing because she didn't know I was Ted's friend. Yes, that's probably it. Ted must have charmed this irritable old concierge, just as he's charmed every woman he's ever met, and now she's eating out of his hand.

I was slightly out of breath as I reached the third floor landing and knocked on the door of number 42.

The door opened.

"Ted," I almost said. But the querulous look of the *Inspecteur de police* met my gaze, and silenced me.

"Ah, monsieur, vous connaissez le professeur Porter?" I stared blankly at the tall man in the doorway. He stared back.

"I don't speak French," I said. "Do you speak English?" He looked puzzled. "Je ne parle pas français," I repeated. "Parlez-vous anglais?"

He looked annoyed, as though offended both by my ignorance and my abominable accent. "A little, yes," he said in heavily accented English. "You know the Professor Porter, no?"

"Yes."

"It is so sad."

"What's sad? What's happened to Ted? Where is he?"

He seemed surprised. "Sorry, monsieur. I thought perhaps you know."

"Know what? What the hell is happening here?"

He paused, and then spoke quickly, as though to get it over with. "The Professor Porter is dead, monsieur. I am sorry."

I felt my knees buckle, and braced myself against the doorpost. I felt detached from my body and from my voice as I, or someone speaking for me, asked where Ted was and how he had died.

The inspector told me that Ted had died earlier that evening, just after eight o'clock. His body had been discovered by the concierge after neighbors in an adjoining apartment reported hearing loud thumping noises on the wall. They thought their fastidious American neighbor was expressing irritation because their television was too loud.

They thumped back, and then called the concierge to complain. After rapping repeatedly on Ted's door, the old woman used her passkey and discovered Ted's body slumped over the radiator, and phoned the police. They were just concluding their investigation as I arrived.

"Where's Ted?," I asked warily, thinking his body might still be in the apartment.

"We take him to the morgue, monsieur."

On the Rue Morgue, I half imagined from old B movies. "And there'll be an autopsy? So we'll know if it was a heart attack, or whatever?"

"No need, monsieur," said the inspector. "We already know what kill him. It was accident. He die quick. The *Magistrat*—the Investigating Judge—who just leave, he say that the cause of death on the *certificat de mort* will be '*l'électrocution accidentelle*'."

"Electrocution? How? From what?"

"Your friend, he touch the radiator while he try to—how do you say?—recharge the computer. The 'power pack' transformer he plug in, but it have the circuit that is short."

"A short circuit?"

"Ah, yes, that is how you call it. A short circuit in his portable computer. It kill him. I am so sorry."

◀ 2 ▶

The next forty-eight hours were the saddest and most frustrating in all my forty-nine years. The police didn't listen, or didn't care to, when I insisted—loudly, repeatedly, and no doubt annoyingly—that Ted had never owned and would never use a computer. Never. But they had already closed the case and weren't about to reopen it for a frantic and grieving American.

I phoned Grace to break the news. She loved Ted as a friend, mine and hers, and she took it hard. Very hard. For the first time in years, I heard her cry.

Would she break the news to Ted's daughter?, I asked warily. Jessica was my goddaughter, and ideally I ought to do it. But I was far away and feeling overwhelmed. And Grace was there, and better at these things.

"Woman to woman?," I pleaded. Grace agreed, and I felt greatly relieved.

That done, Grace pressed for details. When I told her about the "cause" of Ted's death, the tears dried and her voice changed.

"Impossible," Grace said incredulously. "Utterly impossible. Ted would never even touch a computer . . . "

"I know that," I interrupted. "You know that. I tried telling the police. But they wouldn't listen. They believe that the computer is Ted's. They've already ruled his death an accident. I don't know what else . . . "

"Get that machine," Grace said in the low clipped voice that she used when she was hell-bent and determined. "Pack it up. Carefully. Not your usual slap-dash job, Jack. Send it to me, Fed Ex, right away. We'll have it analyzed."

"For what? Fingerprints? But everybody—cops, and everybody else—they've had their hands all over it."

"No, Jack. Not fingerprints. I want that lap-top taken apart. I want them to pick its brains, to examine the memory, the hardware, the software, the contents of the hard drive, the power pack. Everything. And *now*, Jack. No delays. Promise me."

Grace had never, in our eight years together, spoken to me like that. She wasn't asking. She was demanding. Exacting a promise.

I promised.

The French police bureaucracy was like none I had ever encountered. The NYPD looked like helpful pussycats, compared to their Parisian counterparts. I remembered Ted saying that there were no bureaucrats like French bureaucrats, and that even the old Soviet bureaucracy looked benign and helpful by comparison. After protracted arguments and negotiations, including a not-so-veiled threat to take up the matter with the American Embassy, a listless deputy inspector named Bouchard signed a release form. I took it to the basement property room of the Préfecture de Police on the Rue Pigalle. A tiny wizened clerk in a shiny gray suit made me sign four different forms, in triplicate, before releasing the lap-top computer to me. He also handed me a plastic zip-lock bag containing the contents of Ted's pockets, and motioned to me to open it so that (I think he said) I could sign another form saying that everything was there and nothing was missing. I unzipped the bag and dumped the contents onto the counter.

The first thing that tumbled out was a familiar object from long ago—the shiny black arrowhead that Grandma Della had given me for my tenth birthday, and that I had given to Ted on his fortieth. Apparently it hadn't worked for Ted as it had for me. I slipped the arrowhead into my pocket as I examined the other items. Two sets of keys I recognized immediately, because I had matching sets: the front-door key to his house in Princeton and the master key to the flat we'd bought in north Oxford several years ago as a rental property. The third set, which was newly familiar, were the keys to his Paris apartment. There was a black pocket comb, a monogrammed white handkerchief—Ted never used Kleenex—an old Hamilton wristwatch with a scuffed brown leather band, a bright red Swiss Army knife, a small silver cigar cutter, a military-green U.S. passport, a lemon yellow matchbook from the Parisian restaurant Taillevent, two pink ticket stubs from the Paris Opera, and a well-worn black leather wallet. I didn't want to open Ted's wallet, but the little leprechaun of a clerk insisted. Okay, I thought, here goes. New Jersey driver's license, check. Princeton faculty I.D. card, check. American Express and Visa cards, check. Currency and change totaling just under 400 francs, check. A gold wedding ring. Check? What's that doing here?, I wondered. It was with some reluctance that I unsnapped and opened the photo compartment. There were back-to-back color pictures of Jessica—one as a girl of five or six, smiling a gap-toothed smile and hugging Simon, their large and long-departed black Lab; the other was a much more recent photo of Jessica clad in her tomboy tee shirt and jeans, sitting atop a weathered wood-rail fence and looking pleased with life. The next picture surprised me. Surprised me, that is, because it was there at all. It was an old black and white photograph of Anna and Ted, taken at their wedding. His right arm was encircled with hers, both holding champagne glasses, and each smiling—no, beaming—broadly at the other. They looked so young and so happy and hopeful that I could hardly bear to look. But there it was, in black and white. They had been happy, once. Once upon a time, as the fairy tales say.

A wave of sadness swept over me as I returned the wallet and other items to the plastic bag, thanked the clerk, and started to leave.

"Le certificat, Monsieur," the clerk admonished with a scolding wag of his bony index finger as he pushed the triplicate form toward me.

I pretended to read the long closely printed form before signing it without quite knowing what I was signing, and then carried my packages up the spiral steel staircase from the basement property room to the second-floor offices of the *Bureau d'enquête criminelle*. The large noisy room was divided by moveable partitions that looked like they hadn't been moved in years. It smelled disagreeably of scorched coffee, stale cigarette smoke, and disinfectant. I looked for, and finally found, the lugubrious, bloodhound-faced deputy inspector. Bouchard listened impassively as I thanked him for his help in getting the computer released to me. But he heard nothing else I had to say. My vocal and ever-hardening suspicion that Ted had probably been murdered fell on deaf, or at least indifferent, ears. I pressed my case again.

"Ted couldn't have been killed by his computer because he didn't own a computer. He *wouldn't* own a computer. He wouldn't even *use* one. It would be completely out of character—don't you see?" The deputy inspector with the sad droopy eyes obviously didn't see—or, if he saw, simply didn't care. I pressed harder. "Not owning, or even using, a computer is—it was—a matter of pride and principle with him."

"But monsieur"—Bouchard addressed me as though I were a slightly backward child—"the computer, it have his name on it. You see," pointing to a cheap stick-on plastic tag that read "T.M.J. Porter."

He didn't understand, or pretended not to, when I pointed out that the initials were scrambled and explained that Ted would never mark anything belonging to him with a plastic tag and that, in any case, I repeated, he would never count a computer among his belongings.

"The computer, everyone use them now," Bouchard said with a world-weary gallic shrug. "Your friend, too. He find it useful, no?"

No, of course, no. But it was no use explaining. An American was found dead in Paris. A convenient explanation lay close at hand. Accidental death by electrocution—and from a faulty Toshiba Notebook lap-top, no less. No Frenchman dead, no French machine at fault, *ergo* no problem. Very convenient. Close the books. Move on to the next case.

The more I objected, the more I raved, the more I felt like a loony in a padded cell. The bloodhound-faced Bouchard and others who dropped by his shabby gray cubicle heard me, saw me, paid a curious kind of attention. But no one listened. *I* was the curiosity.

Voices both sympathetic and condescending whispered within earshot, in almost inaudible French. "l'Américain," they called me, their tone marked by a mixture of pity and irritation. They weren't without sympathy for *le pauvre Américain*. But mostly they wanted me out of there so that they could do other, more important things. Like talking incessantly while drinking cup after cup of impossibly strong coffee.

Finally I took the hint.

The Toshiba lap-top under my arm, I left the Préfecture de Police on the Rue Pigalle and began walking toward the Rue Clauzel. The rain had ceased but the skies were gray and the streets still wet. Passing cars and trucks splashed hapless pedestrians, some of whom carried at their sides opened umbrellas, deploying them much as medieval knights had once used their shields in the *tournoi de combat*. This produced a faintly comic effect as the umbrella shields deflected splashing water onto other, unprotected passersby, who then directed their curses at these modern but horseless and distinctly non-chivalrous *chevaliers*.

Poor Ted, I thought. He had nothing and no one to protect him. No shield, not even an umbrella to deflect the misfortune that had rained down upon him in his final hour. I had arrived too late to be of any assistance, and the police were of no help at all. So, unable to reach the police, I reached into myself. I saw that I must do what they would not or could not do. Some "person or persons unknown," as the old police blotters used to say, had killed Ted. I had to find out who would want him dead, and why.

Motive, means, opportunity: the venerable pulp detective fiction trio suddenly became both real and urgent.

The first and greatest was motive. Find that, and all else follows.—Doesn't it?

Actually, I didn't know. I'm not—I wasn't trained to be—a criminal lawyer, and I don't think like one. Now I had to learn. Fast.

First of all . . . What comes first? My law school training was of no help here. I tried recalling the good and bad—mostly bad—detective stories I'd read for distraction and amusement since my undergraduate days. Gone were the amusement and distraction. This was deadly serious. Think, man. *Think.*

Enemies. Yes, that's it. Did Ted have enemies? Of course he had. Lots. He had rivals in intellectual and amorous combat—scholars he'd bested in academic competition, and lovers he'd displaced and replaced. But none, so far as I knew, would wish him dead. Well, they might wish him dead, but they wouldn't kill or have him killed. Humiliated, yes. Castrated, perhaps. But dead, no.

Clues, I needed clues. An idea. An inkling. Something. Anything. Again, think.

Ted's files seemed a logical place to begin, if only because they were all I had to work with.

Arriving at the apartment building on the Rue Clauzel, I let myself in with Ted's key and then tiptoed past the concierge's door. She had no objection to my staying in Ted's apartment, and even seemed to welcome my presence. But every time I saw her she caught and cornered me, volubly expressing her condolences for my friend's death and rattling on in impossibly fast French about lots of other things I couldn't understand very well, or at all. The little that I could comprehend sounded unabashedly racist—about the *Japonais* who had no respect, thought they owned France, were threatening something-or-other, and so on, *ad infinitum et ad nauseam*. The garrulous old crone was probably an avid supporter of the National Front, led by Jean-Marie Le Pen, the rabidly racist "French Hitler," I thought with a shudder as I ducked undetected up the stairs to number 42.

3

I approached Ted's study reluctantly. To invade anyone's privacy is bad enough. To invade a friend's inner sanctum is worse, and a dead friend's well-nigh unforgivable.

Forgive me, my friend, for what I am about to do, I said to myself. Grasping my coffee cup tightly in one hand and my arrowhead in the other, I entered Ted's *sanctum sanctorum.*

It was a small room, about twelve feet square, with floor-to-ceiling bookshelves on three walls. A polished mahogany writing table abutted the far wall overlooking the street below. Light entered from a leaded-glass skylight above and a window behind the desk. A dusty shaft of late afternoon sunlight fell near the back of the desk, illuminating two framed photographs. One was a color photograph of Ted's daughter Jessica. She wore khaki shorts, a red tee shirt, and yellow rock-climbing harness, from which dangled a shiny silver 8-ring. A coil of brightly colored climbing rope was draped diagonally from her left shoulder to her right hip. Her blond hair looked like a halo against the dark basalt background. She looked healthy, altogether American, and decidedly wholesome.

The other picture was a black and white photograph of a young woman I'd never seen before. Hauntingly beautiful, dark-haired, Mediterranean, sultry like the young Sophia Loren, wearing a low-cut white dress and holding a cigarette. Greek, I guessed, or maybe Italian. Who, I wondered, was she? I tried to concentrate on other things, but my gaze kept returning to the woman in the black and white photo.

Her presence proved so distracting that I finally turned the photograph around.

At the edge of Ted's desk I saw a series of books, lined up like soldiers: Maurice Cranston's three-volume biography of Rousseau, four thick volumes of the blue-leather and gold embossed Pléiade edition of Rousseau's *Oeuvres Complètes*, a dozen volumes of the *Correspondance Complète de J.-J. Rousseau*, books by Maurizio Viroli, Joan McDonald, James Miller, Judith Shklar, Patrick Riley, Robert Derathé, John Charvet, and Robert Wokler on Rousseau's political philosophy. Most were signed by their authors with respect, affectionate regards, etc. Ted's tortoise-shell reading glasses and his black and gold pen lay next to a bottle of blue-black ink, now nearly empty. How many bottles, I wondered, had it taken to turn out the 627 legal-sized pages of meticulously handwritten manuscript that lay on the left side of the small table? As I touched it I felt Ted's presence in the paper and ink, and the care he put into everything he wrote.

Letters. Ted was the last, the only, person I knew who wrote *letters*. He rarely phoned, never faxed or e-mailed; but he wrote wonderful letters. Long, short, funny, sad, sometimes serious letters. I always thought it a peculiar habit. But I saved them all. Read and even reread them. Some still made me wince, others made me laugh out loud. And now that Ted was gone, I'm glad he wrote them. He left something I could keep. Something of himself, something tangible, and more than a memory that would fade with time.

The manuscript in my hands was, in its way, even more material. Not a private letter but a public document. A going naked in public, risking ridicule and criticism from friends and strangers alike. A wager. A dare. The fruits of Ted's reading, writing, and thinking about Jean-Jacques Rousseau, the eighteenth-century thinker he'd always admired, frequently found perplexing, and sometimes seemed almost to despise. "*Rousseau's Ghost: A Study of the Real Influence of an Imaginary Thinker* [tentative title]," it said on the first page. It was, Ted had told me before he left for France some six months earlier, to be a critical examination of the various misinterpretations and myths that had long surrounded what he called *le Rousseau imaginaire*, "the imaginary Rousseau": Rousseau the fomenter of the French Revolution, Rousseau the Romantic, the Noble Savage, the philosopher of radical individualism, the prophet of totalitarianism, and others. Ted believed that this ghostly figure had long haunted political theory and had wielded more influence than the real Rousseau. He hoped to exorcise the ghost by showing the sources and the consequences of the various interpretations or, as Ted maintained, misinterpretations.

The second page contained only a dedication:

For D.D.

I tried putting a name to these initials. David D_____. Donald D_____. Doris D_____. Dorothy D_____. Nothing worked. Nothing, that is, except Della Davis, my Grandma Della Bird. A flattering thought, though Ted would have no reason to dedicate a book about Rousseau to my late grandmother. I had no idea who D.D. might be.

The third page consisted solely of two short epigraphs. Both, as one might well expect, from Rousseau. And both, unsurprisingly, in French:

> . . . il y a encore plus de lecteurs qui devraient apprendre à lire, que d'auteurs qui devraient apprendre à être conséquents.
>
> Rousseau, *Jugement sur la Polysynodie*

> . . . je ne sais pas l'art d'être clair pour qui ne veut pas être attentif.
>
> Rousseau, *Du Contrat social*, III, 1

I did my best to puzzle them out. The first means something like, "there are still more readers who should learn to read, than there are authors who should learn to be consistent." The second epigraph says that Rousseau doesn't know the art of being clear for those who aren't willing to be attentive.

Yes, that would make sense. Each epigraph captured Ted's point precisely: Rousseau's readers—friendly and hostile alike—had been careless, insufficiently attentive to the subtleties and nuances of (as Ted had written earlier and elsewhere) "this confusingly careful writer, this contrarian master of paradox." His critics were quick to accuse Rousseau of contradicting himself or to condemn him for holding views that he never held. His uncritical admirers were equally quick to accord scripture-like status to his every utterance. Together they had created this most influential of ghosts.

Turning to the fourth page of Ted's manuscript, I began to read, and, thankfully, in a language I could understand. Pages four through six formed the preface, which followed the usual academic formula. Ted thanked Professor M. of the Sorbonne, Professor S. and the late Professor DeJ. at Geneva, Professor Emeritus W. at Berkeley, the late Professor S. at Harvard, Professor M. at Dartmouth, Dean G. and colleagues V., K., and R. at Princeton, and other friends and fellow scholars in France, Britain, the United States, and Japan. He expressed his gratitude for support from the American Council of Learned Societies, the National Endowment for the Humanities, the Society for Eighteenth Century Studies, and the Woodrow Wilson International Center for Scholars at the Smithsonian Institution in Washington, D.C. He thanked libraries and librarians in London, Paris, and Geneva. He expressed his "very great admiration for Professors Masters' and Kelly's excellent English edition and translations of Rousseau's *Collected Writings*" but then added that "all translations are my own, from those two towering monuments of modern scholarship, the unsurpassed Pléiade edition of Rousseau's *Oeuvres Complètes* and the late Ralph Leigh's magnificent fifty-volume edition of the *Correspondance complète de Jean-Jacques Rousseau.*" For the convenience of his readers, he said, "footnotes include reference to the original French, followed by the English translation from the *Collected Writings.*" And then, after the usual academic pleasantries and courtesies, near the bottom of page six, something less formulaic: "I owe a deep and unrepayable debt to Mlle. Danielle Dupin for research and other assistance." This name was new to me. But not the initials: Danielle Dupin must be the "D.D." to whom *Rousseau's Ghost* was dedicated. I didn't even know that Ted had a research assistant. Was she based in Princeton? Or Paris? Or perhaps both? And to what "other assistance" might he have been referring? Did this mysterious Mlle. Dupin bring him his lunch? Or make his bed? Or share it? The preface ended on an even more cryptic and ambiguous note. In the lower right-hand corner Ted barely had room to write:

Paris
May Day 1997

In his interpretations of Rousseau and other political thinkers, Ted had a penchant for paying particular attention to prefaces, footnotes, and other things that were (as he put it) "both outside and inside the text." Okay, I thought, I'll try applying the same approach to his text. The very last words in the preface refer to the date. Last Thursday. Six days ago. May the first. May Day, the international workingman's holiday, celebrated by labor unions in France and around the world. Perhaps, I mused, Ted meant to signal his feelings of solidarity with the working class. That would be consistent with his view that "real" conservatives—among whom he counted himself and Wendell Berry and almost no one else—must be critical of the kind of modern corporate capitalism which he had described in an article in *The Nation* as "among the most destructive and disruptive forces that the world has ever seen. GATT, NAFTA and the other alphabetized free-trade agreements are radical, large-scale, and uncontrolled experiments with people's lives, their communities, and the natural environment." Ted was therefore a strong supporter of labor unions and anything else that might serve as a brake or check on this most productive and destructive of economic engines. He was a disillusioned Democrat who despaired of our Oxford classmate who now occupied the White House. Perhaps his "May Day" sign-off was a barbed inside joke.

I chuckled at Ted's cleverness. But then I felt an almost physical shudder when I remembered that May Day also has another, more ominous meaning: Mayday—the international distress signal. Was Ted signaling, consciously or perhaps unconsciously, that he was in danger? Or was I reading beyond the plain meaning of the words on the page, finding ghostly "meanings" that weren't really there? This "interpretation" business, bad enough in the law, is even worse in political theory. I was glad I had chosen the lesser of two evils.

I rubbed my eyes and took a sip of scalding coffee to bring me back to my senses before turning to page six, where *Rousseau's Ghost* finally got going. The first thing that struck me, as with everything Ted wrote, was his wonderfully lucid prose. The style was the man: direct, elegant without being pretentious, full of well-turned phrases, *bons mots*, witty asides, deft descriptions of people and events, and utterly lacking in the latest—or any—academic jargon.

"Professors are bad writers," Ted once wrote to me, "and French professors are the worst. Well, second-worst after the American professors who imitate them because they can't write anyway and, besides"—here I could almost hear him chortling—"they've got bad cases of Paris Envy. French writers," he went on to say, "once valued and practiced lucidity. Montaigne, Descartes, de Tocqueville, Duhem, Valéry were models of clarity and precision. It all started with Sartre, you see. Old Jean-Paul wrote like a German. *Being and Nothingness* reads like a book badly translated from opaque German into unreadable French. He wrote it during the German occupation. Unfortunately the German occupation of France didn't end in 1945. It continues to this day. Look at Jean Décon. Damn lot of puffing and blowing. He could have been a great philosopher instead of a trend-conscious *savant* pushing the philosophical flavor of the month. What a loss. One of his critics got it about half right when he said that 'M. Décon is forced to write ever more obscurely, in order to conceal the fact that he has absolutely nothing to say'. I mean, why do you think Décon & Co. are always in the U.S. of A.? It's because they're passé in Paris, and his American admirers and hangers-on haven't heard—or don't want to hear—the latest news from the French literary and philosophical front."

Ted was hardly averse to all modern French philosophers. He had great respect for Michel Foucault, "who finally learned to write before he died." He explained that Foucault's early books were prolix and jargon-ridden but that his last ones—the three-volume *History of Sexuality* in particular—were spare, lean, and eminently readable. Virtues all, in Ted's view.

Foucault. Décon. These were names I had heard but authors I had not read. Names from the *New York Review of Books* and other journals I still subscribed to out of habit, but, because of my busy schedule, only rarely read nowadays. But I knew about them through Ted, and Ted knew them all. He had debated with them in person and in print. On one famous occasion he had debated Jean Décon, taking issue with Décon's claim that we live in a world of "representations" which are many and varied but without truth-content.

"For Décon," Ted wrote to me in one letter, "reality is like Gertrude Stein's Oakland: there's no there there. It's all 'representation', and representation is all we have. And because the thing represented cannot be known directly but only through its various representations, we therefore cannot say that one representation or interpretation is better, or truer, or more accurate than another. All that we can know is that one representation *differs* from another. Long live *différence*, the multiple and conflicting representations of whatever is being represented. And so for Décon there can be no misrepresentation, no lies, no truth, no certainty. Fact is fiction and fiction, fact. More or less."

Ted was deeply troubled by what he saw as the pernicious political and moral implications of such a thoroughgoing relativism and radical skepticism. "Propaganda. Big lies and half-truths. They're all 'representations' to Décon and his ilk." On this view, Ted continued, the "Holocaust revisionist" historians who claim that the Holocaust never happened—that it was Zionist propaganda—could not be faulted for their interpretation. Their representations of events were no better, and no worse, than Raul Hilberg's in *The Destruction of the European Jews*. "Hilberg was a historian—meticulous, precise, painstaking, and truthful—and the revisionists are Neo-Nazi propagandists and liars. If we can't make *that* elementary distinction, we might as well pack it in and prepare for the new Dark Ages. Pack your bags, Jack: the barbarians are already inside the gates, and damned if they aren't all professors. Not of history, thank heaven, but of English and of something called Cultural Studies (don't ask me what that is; I don't actually know; nor, I think, do they—though they do manage to put the 'cult' into 'culture'). Décon is their guru, and they his mindless acolytes. They'd follow him anywhere, including the death camps, which are of course only another 'social construction' on their telling."

I could see why some of Ted's colleagues took exception to his hard and flinty take-no-prisoners attitude. Behind his back Ted's more trend-conscious colleagues rolled their eyes. But not to his face. Never, ever to Ted's face. For they knew, or at least feared, that he could verbally filet and skewer them as deftly as a master chef deals with chops and cutlets.

And so I ventured none too bravely into unfamiliar territory. Surely, I suggested, Ted's view of Décon was something of an exaggeration. Décon was Jewish, wasn't he? He'd hardly side with Neo-Nazis.

"Oh, but he has. Not with Neo-Nazis but with real honest-to-god Nazis. The original article." Ted told me about Décon's defense of Paul de Man, the Belgian-born Yale literary critic who had been a Nazi sympathizer and supporter before and during World War II, and about Décon's defense of the German philosopher Martin Heidegger, who had been an early and enthusiastic member of the Nazi party and had never recanted his efforts on behalf of Hitler and his thugs.

So Ted's debate with Décon was, for him, more than an academic exercise. He aimed to undermine Décon's philosophy—"the kind of philosophy," as Ted's friend John Searle once quipped, "that could give bullshit a bad name"—and in a way that would be both personal and public.

Ted had invited Décon to Princeton to give a series of seminars and, as the invitation said, "to defend his views in a public forum." Always the perfect host, Ted had rolled out the red carpet for his distinguished guest. Although famous for his hospitality, he was also known to be unsparing in his criticisms of views he believed to be mistaken or pernicious, or both. And to Ted, Décon's were both.

On the night of the debate, Betts Auditorium was packed to overflowing with faculty and graduate students whose baggy sweatshirts announced none too subtly that they'd come from as far away as Cambridge to the north and Chapel Hill to the south. The buzz subsided as Ted led the distinguished-looking white-haired Décon onstage, seated him at a table, and approached the lectern. I didn't know it then, but Ted's strategy was simplicity itself, and worthy of Clarence Darrow and the other great trial lawyers I'd long admired. After graciously introducing his guest and welcoming the audience, he offered what even I knew was an embarrassingly inaccurate, in fact flat-out false, summary of Décon's views on truth and representation.

"Monsieur Décon holds that the meaning of any text is indeterminate to all readers, himself and his acolytes excepted. He believes it possible, through the method that now bears his name—Déconstructionism—to discover its author's intentions and thus to discern the real or original meaning of the text, revealing its essential unity and coherence, and thus the fixity and stability of its signifiers."

Members of the audience shifted uneasily in their seats. Many were whispering. Someone hissed. And when at last Décon himself objected, Ted turned to him and asked: "Are you saying, Monsieur Décon, that I've misrepresented your views? That I'm being untruthful?"

Décon said yes.

And Ted said: "*Bingo*!"

After a moment of stunned silence, the audience howled and clapped, and only Décon seemed not to have grasped the point that, lacking at least some conception of truth and falsity, of truthful and false "representations," his philosophy was incoherent and self-subverting.

"What is this 'bingo'?," Décon asked plaintively.

Ted could always make me laugh. I laughed then, and I was laughing now. My dear friend dead, and I'm laughing and coughing and laughing some more, so hard that tears of laughter and loss came together.

The tears were still warm when I heard a knock at the door. Before I could answer, a key turned in the latch and the door opened. There, framed by the doorway, was the woman from the black and white photograph on Ted's desk.

4

"Hello," she said in slightly accented English that sounded smoky and warm. "You are Jacques?"

"Jack, yes. I'm Jack Davis."

"Ted's friend. He speak often of you."

"And you," I stammered. "Who are you?"

"Forgive me. I am Danielle. Danielle Dupin. Ted, he is my friend, too. You and I, we have much in common. We both love him. We miss him. It is so sad."

So sad, I thought. Are the French incapable of anything but the most banal expressions of grief and loss? Sad, indeed. Damn stupid awful shame and sorrow is what it is. Crime. Murder, maybe. But I caught myself, and said nothing. She seemed to sense something amiss as she moved toward me, taking both my hands in hers.

"I am sorry," she said, pressing my hands and pulling me close enough to smell her perfume. "Ted is your old friend, and my new one. You know him much longer. We are not equals. You love him more."

"You love Ted?," I asked. Then I corrected myself. "You loved Ted?"

"We are lovers, yes. For five months now."

My mind reeled. Ted was always attracted to women, and they to him. But Ted was forty-eight and Danielle was perhaps all of twenty-three or four. Half his age. Nearly his daughter's age, for Christ's sake.

I was no innocent in sexual matters. But I was sometimes shocked by the sexual escapades Ted had had and told me about, with all names except his changed to protect the not-so-innocent. He'd laugh and say, "You can take the boy out of Oklahoma; but apparently you can't take Oklahoma out of the boy."

Ted dead, and now this. Danielle. Ted. Lovers. No wonder he had thanked her in his preface for "research and other assistance." That "other assistance" must have been extraordinary. I didn't know whether to be shocked or simply awed. Danielle Dupin was stunningly beautiful. A cascade of curly dark brown hair fell far below her shoulders, framing a face that few photographs—and no words of mine—could capture. A face both strong and beautiful. Greenish-gray eyes, light olive skin. A strong nose and high cheekbones set above full red lips that showed something between a smile and a pout.

"I'm sorry," I said. "I didn't know about you. Ted didn't tell me."

"Ted think you might be, ah, shocked. Worried. He say you might not understand. You are, he say, ah—what is the word?—conservative. You are conservative, no?"

No, I thought, probably not. With a married Chinese Catholic mistress-lover, or whatever my conservative relatives might call her, not bloody likely.

She smiled. "Ted, he knows you well. You are conservative. And maybe a little shy, perhaps?"

"A little, yes," I said. Then I almost laughed. "A lot, actually."

She laughed, and turned on the lights.

Danielle, who clearly knew her way around Ted's apartment, made tea and then told me about herself. Danielle Dupin's mother was Algerian, her father a prosperous French physician. She grew up in St-Germain and had as a teenager studied piano and ballet, showing some talent for both. "But not enough to pursue either of them professionally." She had been a student at the Sorbonne, leaving to live for a time in Italy "with the only man besides Ted I ever loved." Later she studied in England, at Pembroke College, Oxford. It was in Oxford that she'd met Ted, at an eighteenth-century studies conference, while working as hostess and translator.

Ted didn't need a translator. But in his middle age he was at last, and for the first time in his life, lonely. He needed a friend who might become a lover. Four years ago he had divorced his wife of twenty-four years, after a long separation and a time of troubles that had no end, in a marriage that seemed to have no future. He had asked Anna for the divorce, and after a long and anguished silence she had finally agreed.

Anna had, to all appearances, been the perfect wife. "An English rose," Ted used to say, perhaps a little too charitably, "entwined with a thorn." He had been a thorn in her side, preoccupied with his work and, in the last troubled years of their separation, with other women. I never knew whether she drove him into their arms, or whether he drove himself. I always liked Anna, though I never quite broke through her British reserve, and found her more cordial than warm. He had stayed with her, I thought, because she bore them a daughter whom Ted loved to distraction.

Jessica was my goddaughter. She looked like her mother and behaved like her father. Willowy and rosy-cheeked, she was always a tomboy, torn between being feminine and fiercely independent. Fierce independence finally appeared to be winning, much to her father's delight and her mother's dismay.

"Theodore," Anna would ask, "what *are* you going to do about that girl?"

To which Ted would always laughingly reply, "As little as possible." But he wasn't joking. As a teacher and a father, he hated what men—fathers and teachers and fellow students—did to young women, and he was determined that his daughter would not fall afoul of any of the traps that awaited her, however attractive the bait. If you had dared to ask Ted if he were a feminist—or any other "ist"—he would deny it with his most withering sneer. And yet I knew women who swore that Ted was, by instinct and principle, a practicing feminist. Of course, no one would dare say that to Ted's face. He hated labels, isms, ists, and other boxes. And, above all, he loved his daughter.

But did he love—I mean, had he loved (for I must now speak of my friend in the past tense)—Danielle, a young woman almost his daughter's age?

I didn't know. I wasn't sure I wanted to know. But I found myself wanting to know more about, and to be with, Danielle Dupin. We talked into the night, sharing memories of Ted. She and Ted had had fun, she said, more fun than she had ever had with any man. They had worked together, laughed a lot, shared secrets, and ate and drank well. And made love.

"Ted was a lover of women. I mean, not that he was a lover only in the sexual way, but he really love women. All women. He like them. He enjoy their company. Mine too, I think," she added with a slightly saucy smile.

She asked me about myself. I told her how I had grown up in Oklahoma, the only child of quarrelsome alcoholic parents, and sent at age six to the farm to be raised by my maternal grandparents, how I was always too tall for my age, physically awkward and not very good at sports, not even basketball. But I worked hard at that, and everything else, and went to Oklahoma State University on a basketball scholarship and did well enough in my studies to be nominated for a Rhodes Scholarship. Which I eventually got, I was later told, because they wanted a few Rhodies who weren't WASPs or Jews from the East or West Coast and everywhere in between. And my being one-quarter Cherokee (on my father's side) apparently didn't hurt either. I was worried and wary and ambivalent about leaving everything old and familiar to go to Oxford, where I didn't expect to fit in. And I wouldn't have, except for one happy accident. I met Ted, who had just graduated from Dartmouth at the top of his class. Despite—or maybe because of—our differences we had hit it off almost immediately. From my first sighting of Ted at Rhodes House I thought him the most exotic human I'd ever encountered. His manner, his dress, his speech, his high spirits set him apart from everyone else. I later learned, to my astonished amusement, that Ted had thought me exotic. And, by New England and Oxford standards, I suppose I was. I had arrived at our first reception at Rhodes House wearing a string tie, freshly pressed jeans, checkered shirt and newly polished cowboy boots. Everyone else wore black tie and dinner jacket. I didn't exactly look like a scion of the Eastern Establishment. Or of any other establishment, for that matter.

That was clear enough to everyone, including the self-important young fop of a fellow Rhodes Scholar who greeted me by saying, in an affected British accent, "Hello there, Chief. But what's this? Why is an Indian dressed as a cowboy? I say, how *did* you get to Oxford? Under the Indian or the cowboy quota?"

Someone laughed nervously. And then a silence that seemed to roar in my ears. My face flushed. I was speechless. But Ted wasn't.

"Neither," Ted said, stepping between us. "He got here by dint of hard work and being both decent and smart, which is more than I can say for you. The only quota I'm aware of is the very special place reserved each year for a single ass. But, what's this? I hear only the braying. Where, pray, my good ass, are your ears and your tail?"

Everyone guffawed as the red-faced ass, imaginary ears burning and invisible tail tucked tightly between his legs, retreated into the farthest corner of the large reception room.

"Hello," Ted said, extending his hand. "I'm Porter. Ted or Teddy, take your pick." I started to introduce myself, but he continued, "I know who you are. You're Davis. From Oklahoma. And don't mind him," he added, nodding toward my tormentor. "Fancies himself as another William F. Buckley. But once the hot air and gas escape, he'll come around. With the right encouragement he might even become a halfway decent human being." And, to my great surprise, he did. The very next day, my tormentor apologized, first by note and later in person. He then took me to The Turf for a pint. From that day to this, Brad—Bradford Breckenridge III—and I have been friends. Somehow I suspected that all this was Ted's doing, although he denied it.

Ted and I soon became fast friends, in both senses of "fast." His love of life was infectious, and I caught it. It was in his company that I learned to savor single-malts and wine that came from bottles with corks instead of screw caps. To dine instead of eat. To smoke good cigars. From Cuba, no less. To dress with some sense of style and color. To talk to, and be with, women. Not girls or coeds, but women. Smart, sophisticated, sometimes beautiful women. Not bad for a shy boy from the boonies. I came to love Oxford, and left a different man.

I rambled on as Danielle listened with an interest that looked genuine, often touching my hand and smiling in a way that seemed somehow to warm me inside and out.

In Ted we had a common bond. My old friend, her new lover. Now he was lost to us, leaving only memories for us to recall and savor. And we did. Together.

It happened fast. Too fast, really. I don't know how or why exactly, but within the space of several hours I was beginning to feel, for the first time in my life, the full force of temptation, the lure of sin, the lust of the flesh. With Danielle I felt giddy and afraid, bold and wary, ashamed and confused. And when I thought of Grace, guilty too. Danielle was half my age, and my dead friend's lover. Shame, I heard an inner voice say. Slow down, another voice said. Catch your breath. Be reasonable. Don't do anything rash.

And yet, for all that, I wanted to touch Danielle, to hold her, to breathe her perfume deep into my lungs, to feel her body pressed against mine. At the same time I wanted to push her away, to distance myself, to immunize myself against a virus that I wanted desperately to catch.

I understood Odysseus's relation to the Sirens.

Dealing with the material and bureaucratic side of Ted's death was emotionally wrenching and physically exhausting. I was relieved to have Danielle's help in filling out the forms and securing the seemingly endless stamps and signatures that the French bureaucracy of death required.

Finally, four days after my arrival in Paris, we sent Ted's body back to the States. Embalmed and packed in ice, his final trip across the Atlantic was not what he would have wished. His ignominious crossing made me all the more determined to discover who might have wished him dead, and why.

I felt frightened and alone and in need of help. An American stranger in a strange French land. Did I dare trust Danielle?

God knows I wanted to. I wanted to trust her, to confide in her, to let her know my darkest suspicions, to open myself to her in every way. On the other hand, though, I remembered Ted's telegram: "Trust only you." Hard as it was, I would for the moment keep my own counsel.

I was sitting at Ted's desk, about to resume my reading of *Rousseau's Ghost*, when the phone rang.

"Jack?," a familiar voice said. It was Grace. I was glad to hear her, and a little apprehensive too. Danielle was in the adjoining room, sorting through and packing Ted's clothes and other belongings.

"I know you're worried and that you've been busy. But I'd hoped to hear from you before now. Are you okay? Do you want me to come? It'll be difficult to get away, but I'll come if you want me to. I might be able to help."

"No," I said, a little flustered. "No need. I'm trying to tie up some loose ends here."

"Are you really okay? You sound a little strange."

"I'm just tired, that's all. Tired and frustrated."

I told Grace about my encounters with the French bureaucracy, the delays and dead-ends, the difficulties involved in securing the release of a dead friend's body and what the police claimed was his personal computer.

"And you did this all by yourself?," Grace asked. "Speaking French to all those officious French officials? Jack, I'm impressed."

I'd been found out, and I knew it. Grace knew me so well it was scary. I fessed up. I told her about Danielle, about Ted's relationship with her, about how she'd helped me, and that she was there now, in the next room.

There was a silence on the other end of the line.

"Jack," Grace said at last, "please be careful."

I couldn't tell whether she was jealous or worried about my safety, or maybe both. Grace had always said that since we weren't married I had none of the obligations of a husband. I wasn't bound, but I felt tied to her by affection and habit and friendship. And, insofar as she would let me, by love.

"Jack, are you there?"

"Yes, sorry. I'm here."

She told me about breaking the news to Jessica. In person, at her apartment. As with all who grieve the loss of a loved one, Jessica's reaction was now proceeding in grimly predictable stages. First, denial. Jessica had initially insisted that there must have been some mistake, that her father couldn't be dead. Then blame. Who had done this? Why had it happened? Whose fault was it? Grace wisely did not reveal my suspicions, and said only that the Parisian police had ruled it an accidental electrocution because of faulty wiring.

As for acceptance, no. Jessica could not accept her father's death. Not yet. That would be slower and much more painful in coming. He was her father, her favorite parent. And now he was gone. Forever. A memory. A ghost.

This was hard going for both of us. We both wanted to cry, but didn't. Trying to stem the flood, Grace and I talked about other matters. About the firm, my partners, the clients who were concerned about or offended by my absence, demanding to know where I was, threatening to take their lucrative business elsewhere.

"Don't worry about it, Jack," Grace soothed. "I told them that your brother had died unexpectedly and that you had gone to France to take care of his affairs. It was the smallest of white lies."

But of course it wasn't a lie at all. It was closer to the truth than most literal truths. In all the ways that mattered Ted was my brother. Not by blood but by choice.

As for going to France "to take care of Ted's affairs," I winced at the double meaning. That Ted had had an affair with Danielle, I did not doubt. Whether he loved her, I did not know. Whether I was about to embark on an affair with Danielle, I dared not guess. But already I was harboring hopes.

"Jack, there seems to be a bad connection. You're fading in and out. I can hardly hear you." A low hum turned into a loud crackling sound.

"You're right," I said. "Perhaps I could call you tomorrow." The crackles became loud pops punctuated by buzzes.

"What?"

"I'll call you tomorrow," I shouted.

"No, Jack. Don't do that. Use your lap-top. Get on the Internet. It's more secure than the phone. And let's use our language from now on."

"Our language" was short for the pidgin Chinese and English that Grace and I used when we didn't want anyone eavesdropping. Mostly we used it in faxes and e-mail messages that we didn't want to be intercepted or, if intercepted, understood. Hackers might break into our firm's computer; they might read the confidential memos from one partner to another; they might tap into files and legal briefs; they might even intercept a message from Grace to me, or from me to her. But they would never understand it. Ever.

Our language was a little like pig-Latin, but in an unlikely combination of Chinese and Okie that we called "Chokie." We used abbreviations of words in English and transliterated Chinese, turning them back to front, arranging sentences so that the verb came first, followed by the noun or subject and then any modifiers. The result was a bizarre but intelligible argot comprehensible to us and, better still, to no one else.

Although I had no talent for foreign languages, I felt flattered and honored when Grace brought me into her small familial circle by teaching me a few words of Mandarin, and then a few more, until I had acquired a small but usable vocabulary. I reciprocated by teaching her some Okie terms and expressions (including my grandfather's favorites, such as saying that an unattractive person "could give ugly a bad name" and calling someone he disliked or disapproved of "the south end of a northbound horse"). And these we combined in an ersatz language that no one but us could understand. And that's just the way we wanted it.

Chokie proved indispensable around the firm. Memos, faxes and e-mails in Chokie were indecipherable by anyone but us. On some occasions, when a message was misrouted or intercepted, the recipient simply saw the sort of incomprehensible garble that suggested a programming or syntax error. What others saw as garble, the two of us read and understood. It shut others out, and it tied us together. Grace and I constituted a Secret Society of two.

Our secret language grew out of Grace's and my childhoods and our shared adulthood. As a child she had, until age five, when her family arrived in the States, spoken only Chinese. Mandarin, more precisely. After that her father, hoping his family would be accepted and eventually assimilated, had forbidden the children to speak anything but English. He was a stern man, and punishments for infractions were swift and harsh. But sometimes—when she was sick in bed with the measles, or had to stay home with the flu—Grace and her grandmother would whisper confidences in the now-forbidden tongue. Mandarin was her "comfort language," the tongue that cooled and soothed a young girl's fevered brow and stilled her fears, that brought her close to her grandmother, and both closer to their ancestors.

Even now, Grace's spoken English, excellent as it was, had certain Chinese inflections and carried detectable but ever so slight traces and accented remnants of her ancestry. Her English, both written and spoken, had a degree of precision, clarity, and dignity that few native speakers now possessed. I recall Ted saying that the best English prose was now being written by non-native speakers: Rushdie, Ishiguro, Naipaul, and others. And, he added, this—despite all the media hype—was hardly new: he was a great admirer of Joseph Conrad, a Pole, and of the German-speaking emigrés Arthur Koestler and Karl Popper, all of whom wrote about important issues in exemplary English prose. "Our thoughts can be no clearer than the language in which they are expressed," Ted often said. "Muddy prose, muddled thinking." The clearest and most precise prose, and therefore thought, came from the intersection of, if not the clash between, different cultures and languages.

As for myself, I never even knew that I belonged to a culture or had an accent until I left Oklahoma for Oxford. There I became acutely aware of accents—my own and others'—and quite adept at detecting regional accents in Britain. Cornish, Cockney, Yorkshire, Scots, Welsh, and others seemed like badges of identity, worn proudly by some and half-hidden by others. British accents, I discovered, reveal a great deal about the speaker's region, class affiliation, ethnic background, education, and much else besides. Ted and I used to make a game of guessing where Britons came from, what class they belonged to, and the other badges by which people are classified, categorized, deferred to, or dismissed outright.

Not that our own, supposedly classless society is any more generous or less judgmental. Easterners and northerers think that southerners are dumb simply because of their slow drawling speech. On this scale, I suppose, Oklahomans are only borderline retarded.

Following Grace's advice, I hooked up my modem and got on the Internet. Fortunately that was easy to do, since Ted's apartment was owned by his university and rented to faculty members on leave in Paris. It was equipped with a second phone line for Internet communication, with a direct line to the server.

My first e-mail message told Grace that I had sent her the lap-top computer, with faulty power pack, via Fed Ex yesterday afternoon. I confessed that I had delegated the task to Danielle, because I was so inept at wrapping packages. Almost immediately came Grace's reply, in Chokie, saying that she had received the package that morning and that it was already on its way to the lab for analysis.

I didn't know what she expected to find. For that matter, I didn't know what I expected to uncover. So far I had discovered nothing out of the ordinary in Ted's manuscript. Maybe I was looking in the wrong place. Or maybe I was distracted by Danielle.

6

"Jacques, it is late. You are tired. You need to sleep now."

I felt Danielle's hands on my shoulders. Thumbs on my neck, she massaged gently but firmly with fingers that seemed surprisingly strong. I closed my eyes. This time I didn't pull away.

She had remade Ted's bed. Cream colored satin sheets and feather pillows. A down comforter. Soft light from a small electric lantern above the bed. A slight scent of something I almost recognized.

Danielle was right. I was tired. I wanted to sleep. But not just yet. And not alone.

"Good-night, Jacques," she said, as she pulled the satin sheet and then the duvet up to my chin. "Sweet dreams."

I felt her full lips touch my right cheek, then my left. I wanted and waited for her lips to touch mine. But they did not.

She turned out the light and moved toward the open door.

"Danielle?," I asked. Or implored.

"Yes?," she said, turning sideways. The light from the next room shone through her blouse, silhouetting her breasts.

I felt tongue-tied. "Sweet dreams," I said lamely.

"You too." The door closed and the room went dark.

I heard rustling noises in the next room. The hall door closed. Soft footsteps disappeared down the hall. And then silence.

Where had she gone? I didn't know where she lived, or very much about her. I wanted to know more. Much more.

At long last—I don't know how long—I fell into a fitful slumber. I saw policemen. A sparking computer, connected to an electric chair with Ted strapped in it. Leering dark figures around the edges, with faces I tried desperately but unsuccessfully to identify.

Pale light crept through a crack in the heavy curtains. It was early. My watch said 5:42. I was still tired, but I couldn't sleep. I got up, went to the kitchen, made coffee. A newspaper came through the mail slot. *Le Monde*. I looked at the headlines, making out every other word. Trouble in Rwanda. Bleak prospects for the Israeli-Palestinian peace accord. A nationwide general strike threatened by the CGT and other powerful French labor unions over proposed cuts in social services. And on a back page an obituary for Ted, with a pencil-sketch picture that made him look rather more stern than I or any of his friends would recognize. It was a gracious and appreciative farewell from perhaps the most prominent Rousseau scholar in France, recounting the record of Ted's scholarly achievements and awards, and concluding on a personal note about Ted's *bonhomie*, his *joie de vivre*, and his love of French letters.

And his love of French women, I thought, as I wondered where Danielle might be.

I took my coffee into Ted's study and sat down to resume my reading of *Rousseau's Ghost*. I paged through to the end, scanning chapter and section headings, trying to get a sense of the whole. A page appeared to be missing. Page 241a was followed by page 242. I couldn't find a page 241b to bridge the gap between the sentence that continued from 241a but wasn't resumed on 242. Stranger still was a large gap in the numbered footnotes. The last footnote on page 241a was number 41, and the first on 242 was 42, which was crossed out and replaced by footnote 67. Which meant that twenty-five footnotes were unaccounted for. It seemed unlikely—impossible, even—that one page would contain that many footnotes. Which suggested that more than a single page was missing. Then, somehow—I don't know how, I must still have been half-asleep—my hand hit my coffee cup, which overturned, spilling its contents in a steaming black cascade across Ted's desk and down to the floor below.

"Damn and blast!"

I grabbed Ted's manuscript, setting it none too gently to the side before running to the kitchen for a towel and back to the study to mop up the mess. I wiped the desk top and then crawled underneath to sop up the rest. Too tall for these cramped quarters, I hit my head, hard, on the bottom of the middle drawer.

A small diary, hardly larger than a postage stamp, fell to the floor.

I was still wiping coffee from the floor and from my fingers as I opened the miniature diary. No names, just initials and abbreviations. Addresses. Dates. Even the odd phone number. This was not Ted's main diary, which was filled with tasks to perform, people to meet at certain times and places, and written in his usual bold script. The small diary consisted of no more than a dozen pages, and Ted's handwriting here was small and cramped. As I paged through it a curious entry caught my eye. Across facing pages was written, in Ted's characteristically bold hand, "**Inst pol?!?!**," underlined three times, and, underneath, a series of numbers and letters—d4g20d15g9d13—that made no sense, except perhaps as some sort of code, and a date some two weeks earlier. The last entry was equally mysterious: "V.D.," followed by a Paris phone number. Venereal disease? A V.D. clinic? Could Ted have needed their services? It seemed so unlikely, so uncharacteristic. But not impossible. Perhaps Danielle had given him something unwanted, unwelcome . . . This was too disturbing, too painful, to contemplate. I had to do something. To act.

I screwed up my courage and reached for the phone, dialing the number following "V.D." I had to get to the bottom of this one. The phone rang five times, followed by a click. A recording of a woman's voice answered. "Bonjour. Vidéo Date de Paris. Nos heures d'opération sont. . . "

I hung up, dumbfounded. Ted using a video dating service? That seemed even less likely than Ted needing the services of a V.D. clinic. He would never use a dating agency. Would he? No, of course not. If nothing else, his pride—and his aversion to television and video—would preclude that possibility. And so, surely, would his relationship—his affair—with Danielle. Still, there it was in his diary. I didn't know what to think. It just didn't make sense.

Not that the preceding entry made any more sense. Somehow—perhaps because it was written in Ted's bold hand and underlined—I felt that this was what I'd been looking for. The problem was, I had no idea what I'd found, or what "Inst pol" stood for, still less what the code might mean. I guessed it had something to do with what Ted was working on and that it must therefore have some connection with Rousseau. But what, I didn't know. And why it mattered, I hadn't a clue.

I suppose I could have asked one of Ted's French associates and fellow Rousseau scholars. But I wasn't in a very trusting mood. Ted had died—been killed—in France, probably by some Frenchman. So I wasn't about to confide in any Frenchmen.

French women were perhaps a different matter. I thought I should tell Danielle what I had found. Maybe she would know what it meant. On the other hand, I felt foolish. It might mean nothing at all, and would serve only to reveal my ignorance. Or, if it did mean something, anyone who knew about it might be in some danger. If so, I had already exposed myself. Why should I also expose Danielle? Or—I felt horrified even as I considered the possibility—maybe Danielle's not to be trusted. Maybe she's . . . no, that's absurd. Even so, I'd better lead with my brain, not my crotch. Again Ted's words came back. "Trust only you." And so again, albeit reluctantly, I resolved to keep my own counsel.

Hands in my pocket, I paced back and forth across Ted's study, fingering my newly recovered arrowhead and wondering what to do. Wondering what Grace would do. Or what Ted would do.

Then I remembered Jeremiah Altmann. Sir Jeremiah, as he now was. My former tutor and Ted's old friend at Oxford. He was the leading English—arguably the leading European—historian of ideas, and an expert on Rousseau and almost any other political theorist you might care to name. And an original and influential political theorist in his own right. Perhaps he would know. And if he didn't, probably no one would.

I called U.K. directory inquiries to get his number. It was unlisted. Then I phoned the porter's lodge at Christ Church, Oxford. A rather huffy college porter told me that they didn't give Sir Jeremiah's, or any other don's, telephone number to strangers.

But I was no stranger, I protested. Sir Jeremiah was my old tutor. I needed to speak with him, and right away. It was urgent.

My protests were to no avail. I would have to call on Sir Jeremiah in person, much as I had as an undergraduate, some twenty-five years earlier. I half trembled at the thought. I had not, to say the least, been a stellar student. Barely adequate, in fact. It was my early acquaintance with political theory that had convinced me that my talents lay elsewhere. I began packing my bag.

Just as I finished writing a note to Danielle she suddenly appeared.

"This is for you," I said, handing the note to her. "I've got to go to England on business. To Oxford. To see my old tutor and a close friend of Ted's. I'll be back in a few days."

Danielle skimmed the note and then looked sweetly at me. "Jacques, take me with you. I have not been back to Oxford in more than a year. We can go together. It will be, ah, nice," she said, putting her hands in mine. We agreed to meet at the Gare du Nord in half an hour.

In my haste I left my lap-top behind.

At the Gare du Nord we considered taking the EuroStar Express up to and through the newly completed Chunnel. It would be faster than any alternative. But somehow the idea of travelling through a tube under the English Channel didn't appeal to my more claustrophobic side—nor, fortunately, to Danielle's aesthetic sense. Besides, it was a beautiful sunny day—ideal weather for crossing the Channel the old-fashioned way, by ferry.

We boarded the slower but still high-speed SNCF express train which whisked us toward Calais at well over 100 m.p.h. Not exactly Amtrak, I thought, as we sped through the pine forests and flat farmlands of northern France. Whatever their faults, the French at least know how to run a railroad.

We had lunch on the upper deck of the Channel ferry Sterne Invicta. Gulls squawked above, circling the white stacks belching black diesel exhaust. The wind was brisk, blowing Danielle's hair, revealing soft delicate ears pierced in several places and laden with large round earrings that glistened in the sunlight and seemed almost to tinkle in the breeze.

For a moment I forgot why I was there or where I was going or that Ted was dead. Danielle seemed to live so much in the present that the past seemed somehow long past and the future far away. Only now mattered.

Perhaps it was the wind or the wine, or both, combined with her presence on that sunny deck. Or perhaps it was a middle-aged man's grasping for some semblance of lost youth. But I leaned across the table and kissed Danielle. Gently at first. And again, when she responded, harder and more insistently.

Her mouth tasted of wine and brie. Out of the corner of one eye I saw a Japanese tourist taking our picture. Instinctively I recoiled in embarrassment.

Danielle drew back, smiled, and then laughed.

"Jacques, you amaze me. Perhaps you are not so conservative."

Perhaps I wasn't. I wasn't sure what I was anymore. A conservative out of control, maybe. I had had several lovers but I've loved only one woman, I said. And then I told her about Grace.

In telling Danielle about Grace I felt unburdened, as though a load of bricks were being lifted off my body, brick by brick. I told her how Grace and I had first met, how we were almost immediately attracted to each other, how she didn't reciprocate because she was already married. Her husband, nearly fourteen years her senior, was a dull but decent man and the son of her father's American business partner. Grace's marriage at age nineteen had been arranged several years earlier by her father and his partner, who expected that the two would come to love each other. They didn't. From the beginning they quarreled. First about Grace's education: he didn't want her to continue her undergraduate studies at Berkeley. She won that battle, graduating with honors just before her twenty-first birthday. She wanted to go to graduate school at Stanford, where she'd been offered a generous fellowship; he wanted to move to New York to get into the lucrative security business and support his housebound wife. With help from her father, her new husband won the war; they moved east; Grace gave up her hopes of graduate school and an academic career and settled none too happily into the role of housewife. After nearly two years, her father died. Feeling freer to assert herself, Grace insisted that she be allowed to take a job outside. Her husband resisted, but, no longer able to turn to his father-in-law for support, he finally relented. Grace became a secretary, and soon thereafter a legal assistant, at Anderson Davis. Grace proved to be so good at her job that I suggested she go to law school, at the firm's expense if necessary. Her husband said no. The marriage turned from bad to worse. But, being unwilling to offend her dead father or her church, Grace resolutely refused to consider divorce. Desperately unhappy, she at last turned to me. First for friendship, and later for love. Thus began our "arrangement."

It had not been without its troubles. We saw each other mainly at the office, where we were always, and often frustratingly, on our best behavior. Otherwise a stolen late afternoon or early evening, and very rarely an entire weekend, was all we could manage. I wanted to see much more of Grace, and she of me; but her marriage, and her sense of decorum, made that difficult, if not impossible. I had been faithful for nearly eight years. But lately I had begun to chafe under this regime of propriety. Weekends were the worst. I occupied myself mostly with work and, less often, tinkering with the 1925 Bugatti roadster that I had spent several years restoring to its youthful perfection. Sunday drives through Central Park and along Riverside Drive would have been much more enjoyable if Grace could have joined me. But she couldn't. Or rather wouldn't. I felt frustrated, she felt guilty. Lately we had not been doing very well. Something had to give. But whenever I contemplated the possibility of ending our "arrangement" I experienced a despair so deep that I felt physically ill. The result was that I—we—drifted, did nothing, took no action at all. Love in limbo.

"It is sad," Danielle said. "But it is life. This love, it cannot be in marriage. But some love—sometime the best love—it is not in marriage. Sometimes it is long. Sometimes it is short. Love we take when we find it. Ted and I, we are lovers for a short time. But we love so well that the time it does not matter."

She looked wistful, and wise beyond her years.

I pulled Danielle close as the ferry docked at Dover. Ever so gently I kissed her right cheek and then her left, feeling her loss and mine as one single awful absence.

On the train to Oxford we were both uncharacteristically quiet. Danielle seemed far away, and I must have seemed preoccupied. I was preoccupied. I gazed out the window as the train rolled and swayed through the green English countryside where sheep grazed, cars stopped at railway crossings, ruddy-faced children with chapped knees and wearing school uniforms waited on station platforms. I thought about Ted, about Sir Jeremiah, and what I could say to him that would not make me look like an utter fool. Nearly fifty years old, quite successful in my way, and I was feeling like an undergraduate again as I remembered our first meeting, more than twenty-five years ago.

It had been with some trepidation that I climbed the ancient wooden staircase to Altmann's rooms, and knocked on his door. The wait seemed interminable. Then the door opened. I was surprised by what I saw. Somehow, no doubt because of his towering reputation, I had expected him to be tall. He wasn't. He was short, stout, balding, with a countenance that seemed both fierce and friendly.

"Come in, Mr. Davis. Come in. Altmann's my name," he said in very rapid and slightly accented English as he shook my hand vigorously. "Do have a seat. Over there, if you please," he said, motioning me toward the larger and more comfortable of the two overstuffed armchairs in his large book-lined study.

"Now," he said, settling into the other chair, "tell me about yourself. You're an American, I believe. From where do you hail?"

"Oklahoma," I stammered. "A small town. You've probably never heard of it. Durant. Durant, Oklahoma."

"Ah, yes. Oklahoma. Will Rogers. A genius. Roosevelt was very fond of him, a great admirer."

I learned then that Altmann's thinking—and his conversation—was prompted by association. One thing reminded him of another, and that of another, and so on, in an endlessly interconnected display of memory and erudition that seemed both extraordinary and normal. Normal for him, that is, and for no one else. And I was reminded that as a young man during World War II Altmann had held a minor diplomatic office in the British Embassy in Washington which by force of character and intellect he had turned into a position of some importance. He became a favorite of Roosevelt's and Churchill's, and something of a secret go-between, or "back channel" in diplomatic lingo.

This man, a refugee from Russia and a Jew, who had played no small part in twentieth-century politics, was no politician. He was first and foremost a scholar intrigued with, perhaps preoccupied by, the history of ideas. Not ideas in the abstract, but ideas put into practice by political parties and movements. Ideas and beliefs that had produced the twentieth century and all its horrors.

"Our century," he observed in a famous essay, "is the stage on which scripts written by earlier, and especially nineteenth century, theorists have been acted out. The well-intended theories and fictions of an earlier age have become the all-too-real terrors of our time. We have thought and argued and marched, by and large, under the banner of their age, which they fancied as an age of science: or, perhaps one should now say, of pseudo-science. The 'scientific' racism of Gobineau gave rise to the gas chambers and ovens of Auschwitz. Marx's 'scientific' socialism gave rise to the Gulag. Ideas—good, bad, or banal—have consequences. And the goodness, badness, or banality of these ideas has little to do with their authors' intentions and everything to do with their final fruits, some of which are poisonous beyond belief and even perhaps beyond their authors' worst imaginings."

The terrors of the twentieth century were due, Altmann argued, to the misbegotten attempt to make an imperfect world—and the imperfect beings who inhabited it—perfect. The vision of a perfected world in which like-minded equals agreed about everything and marched together in agreeably harmonious lock-step was Altmann's idea of hell. Against the millenarian and utopian idea that "the crooked shall be made straight," he liked to repeat Kant's dictum that "From the crooked timber of humanity, nothing straight can ever be made." And that, for Altmann, was neither an expression of cynicism nor a counsel of despair, but a plea that we recognize and appreciate the wondrous and irreducible plurality of human cultures, communities, individuals.

Altmann seemed somehow to grow taller as he talked in a torrent of words, on every subject imaginable, and almost as though he had known Tolstoy, Kant, Herder, and a hundred others personally, indeed intimately. My weekly tutorials were a bracing experience for which I was not fully prepared and whose full meaning did not occur to me until much later.

I was a mediocre student in Altmann's subject, and I knew it. And I know now what I only suspected then: that his judgments of my weekly essays were more generous than just, and meant to encourage an easily discouraged boy who felt unsure of himself, and very far from home.

My new friend Ted Porter was a student of an altogether different calibre. Smart, eager, confident, and already uncommonly well-read, he delighted Altmann and the other dons in a way that I envied but could never hope to match. He took issue with their interpretations of various political theorists, advanced his own original views, and impressed people who were hard to impress.

Now, nearly thirty years after our first meeting, my old friend Ted Porter was dead. And I was about to meet again with our former tutor to try to enlist his help in solving a mystery, the murder of our mutual friend. Or maybe not. Perhaps he would refuse. For all I knew, Altmann might well agree with the Parisian police that there was no mystery to be solved, because there was no murder. Perhaps he would agree with them that I had become unhinged. Maybe I had.

I felt very cold, and must have shivered visibly.

"Jacques, you are trembling and pale like a ghost. What is wrong?"

"Oh, nothing," I lied as the train pulled into the Oxford station.

8

We took a taxi to Christ Church. The college seemed almost to shimmer and glow as the Cotswold stone caught the late afternoon sunlight. The driver waited on St. Aldates while I ducked into the porter's lodge under Tom Tower, carrying a note for Sir Jeremiah, explaining my purpose, asking to meet him as soon as possible, and giving the phone number of Ted's and my apartment in north Oxford. The lodge shook six times as Great Tom—the massive bell in Tom Tower—tolled the hour. Looking a little skeptical when I told him that my note must reach Sir Jeremiah today, or tomorrow at the latest, the assistant porter placed it in a slot bulging with mail and messages.

"E's not been in today, sir," he said. "Just back from Italy, 'e is. But I'll see that 'e gets it."

I thanked the assistant porter and rejoined Danielle and our talkative taxi driver, who was in the middle of some long tale about the drunken and destructive misbehavior of undergraduates during Eights Week—when college rowing teams compete against each other—and how the police turn a blind eye to "the toffs" and how his children would never be allowed to get away with such things, and on and on.

College against college, and Town against Gown, I thought. The old animosities persist. Somehow it seemed an oddly comforting thought. Seeing as how my whole world had been upended of late, I welcomed permanence and continuity in almost any form.

We drove past the Parks, up the Banbury Road, past North Parade and Park Town and into Wycliffe Close, near Summertown. Ted and I had bought a condominium here several years ago, and had done reasonably well in renting it to visiting academics, mostly Americans. Ted often stayed here when it wasn't occupied, but I had seen it only twice since we'd bought it in 1979. Fortunately, the next renter wasn't due to move in until the following month, so Danielle and I had the place to ourselves.

The flat was, by north Oxford standards, both modern and modest. It had two bedrooms, one bath, a large living-cum-dining room, a tiny kitchen, and a small study. Ted chortled when I described the decor as "Motel 6." But it was warm and cozy, and the beds comfortable.

"You take the master bedroom," I told Danielle. "I'll take the guest room."

She hesitated for a moment, smiled, and, picking up my bag and hers, put them both in the larger bedroom.

"I am remembering your kiss, and thinking how nice it was, and wondering if there might be more," she said, stepping out of the bedroom.

Danielle put her arms around my neck, pulling herself up and me down toward her. Our lips met. This time there was no table between us, no Japanese tourists to gawk at the sight or, worse, to take pictures. Her kisses were warm, welcoming, eager. I began unbuttoning her white silk blouse.

The phone rang.

"Mr. Davis?," a familiar voice from long ago said. "Altmann here. Got your note. Very sad about Teddy, very sad indeed. Heard the news from several of our French friends. He'll be sorely missed, I can tell you."

I tried to catch my breath, to breathe normally, and thanked him for ringing so promptly, and asked if we could meet, and soon.

"I'm afraid I'm rather busy at the moment. I've just come back from Italy, you see, and . . ."

"Sir Jeremiah," I interrupted, surprised at my own boldness, "this is important. Very important. I can't say just why over the phone, but, believe me, it is. Could we meet tomorrow? For Ted's sake."

There was a shuffling sound on the other end of the phone.

"Very well, Mr. Davis. Tomorrow it is. Come round to my rooms at half past six. We'll have a drink and dine in college, shall we?"

I stammered my thanks, and rang off.

Danielle looked puzzled.

"Why must you meet Altmann? What is so important?"

"Loose ends," I dissembled. "Things I need to talk about."

"What things?"

"Private things."

"A secret, then? You would keep a secret from Danielle? Perhaps Danielle will keep a secret from you," she teased as she made to rebutton her blouse.

"Stop that," I ordered in a tone of mock command. "Please," I added, now pleading in earnest. If she had been Mata Hari and I an Allied general, I'd have given her every military secret she asked for, and more. Just for starters. Is any force of nature more powerful than sexual desire? Why else does the Black Widow's mate go willingly, and even eagerly, to his death?

Danielle left her blouse unbuttoned, revealing dark chocolate nipples high on olive breasts beneath a bra that seemed too sheer and almost too small to contain them. She turned, and walked into the bedroom.

I followed, obediently, eagerly.

Danielle's skin was soft, her body supple and warm, her hands skilled, her tongue talented and versatile. She made love like no woman I'd ever been with. Every part of my body shuddered and shivered and tingled. We were on a raft in white-water rapids, borne along on undulating currents of erotic energy, ebbing and surging by turns.

I was in the middle of a middle-aged man's most ardent fantasy.

And all I could think about was Grace. I saw her dark almond eyes, her inquisitive face with its wan sad smile, her shoulder-length straight black hair now flecked with gray. She was wearing her red silk kimono.

The kimono was a standing joke. I'd bought it for her birthday at Saks shortly after we had become lovers. At the time it seemed to me, well, oriental. Eastern. Exotic.

"And Japanese," Grace added, a little coolly, as she opened her present. "Really, Jack, you sure know your way to a Chinese woman's heart."

I was mortified by my gaffe and wanted more than anything to take it back and start over, but she wouldn't let me. Grace shook her head and laughed, slid out of her dress and donned the red kimono. She strutted and twirled like a model on a runway, and bowed low and called me Samurai-san.

"Unsheathe your sword, Samurai-san," she said softly. And, wrapped in red silk, we made love.

"Jacques, is something wrong? You seem not so pleased. What do you wish me to do? Just say, and I will do it."

"It's not you, Danielle. It's me. I'm not myself. Or maybe I am, and that's the problem."

"You think of your woman in New York?"

"Yes."

"But we are in Oxford, many miles away. Many. We are here, alone. Just us. No one else."

But of course we weren't alone. And three's a crowd. Four, if you count Ted.

"I'm sorry, Danielle. I wanted—I want—to make love to you. But I can't. I'm feeling guilty."

"Guilty?" The word rolled off her tongue as though for the first time.

"I guess I have a guilty conscience."

"Guilty conscience?" Two new words.

I was beginning to sense that Danielle and I lived in two very different worlds. Hers was a world of physical and other pleasures, of actions that didn't carry consequences. Or didn't carry them very far. Mine was a world in which every pleasure produced equal or greater pain, and actions carried consequence upon consequence up to, and for all I knew, beyond, the grave. Danielle danced naked and unashamed; I wore responsibility like a hair shirt. Much as I might want to live in her world, I could never be a citizen. I would always be a visitor and an alien.

Only Ted seemed to live comfortably in both worlds. The contradiction—if that's what it was—didn't trouble him. He was Danielle's lover and my friend. Dionysian and Apollonian, hedonist and ascetic, sensualist and scholar—somehow he had taken out dual citizenship. He moved easily between warring worlds, and was at home in both.

"Poor Jacques, you are tired. Tomorrow will be better. Try to sleep now." Danielle's strong fingers worked their way from my neck, across my shoulders, down my back, over my buttocks, my legs, my feet, and back again. I floated, and finally I slept.

I saw Ted in a forest clearing, sitting on a large stump. He was talking animatedly but almost inaudibly, in French, with a trim man in a dark dressing gown or caftan, sitting on an adjoining stump. Ted was showing a thick handwritten manuscript to the other man, who looked bemused. Ted said something I couldn't understand. Then, suddenly, the other man's expression turned angry. He waved his hand, the wind came up, and the pages of the manuscript were blown away and scattered through the surrounding forest, which then began to burn. Ted made no effort to retrieve the pages as they blew into the burning woods. He sat and watched as the other man walked quickly away and disappeared into the inferno.

I sat bolt upright in bed. I'd seen Rousseau.

9

God, how do the French smoke these things?, I asked myself as I took my first drag from the thick unfiltered Gauloise I'd found after rummaging rather guiltily through Danielle's purse. I lit it with her gold-plated lighter, and put the lipstick, the lighter and the silver cigarette case back into the soft suede bag. I felt dizzy. The cognac didn't help either.

The sense that I had somehow actually seen, and not merely dreamt about, Rousseau and Ted—together and alive—wouldn't leave me. Maybe it was superstition, but I couldn't shake the sense that Grandma Della was right: dreams are imaginary, but they're not unreal—they are every bit as real in their way as the waking world we inhabit by day. My grandmother had never read Freud, never even heard of him, did not know or speak about the subconscious; but she knew by lore and instinct what Freud had discovered slowly and painstakingly. She believed, not that dreams come true, but that they *are* true—that they reveal our deepest desires and aversions, our fears and fantasies, and show sides of reality not readily apparent to our waking selves.

But what dreams show, and how we know it, requires interpretation. And on that score Grandma Della never failed to deliver. For any dream I asked her about, she had an interpretation—sometimes multiple interpretations—of its meaning.

"Silly old Indian stuff," my father would sniff when his mother was out of earshot. "Superstition. Same as that stupid medicine pouch Mama gave you. Kinship with nature and the animals, my ass. It's hard enough just being kin to your own kinfolk. Mama's not educated. She never got past eighth grade. You're a smart boy. You can amount to something, if you don't go falling for all that magical mumbo-jumbo crap."

As I grew older, more educated, more sophisticated, my grandmother's medicine loosened its grip and more or less left me. But now, thirty-one years after her death, it was back, with a vengeance born of neglect.

"Use it," I heard Ted say.

Then I woke up. The room stank of stale cigarette butts and sickly-sweet cognac fumes. My head hurt.

"Breakfast? Or should I say lunch?" Dressed in blue jeans and a white bandeau, Danielle looked as bright as the sunlight streaming through the kitchen window. She had already been to the bakery, the butcher shop, and Budgens' market in Summertown. I smelled coffee. She was scrambling eggs and making toast.

"Drink this," she said, holding out a large glass of tomato juice.

"No, thanks. I'll pass. I'll never drink anything again. Well, maybe some coffee."

"First juice, then coffee. Then you eat. Then you walk and walk."

"No juice, no food, no walk and walk. Just sleep and sleep."

"So you won't dine with Altmann? Shall I ring him now?"

Oh my God, I thought. Altmann. At Christ Church. This evening. Drink. A gloriously sumptuous meal, as always at the House. I felt nauseous.

"Drink this, Jacques. It help the—how do you say?—the overhang."

"Hangover."

"Ah, yes, the hangover."

I drank the tomato juice. Danielle poured a large cup of black coffee. It tasted bitter. A second cup began to bring me out of my stupor. The eggs and toast tasted almost, but not quite, good. Danielle was right. I began to feel better.

She was too kind, or too diplomatic, to mention my failure of the previous evening. I wanted to forget it. I wanted to call Grace and beg her forgiveness. I wanted to make love to Danielle. I didn't know what I wanted.

When, I asked myself, would I ever grow up?

"Now we walk, Jacques. A long way."

The bright sunshine stabbed my eyes as we stepped outside. We walked briskly across the Banbury Road, over to and down the Woodstock Road, and into Aristotle Lane. We arrived at the south-eastern end of Port Meadow, climbed over the stile and walked among and between the cows and horses grazing near the river. Port Meadow is common land, a "Commons" in English law. Anyone could amble or walk their dog or graze their horse there. The meadow smelled agreeably of damp grass and horse manure. The still-narrow and slightly muddy Thames cut lengthwise through the mile-long meadow. A brightly colored houseboat passed beneath as we walked over the old arching iron bridge and up the gravel path to The Perch, Ted's and my favorite pub.

Not yet ready for anything alcoholic, I ordered a pot of tea and we sat in the pub garden. Adults talked and laughed as small children played and dogs sniffed the grass and each other. I remembered the times that Ted and I had sat here as undergraduates, the future still open and bright with possibility. No future was brighter than Ted's. And now it was closed, or foreclosed. Forever.

I was in one of my favorite places. The sun was shining, the grass green, the meadow smells succulent, and my companion sympathetic and attractive. And I felt lonely and sad. I tried not to show anything, but Danielle saw something.

"Is it Ted?," she asked.

"Yes."

"We walk," she said.

And walk we did. Up the pebbled path along the river. Children swam naked in the cold muddy water. Fishermen cast their lines. A remote-controlled model airplane swooped and soared on the other side of the river. A Japanese tourist, camera in hand, took pictures and bowed politely to people coming up the path. Cud-chewing cows on both sides seemed to pay no attention to any of this. Arriving at the Godstowe Lock, we rested and watched as boats going upriver waited for those going downriver to enter, and then leave, the lock. The lock-keeper did a brisk business, skillfully going through motions performed a thousand times before. A boat headed downstream entered a lock full of water. The water was drained, the level lowered, the lock opened, and the boat continued on its way downriver toward London.

"Cheers, mate," a departing boatman called out.

"Cheerio," the lock-keeper answered with a wave.

There was something here that was sorely missing from the life I lived in New York. Something slower, friendlier, more familiar. Not like Oklahoma, but closer to Oklahoma than to New York. The pace, the people, the sense of cheerful cooperation—whatever it was, this was nothing like the New York I'd come to know and accept, and even to enjoy, but not to admire.

We walked and walked. Past the ruins of the twelfth century nunnery and across the river to The Trout, the pub at Wolvercote, at the north end of Port Meadow. Thirsty and more or less recovered, I ordered a pint of their best bitter, and Danielle a half. Swollen by spring rains, the river roared loudly as it narrowed and cascaded over the falls just outside The Trout.

"Jacques," Danielle said over the roar, "there is something we have not talked about."

"Yes?"

"It is Ted. I am thinking that we miss him so much that he get in the way of us. Of our lovemaking. You think of your woman, of your friend, and I of my lover. Your friend, my lover, they are the same. It is all so complicated."

"That's putting it mildly," I said. In reality, I thought, Danielle had mastered, or even exceeded, the fine art of English understatement.

"It does not need to be so," she said, putting down her glass and touching the back of my hand. "Tonight does not have to be like last night. We can be friends, as we are now. Or we can be both friends and lovers. That is what I hope for. What do you hope for, Jacques?"

"A less complicated life," I said.

The answer did not please her. Danielle pursed her lips and stared down at her glass. Then she looked up, smiled a sad smile, and said, "Life, it is always complicated. It never cease to be so until we are dead."

◄ 10 ►

We said little as we walked through Wolvercote, down the Woodstock Road to Summertown, and back to the flat. In less than an hour I was to appear in Altmann's rooms in Christ Church. I showered, shaved, put on my slightly wrinkled white shirt, gray trousers, and navy blazer. I'd brought only one tie, a red and yellow floral print, packed in haste from my minimal office wardrobe. Too loud, I thought. Vulgar, even. But it'll have to do. Worse yet, I didn't have a black academic gown, still the dress *de rigueur* at Oxford high table. I'd sold my M.A. gown when I left Oxford and hadn't worn one since. *Faux pas* without end, I thought. This evening was not going to go well, sartorially speaking. I felt almost as I did when I first set foot in Oxford, nearly thirty years ago. I might as well be wearing a checked shirt with string tie and cowboy boots.

"Jacques, here—I find it in the back of the bedroom closet." Sure enough. Ted to the rescue. It was his M.A. gown, sheathed in dry cleaner's plastic. He kept it here, because it was the place he'd most likely need it.

I unwrapped the gown. It was well-worn, slightly frayed around the collar and sleeves. Just nicely broken in by Oxford standards.

Half an hour to go. Barely enough time for a brisk walk to Christ Church. I needed to clear my head, to rehearse what I wanted to say to Sir Jeremiah. Danielle offered me a drink. I declined. Tucking Ted's gown under my arm, I kissed Danielle good-bye.

I knew where I was going, geographically; but in every other sense I felt unsure of my course and my destination.

As I walked out of Wycliffe Close and down the Banbury Road I remembered the other times in my life when I felt unsure, even panic-stricken. The first was when I was eleven years old. Grandpa Wagner was driving the old Ford tractor, plowing contour furrows on the hilly field on the far western side of the farm. I was perched on the fender above the large back wheel. Suddenly the tractor pitched sideways. I was catapulted through the air, and landed hard in the soft dirt. Grandpa was pinned under the overturned tractor. The only sound came from the engine, still running. Grandpa lay face down. He wasn't moving.

That was the first time I felt The Calm. Everything seemed to move in slow and surreal dream-time. I walked to the tractor, turned off the ignition, reached down and scooped out handfuls of dirt under and away from Grandpa's face. Then I ran in slow motion over to the barbed wire fence and picked up one of the new replacement fence-posts laying alongside, brought it back, placed it under the large left back wheel, and lifted as hard as I could. The tractor moved a little but didn't right itself. I ran back to the fence and found an old bucket which I then used as a fulcrum under the fence-post. Each time I lifted the post, I kicked the bucket, and with each kick gained more leverage. Finally I pushed the fence-post lever down as hard as I could. The old Ford raised on its side, teetered for a long moment, and finally landed upright. Grandpa still wasn't moving, but he had a pulse and was breathing. Blood dripped from his nose. Suddenly the slow motion ended. I ran at top speed over the hill and back to the house. Uncle Fred had just pulled into the driveway.

"Whoa, what's the hurry, boy? You look like you've seen a ghost."

"It's Grandpa," I wheezed as I jumped into the cab beside him. I didn't need to say more. He drove his old pickup at top speed, bumping and bouncing through the west pasture and up and over the hill faster than anyone before or since. When we got there Grandpa was sitting up where I'd left him, wiping the dark blood from his nose with his faded red bandana.

"Close call," Fred said.

"Yeah, I reckon," said Grandpa.

The Calm came over me on only a few other occasions. Once in the Southwestern Varsity championship, with the score tied and two seconds to play in a furiously fast-paced game, a teammate passed the ball to me. I watched as it drifted toward me. I reached out calmly, gradually opening and then gently closing my fingers as the ball settled into my hands. Then I rose languidly into the air, spiralling slowly as I pushed the ball toward the basket. It seemed to hang in the air for a long time, finally falling into the basket as the buzzer signalled the end of the game and brought everything back up to speed. But even that experience pales in comparison to another.

Just before my Rhodes interview in Oklahoma City I excused myself, went into the men's room, and vomited violently, repeatedly, and well past the point where there was nothing else to bring up. I looked at my miserable dejected sickly face in the mirror and decided to withdraw. Nothing was worth this, I thought as I washed my face, slapping myself to restore some semblance of color to my cheeks. I left the men's room, walked down the hall and reentered the anteroom of the third-floor conference room in the newly constructed Murrah Federal Building. I was about to tell the secretary that I was withdrawing my name. As I walked through the door I heard my name called. Putting my left hand into my pants pocket I squeezed the black arrowhead as hard as I could, driving its sharp point into my palm until the pain blocked out the fear. Then everything switched into slow motion. I entered the conference room, smiled, shook hands with the judge from Ardmore, the professor from Tulsa, and another ex-Rhodie from Oklahoma City, and seated myself across the table from them.

I don't remember much about the interview, except that they asked me about my background, my family, my academic and athletic interests, what I hoped to gain from going to Oxford, and a few other predictable questions. Then the judge from Ardmore asked a question that I still remember verbatim. "Son," he said, "Oxford University is a mighty fine university, old and distinguished. But you're young and, as yet, undistinguished. Just what makes you think that you'll fit in, do well, and won't bring the blush of embarrassment to those who send you there?"

The Calm was still with me. "Send me there," I said, wrapping my fingers around the arrowhead, "and I'll get back to you with answers to the other questions."

They sent me there.

And now, after all these years, I was back, and more in need of The Calm than ever. But it wasn't coming.

My pace slowed as I passed the Martyr's Memorial outside of Balliol. Cranmer and the other Oxford martyrs had died for their convictions. Religious convictions. Did I have any convictions, religious or otherwise, for which I was prepared to die? I envied Grace her almost childlike belief in a loving God. I had been raised that way too, although as a Protestant—a hellfire-and-brimstone Baptist, to be exact—but somehow it didn't stick. There were times I wish it had. But I was by temperament an unbeliever and a skeptic.

"Either you hear the music or you don't," Ted told me. "Religious belief isn't like believing that this table is here. It's not really a matter of belief at all, but a kind of sensibility. It's more like being able to discern the melody in a song or symphony. Some people are tone-deaf. All they hear is a lot of noise, all sound and fury, signifying nothing. No melody. You're like that, Jack. But at least you're in good company. Max Weber once said that, where religion was concerned, he was 'unmusical'. He wished he could hear the music that others heard, but he couldn't."

Ted heard the music. Grace hears it still. I envy them their musical abilities. Sad to think there's a symphony that others hear and find inspiring, that I neither hear nor am inspired by. Whatever fledgling religious sensibilities I might once have had were long ago roughly cut out and the wound cauterized by the hellfire breathed by fundamentalist preachers.

I found myself at the east gate of Christ Church. A sign at the entrance read "College Closed to Visitors." The bowler-hatted gatekeeper asked my business. When I told him that Sir Jeremiah was expecting me, he asked my name, looked at a list posted inside the gatehouse, and then let me pass. Once inside I heard the sound of choral music coming from the Cathedral. The Christ Church Choir was practicing for Evensong—or perhaps for another of its world tours. I walked along the gravel path past the Picture Gallery and the colonnaded eighteenth century library on the south side of Peckwater Quad, and then turned right into Killcanon. I trudged slowly up the well-worn staircase. The almost forgotten smell of old wood and fresh wax triggered memories that made me feel young again. And ever so slightly apprehensive.

I paused on the second floor landing to catch my breath before knocking on Sir Jeremiah's door.

11

"Mr. Davis. Do come in. Nice to see you again after all these years." Sir Jeremiah had large hands and his handshake was still firm. He had aged well, I thought. He now had less hair and was rather more stooped than I'd remembered him. He was dressed, as always, in a black three-piece wool suit, which now seemed slightly large for his shrinking frame. From his vest dangled the gold chain of an antique pocket watch. The only other bright color came from the red silk handkerchief that protruded from the left breast-pocket of his suit coat. The lively, darting eyes behind his horn-rimmed spectacles made him look like a horned owl or some other sharp-eyed bird of prey. His eyrie looked pretty much as I remembered it. Dark floor-to-ceiling bookshelves contrasted with the well-worn red and blue Persian carpets. His large wooden writing table was littered with books and papers. The early evening sun shone through the leaded glass west windows out of which I could see some of Tom Quad and the top of Tom Tower.

"Good of you to see me, Sir Jeremiah, and on such short notice."

"Not at all, my dear Davis, not at all. Sherry?"

"Yes, please. A dry one, if you have it."

Moving slowly and deliberately, he headed toward the mantlepiece, removed an upended glass, and then, bending down, reached into a cupboard and took out a bottle of Gonsalves pale.

"Let's see if this one will do," he said as he poured a glass and handed it to me. He sat down.

"You're not joining me?," I asked.

"I'm afraid not. Doctor's orders. No sherry, no port, no brandy, no whiskey; just a little wine with dinner. And no pipe, more's the pity. It's age, you see. Be thankful you're still a young man, and enjoy these things while you can."

At almost fifty I didn't think of myself as young, but Sir Jeremiah, now in his late eighties, clearly did. In his eyes I would always be his pupil, and therefore young by definition. It was, in its way, a comforting thought.

"To your good health," I said, taking my first sip of one of the best sherries I'd ever tasted.

"And yours," said Sir Jeremiah with a nod.

He asked me about myself. What had I done after leaving Oxford? Had I married? Did I like living in New York? I told him I'd gone to Columbia Law School, and into the New York law firm in which I was now a senior partner. No, I'd never married. Yes, I liked living in New York, as long as I could get away from the city for extended periods—the most pleasant of which I'd spent with Ted at his island retreat in Lake Superior.

These preliminaries out of the way, our talk turned to Ted. Sir Jeremiah asked what I had learned from the Parisian police. I told him that the cause of death was listed officially as "électrocution accidentelle."

"From what? An electric kettle? A lamp?"

"A computer. A lap-top computer with a faulty power pack."

Sir Jeremiah leaned forward, his sharp eyes narrowed, and a look of utter incredulity came over his face.

"A *computer*? Teddy wouldn't touch a computer with a barge-pole."

"Precisely. Which is why I'm here. I don't think Ted's death was an accident. I think it was murder, made to look like an accident. And the ruse worked. The Parisian police fell for it. They've already closed the case." I told him about Ted's telegram, summoning me to Paris posthaste, and about its uncharacteristically urgent and even frightened tone. "Not like Ted," I said.

"No, not at all," Altmann agreed, shaking his large head.

"I was going through Ted's papers and came across this," I said, reaching into my pocket and pulling out Ted's small diary. "He had hidden it under a desk drawer. I discovered it only by accident." I said nothing about how my carelessness and clumsiness had aided my discovery. "It looks like mostly run-of-the-mill stuff, except for the last two entries."

I got up, walked over to Sir Jeremiah's chair, and turned on the lamp. "Here," I said, bending down, and holding the diary open to the last page, "is the first puzzle. I rang the number. It turns out that 'V.D.' is short for Vidéo Date, a video dating service in Paris. . ."

"A *what*?"

I had to explain to Sir Jeremiah what a video dating service was. He harrumphed indignantly and mumbled something that included the word "absurd."

I wasn't surprised that he was of no help on this score. The entry about video dating made no sense to either of us. But I hoped he could help solve the other puzzle.

"Here," I said, turning the diary to the preceding page, "is where I need your help. There are these five numbers and the alternately recurring letters 'd' and 'g'—which looks like some kind of code—and above you see 'Inst pol?!?!' underlined three times."

Altmann's eyes darted from left to right, and back again. "Your 'code' isn't a code at all," he said. "It looks like a combination. . ."

"But what about the letters d and g?," I interrupted.

"As I was about to say," he continued a little curtly, "it looks like a combination, perhaps to a safe or a safe-deposit box or locker or some-such. The letters 'd' and 'g' stand for *droit* and *gauche*—right and left. Right 4, left 20, right 15, left 9, right 13. My guess is that there is a safe somewhere, probably in Paris, to which this is the combination." He pursed his lips, looked up, and handed the diary back to me.

Of course it made perfect sense, and I felt a little foolish. In France Ted spoke and wrote in French. "But what about 'Inst pol'? Instant something—instant policy, politics, what?"

"That's even easier," Altmann answered. "Remember Teddy was in France, working on a book about the political philosophy of Rousseau."

"Yes. So?"

"So it seems certain, or at least highly probable, that the abbreviation refers to a work by Rousseau—the *Institutions politiques*—that was to be his *magnum opus* in political theory, on which he worked through the 1750s."

"And this was then published in—when?—the 1760s?"

"No, his *Political Institutions* was never published. It was, as Rousseau himself said, abandoned and destroyed." Rising with some effort from his chair Altmann crossed the room and pulled a thick blue-and-gold leather-bound volume of Rousseau's *Oeuvres Complètes* from a shelf. He opened the book and brought it to me. "Here is what Rousseau himself says." He pointed to a paragraph, clearly expecting me to read it. It was, not surprisingly, in French. I did my best, which was not very good.

"Avertissement," I read aloud, mispronouncing the first word. "Ce petit traité est extrait d'un ouvrage plus étendu, enterpris autrefois sans avoir consulté mes forces, et abandonné depuis long-tems. Des divers morceaux qu'on pouvoit tirer de ce qui étoit fait, celui-ci est le plus considérable, et m'a paru le moins indigne d'être offert au public. Le reste n'est déjà plus."

"So there," said Sir Jeremiah, "now you see what happened to Rousseau's *Institutions politiques.*"

"I'm sorry, Sir Jeremiah, but I don't see. I don't fully understand what I just read. Not just the words, I mean, but the references he's making." I felt like a drowning forty-nine year-old undergraduate, struggling for air.

"Very well, then," he said in his best tutor's voice. "Let's go through it a bit more slowly. What you've just read is the *Avertissement*—the foreword—of Rousseau's *Contrat social*, the *Social Contract*. That is the *petit traité* or 'small treatise' extracted from *un ouvrage plus étendu, entrepris autrefois sans avoir consulté mes forces*, 'a more extended work undertaken earlier without having considered my strength', *et abandonné depuis longtemps*, 'and long since abandoned'. That 'more extended work' was the *Institutions politiques*. 'Of the various portions that could be taken from what had been done', Rousseau says, 'this'—that is, the *Social Contract*—'is the most considerable, and seemed to me the part most worthy of being offered to the public. The remainder', he concludes, 'no longer exists'. That is, except for the extract that we now know as the *Social Contract*, the bulk of the *Political Institutions* no longer exists. Elsewhere—in his posthumously published *Confessions*, for example—he says that the larger manuscript was destroyed."

Sir Jeremiah rose again and walked across the room, taking another blue and gold leather-bound volume from the shelf, thumbed the pages, and found the passage he wanted.

"Rousseau's first reference to the *Institutions politiques* appears in Book 8 of his *Confessions*. It was in the course of long walks around Lake Geneva in 1751 that the plan for the work came together in his head." Sir Jeremiah thumbed through several pages, stopping abruptly. "Here, in the next book—Book 9—Rousseau writes, um, yes, here it is, 'Des divers ouvrages que j'avois sur le chantier, celui que je méditois depuis longtemps, dont je m'occupois avec le plus de goût, auquel je voulois travailler toute ma vie, et qui devoit selon moi mettre le sceau à ma réputation étoit mes *Institutions politiques*.' So you can see," he said, looking over at me, "that Rousseau had high hopes for this . . . Is something the matter?"

"The French. I was having a little trouble following the French." A little trouble indeed. I was having a *lot* of trouble.

"Perhaps I was reading a bit too quickly," he said diplomatically. "In this passage Rousseau says that of the different works he had begun, 'the one on which I meditated for the longest time, to which I attended with the greatest gusto, on which I wanted to work all my life, and which I believed should put the seal on my reputation, was my *Political Institutions*'. So Rousseau quite obviously set great store by this work."

"Which he never finished. But why not? I mean, why didn't he press on if it was so important?"

"That is a rather long and complicated story. Rousseau had planned the book in the late 1740s and had begun to work on it in earnest in 1751." Sir Jeremiah ran his finger down the page as he paraphrased and translated. "After five or six years, Rousseau tells us, he had made little headway. 'Books of this sort,' he says, 'demand meditation, leisure, tranquillity'—three things in rather short supply. He worked in secret, telling no one—not even his good friend Diderot—about it, 'fearing that it might be too radical', he says, 'for the century and the country in which I was writing.' And then his nerve—or his health, which was always a bit dodgey—began to fail him during this, the most productive period of his life. He was pursuing several projects at once, including his treatise on education, the *Emile*, his novel *Julie*, and a major treatise on political theory. He had, as it were, to throw something overboard, lest his ship sink with all his unpublished books still on board."

Sir Jeremiah flipped quickly through a sheaf of pages before pausing. "This is what Rousseau tells us in his *Confessions* about, um, um . . . ah yes, here it is, Book 10: 'mes *Institutions politiques*. J'examinai l'état de ce livre . . .' He looked over at me, frowned slightly, and continued, to my relief, in English. 'My *Political Institutions*. I looked at the state of this book, and found that it still needed several more years' work. I lacked the courage to pursue it, and to put off my resolve until it was finished. And so I abandoned this work after deciding to extract whatever could be taken from it and then to burn all the rest—*brûler tout le reste*'. So, except for the extract that we know as the *Social Contract*, the *Institutions politiques* was long ago reduced to ashes."

"Is it possible that it wasn't—that the *Institutions politiques* still exists?"

Altmann frowned thoughtfully. "Possible? Perhaps. I suppose that anything is possible 'in principle,' as my philosopher friends like to say. But the survival of the *Institutions politiques* is as close to impossible as one can imagine. I very much doubt that this manuscript survives. Two and a half centuries would be a very long time to keep such a secret. If I were a betting man—which, mind you, I'm not—I would wager a very large sum that the *Institutions politiques* met with precisely the fate that Rousseau tells us—that it was burned. Consumed by flames. And that's the end of it."

"But what if this manuscript did survive? What would it mean for Rousseau's reputation and for modern scholarship?"

Sir Jeremiah flexed his generous jowls. "Large questions, my dear Davis, for which I have no answers. We can hardly say what its survival might mean, without knowing what the *Institutions politiques* contained. All we have is that 'short extract', the *Social Contract*. If the rest of the work were up to that standard, then . . ." For once, Sir Jeremiah was at a loss for words.

"Then what?"

"Then it would be very significant indeed. It could revolutionize our understanding and our estimate of Rousseau."

I was leaning forward full tilt. "And?"

"And quite simply, my dear Davis, I doubt that Rousseau would have abandoned and destroyed a manuscript that he thought well of. More likely, he had a poor opinion of its merits, and believed it best to burn the manuscript. Full stop. Any writer worth his salt and mindful of his reputation would have done the same. And Rousseau was a very meticulous writer."

"But suppose—just suppose—it did survive. Purely hypothetically and for the sake of argument. What, if I might put it rudely and crudely, would Rousseau's *Institutions politiques* be worth? Not, I mean, in scholarly terms, but in monetary terms. What price would it be likely to fetch at auction at Sotheby's or one of the other large London auction houses?"

Sir Jeremiah looked as if I'd placed a week-old dead fish under his nose. I half regretted asking the question. But only half.

"It does all come down to that, doesn't it?," he said more in sorrow than in anger. "Money. The 'cash nexus,' as Marx used to say. He was wrong about so many things. But about that he was dead-on. The price of something seems always to be taken—or rather mistaken—for its value. Real value can never be measured, and certainly not in monetary terms—the appalling conceits of modern economists notwithstanding."

"I'm sorry, Sir Jeremiah, I wasn't meaning to imply that I wished to measure the value of Rousseau's *Institutions politiques* in monetary terms. I'm only trying to get some sense of its market value and not, as you say, its real value, which must surely . . ."

"Yes, of course, I do see your point. It's just that . . . Well, the almighty market seems to be not one, but the *only* measure of value in modern Britain, after Mrs. Thatcher and her ilk. It's such a perversion of all that is . . . But forgive me. I am on occasion quite carried away. I am an old man, not really up to or prepared for this return to Social Darwinism and Manchester Liberalism. Whether Mr. Blair and 'New Labour' represents an improvement over the Tories remains to be seen. I, for one, am rather skeptical. But you asked a fair question, and I gave an intemperate answer. Or rather, I failed to answer your question at all." He inhaled, his nostrils flaring, as though his olefactory sense were attempting to adjust to something unpleasant. "What would the *Institutions politiques* be worth in monetary terms? I have no good idea. I would suppose that its value must be in the millions, and quite possibly the tens of millions, of pounds. But that is simply a guess. Certainly no comparable manuscript has appeared on the auction block in recent years. So I suppose one might almost say that Rousseau's *Institutions politiques*, had it survived, would be a pearl beyond price—so valuable that its value could scarcely be measured in monetary terms at all. But, happily, that is pure conjecture, since Rousseau's unfinished manuscript did not survive. It was burned, and there's an end to it."

"But we don't know whether . . ."

"We do at least know one thing for certain, my dear Davis," said Sir Jeremiah, taking out and glancing sharply at his pocket watch. "If we aren't in the Senior Common Room in three minutes, we'll miss dinner." He rose slowly and took his gown off a hook on the wall. I helped him into it and then I donned Ted's gown.

We walked as briskly as my old tutor could manage down the dimly lit staircase, through the north portal past the Deanery and across the impressive expanse of Tom Quad. The last rays of daylight played atop the east wall and the Cathedral spire. I had the sensation of walking inside a large golden bowl, burnished by centuries of sunlight and showers. We went through the south portal, into the Fellows' Garden and then into the dark wood-paneled Senior Common Room, where a group of some ten or twelve dons and their guests had assembled. An illuminated portrait of Christ Church's most famous philosopher looked down on this murmuring assembly. The long lean face of John Locke looked bemused, benign, tolerant.

We were more than five minutes late, but no one had moved upstairs to high table, and I knew why. Sir Jeremiah was on the list, and everyone—Dean, canons, Students (as Christ Church dons are called), undergraduates—would await his arrival.

"Oh dear, I fear I am late," said Sir Jeremiah to the Dean.

"Not at all, my dear fellow. Just in time." The Dean was an imposing figure, tall, slender, with a delicate aquiline face framed by gray hair, and wearing the white surplice of his office as head of both college and Cathedral. "This must be your guest," he said, smiling at me.

"Yes, do forgive me, Dean. May I present my guest, Mr. Jack Davis of New York. My former pupil and a dear friend of my dear friend, Teddy Porter."

The Dean shook and then held my hand. "May I say how very sorry I am about your friend's passing. I did not know him well, but I admired him and his work. He was, as perhaps you know . . ."

The saturnine Senior Common Room Butler interrupted, nodding at the Dean and pointing none too subtly at his watch.

"Ah, yes, we must away," said the Dean. "Mr. Davis, you'll sit with me—if that suits you, Jeremiah?"

"Yes, by all means, but only if I am seated on Mr. Davis' other side." I was beginning to feel distinctly welcome.

"Done," said the Dean. He led the entourage out of the Senior Common Room, up the narrow spiral stone staircase, through the large wooden door and into the great medieval hall. It was, by any standard, an impressive sight. The largest, certainly the longest, dining hall in Oxford. The dark wood-panelled walls were ringed with portraits of notable and famous Christ Church men, including scientists, statesmen, and literary figures such as Lewis Carroll and, more recently, W. H. Auden. Some two-hundred black-gowned undergraduates stood at long dark candle-lit tables, awaiting the seating of those at high table.

We stood with heads bowed beneath the large portrait of a porcine Henry VIII while a pretty Indian or Pakistani undergraduate with a Yorkshire accent recited a Latin prayer. Then, with a sharp blow from the Dean's gavel, we were seated. It all went like clockwork, not a beat being missed.

The Dean turned to me. "As I was saying, or about to say, I did not know Professor Porter intimately, but I formed a very high opinion of him while he was with us. He was, as probably you know, our Falconer-Hamlin Professor in . . .—was it 1993, Jeremiah?"

"No, Dean, it was 1994."

"Ah, yes, 1994 it was. In 1993 we had some fellow from Michigan or Minnesota or one of those places. Can't recall his name. At any rate, Teddy Porter was a great hit with everyone, though I must say the women seemed especially fond of his company." He looked slightly quizzical, either scandalized or more likely, I thought, amused.

A white-coated wine steward filled my glass with a very nice Montrachet.

"Teddy gave a most amusing inaugural address." I looked across the table at the speaker, a trim sandy-haired man about my age with graying temples, blond bushy eyebrows, and twinkling eyes. "For a Falconer-Hamlin Lecture it had a rather salacious title, 'Rousseau's Women'. Teddy began by saying, 'This being a lecture of only one hour, I shall be unable to name, much less discuss, all the women in Rousseau's life; so I shall confine my remarks to only six of the most notable.' His thesis was that Rousseau, who has been so often reviled by modern feminists as a misogynist, was nevertheless inspired by and deeply indebted to a number of women." The sandy-haired man across the table went on to recount Ted's lecture in minute, learned, and sometimes hilarious detail. All at high table were straining to hear, and those who could laughed uproariously, as bemused undergraduates wondered what could be going on. His five-minute monologue made Ted's presence almost palpable and brought his memory back to vivid and vigorous life.

"I'm sorry," I said to the man across the table. "I don't believe we've met."

"Martin Thompson," he said, nodding and raising his glass.

"Jack Davis," I reciprocated, raising mine.

Sir Jeremiah leaned over and whispered, "Our Senior Politics Tutor. Late nineteenth-century British political thought—wrote a brilliant book about the British Hegelians: Bradley, Green, Bosanquet, McTaggart, and lesser lights."

"An admirer?" I asked a little lamely, since none of these names rang a bell.

"Can't stand them," said Sir Jeremiah. "Dislikes the whole lot. I've never understood how anyone can devote his life to writing about thinkers one detests, but Martin manages brilliantly." Clearly, Thompson seemed a man worth knowing.

A cold cucumber soup was served, and then the main course, roulades of poached Scottish salmon topped by a creamy yogurt and dill sauce, with a light overlay of limes and Mandarin oranges. The wine flowed as freely as the conversation, which ranged from Tony Blair and the "new" Labour Party to amusing stories of long-departed dons known for their annoying or endearing eccentricities. Much to my surprise I was having a splendid evening. What might appear from outside to be a formal and even stuffy occasion was, in fact, a warm and cordial encounter of colleagues and strangers sharing stories, good food, and wine, not necessarily in that order of importance. I understood why Ted loved Oxford, and why that love was well requited.

Before I knew it, the Dean stood. The rest of us rose with a noisy shuffling of large wooden chairs. The Dean dismissed the table with the briefest of benedictions—*Benedicas, benedicat*—and we filed back downstairs to the Senior Common Room for coffee and after-dinner drinks.

I had coffee because I wanted to be alert, and because I still had questions to put to Sir Jeremiah. Somehow we had become separated, and I found myself making polite small-talk with people I'd not met before.

"Looking for Jeremiah?" a voice asked from behind. It was Thompson.

"Yes, have you seen him?"

"Just saw him leaving. His driver took him home. He asked me to convey his regrets to you. He was sorry to leave so abruptly, but the meal was a bit rich for him. His digestive system isn't what it used to be. Nor, I must say, is mine. This new chef will kill us all. But at least we'll die with smiles on our chubby faces."

Thompson's cadences, and his impish sense of humor, reminded me of Ted. So too did his dress and demeanor. He had a military bearing and looked very fit. His dark suit, starched blue-pinstripe shirt, and carefully knotted regimental tie could almost have been a uniform. We sat in a corner and talked about the changes that had come to Christ Church since my time at Oxford.

"We now have women undergraduates at the House. I was opposed at first—thought they'd be a distraction. And so, I suppose, they are, though a rather agreeable one overall. But the best thing about having them here is that they keep this lot of loutish oarsmen on their toes. Our women get more Firsts than the men, relative to their numbers. They're really very good, and a delight to teach."

I told Thompson about Ted's daughter Jessica, and how she was having a hard time accepting her father's death. A look of genuine concern crossed his face.

"Terrible to lose a parent, particularly one as young and vital as Teddy Porter." Thompson paused, rolling his brandy snifter between his hands. "Would it help, do you think, if I wrote to his daughter, saying how much I and my colleagues cherished his company and mourn his passing?"

I was touched. "That's very kind of you. I'm sure she would welcome even the briefest of notes. Her name is Jessica. Here's her address." I wrote both on the back of my card and handed it to him.

"Look at the time," he said. "My dear wife will wonder what's happened to me. Do you have a car?" I said I didn't. "Do you need a lift?" I said I did. "Then come with me."

With a loud grinding of gears the blue Vauxhall leapt out of the Christ Church car park and into St. Aldates and the meandering one-way street system behind the Westgate Shopping Centre, between Worcester and Nuffield colleges, along Beaumont Street and up the Banbury Road. As we sped past North Parade and then Park Town to Bardwell Road, Thompson said, "That's where I live. You must come to tea and meet my wife." I thanked him for the invitation and told him I wasn't sure how much longer I would be in Oxford, but would come if I could. The blue Vauxhall careened around the corner and into Wycliffe Close. The speed of the ride reminded me of an earlier trip in Uncle Fred's pick-up.

I thanked Thompson for the ride and said good-night. As I entered the building I thought of Danielle lying sleepily in bed, awaiting my return. I had had enough good wine to shed my inhibitions. "Perhaps tonight . . .," I thought as I unlocked the door.

12

The lights were off, the flat completely dark. I flipped the hall light switch. "Danielle?," I called out. No answer. I tiptoed into the dining room, then the bedroom. I turned on the bedside lamp. And there she lay, like a young girl at rest, her face serene, her dark hair tousled, one breast half bared but the rest of her covered by the disheveled sheets, as though she'd thrashed through a nightmare, now happily ended. I turned off the light, crept into the bathroom and brushed my teeth. In the darkened bedroom I undressed and crawled into bed beside Danielle. The fingers of my right hand ran through her thick curly hair; the fingers of my left touched her knee, moved up and between her downy thighs, and felt the slightly moist pubic hair where they came together.

Alive and aroused, I felt myself ready to enter her world, if not as a citizen then at least as an eager visitor. My inhibitions had been shed. I wanted Danielle as I had never wanted any woman, and all the consequences be damned. My tongue caressed her ear, her lips, her nose, her eyelids.

Her eyelashes fluttered. I felt her eyes open, and kissed her hard. But still she didn't move. She had told me she was a deep sleeper, hard to awaken. I tried hard to wake her. I shook her, whispered and then shouted her name. Nothing. I turned on the light.

Danielle's eyes were open. She was dead.

I gagged, and ran to the bathroom, barely reaching the toilet bowl before vomiting cucumber soup and chunks of salmon. I couldn't stop shaking. I wrapped myself in a blanket from the guest room. Although temperature wasn't the problem, I continued to tremble like someone suffering from hypothermia.

The police. I had to call the police. But I could hardly talk. And in any case what would I say? "Here is this young French woman, half my age, my dead friend's former lover, whom I've known for less than a week. We're sharing this flat, this bed, and we've been lovers, more or less. Now she's dead in my bed. But not to worry: I didn't kill her." I tried saying it aloud. All that came out was a low chatchatchattering sound.

Then The Calm came over me. Of course I had to call the police. And of course they would suspect foul play and—equally obviously—I would be their prime suspect. So my first call would not be to the police. To put it crudely and self-interestedly, I needed an alibi, someone to vouch for my whereabouts, so that the police could get on the trail of the real killer. And who might that be? I had no idea, save for two fundamental suspicions: first, that whoever killed Danielle had also killed Ted; and second, that I was almost certainly next. Someone who had had it in for Ted was now killing those closest to him. Had I not been at dinner at Christ Church the killer would doubtless have scored a double hit. I pulled the blanket tightly around my torso.

Somehow I knew what to do. In slow motion I re-entered the bedroom, pulled the sheet back and looked for marks—bruises, wounds, anything—on Danielle's body. My untrained eyes saw nothing but a beautiful body emptied of life. Her big toes seemed slightly bruised—the result, I thought, of wearing sandals on our walk through Port

Meadow, and doubtless stubbing her toes on the rocks and pebbles protruding from the dirt path. Odder still, and unlike last night, Danielle had gone to bed tonight still wearing her bright bangly bracelets. Most obvious and distracting of all, Danielle's eyes were still open, staring, vacant. I pulled the sheet up over her head. Then I looked around the flat for signs of a forced entry, a struggle, anything out of the ordinary. Doors and windows closed and locked. Nothing broken. Everything seemed to be in its place. Finally I turned the pages of the Oxford telephone directory to the T's, to Thompson, M.S.P.

"Hello, and do you know what time it is?," a distinctly irritated male voice answered.

"I'm sorry. I know it's late, and I hardly know you," I replied, "but I don't know who else to call."

"You're the American—Davis, is that you?"

"Yes."

"What's the matter, man, are you ill? Did our chef get to you, too?"

"I wish it were that simple," I said. "No, I'm not ill. I don't know how to tell you this, and on hearing what I have to say you might wish to hang up. And I wouldn't blame you if you did."

"This sounds serious. Do go on."

"After you dropped me off tonight, I found a dead woman in my flat."

"A what?"

"A woman. A dead woman."

"How did she get in there?"

"She was already here. You see, she . . ."

"Already there? I'm afraid I don't . . ."

"She shared the flat with me."

There was a pause. "I see," he said, clearly not seeing.

"It's a long story. She is—she was—a young French woman, Ted's friend, his lover, actually, and my new, um, friend, here to help me sort out some of the details of Ted's death."

"I see. And now she's dead."

"Yes."

"You must ring the police."

"I know. I wanted to call you first. I'm not sure why. It's just that you seem, I don't know, solid, trustworthy. I'm sorry. You remind me of Ted."

A long embarrassed silence followed.

"Ring the police. I'll get dressed and be there in ten minutes."

Thompson and the Thames Valley Police constable arrived at almost the same time.

Even in his well-pressed black uniform P. C. Barton looked too young—or perhaps too innocent—to be a policeman. Bright reddish-orange hair, freckles, not yet thirty, I'd guess. He took my name and address, then Thompson's. He asked to see the body. I led him into the bedroom. Thompson waited in the dining room.

"What time did you find the body?," Barton asked matter-of-factly as he pulled the sheet back from Danielle's face. Her eyes were still open. He closed them.

"Sometime around eleven," I answered.

"Could you be more precise, sir?"

I leaned into the hall and called to the dining room. "Martin, what time did you drop me this evening?"

"About ten to eleven. I got home just as the clock struck the hour."

P. C. Barton made a note in his black spiral notebook. He looked up. "What is the young woman's name?"

"Her first name is Danielle. Last name Dupin."

"Would you mind spelling that, sir?"

"Dupin. D-U-P-I-N."

"Present address?"

"Sorry, I don't know. Somewhere in Paris. But she was a student at Pembroke College a year or two back, so they might know."

"Nationality?"

"French."

"Next of kin?"

I hesitated, because I didn't know.

P. C. Barton looked up and asked sympathetically, "Would that be yourself, sir? Is she your daughter?"

I felt a fierce stabbing pain under my ribs. "No, she isn't my daughter. She's my . . . my friend."

"Your friend?" He looked distinctly skeptical.

"Look," I said, "it's really rather complicated. Danielle Dupin is my friend because she is—she was—the girlfriend of my old friend Ted Porter."

"And where might I find this Mr. Porter?"

"You won't. He's dead."

"I'm sorry, sir," P. C. Barton said, putting his notebook down, "but this is a bit confusing. Now this Mr. Porter—when did he die?"

"Almost a week—six days—ago. In Paris."

"And Mr. Porter's death was due to . . . what?"

"Electrocution," I said with my best poker face. "Accidental electrocution." To tell the whole truth as I suspected it seemed somehow unwise. "Ask the Parisian police."

"Right. You can be sure we will. Now, let's see. Mr. Porter dies in Paris. And less than a week later his . . . his young woman dies in Oxford, in the flat—in the bed—of his friend, that is, of yourself. Am I right so far, sir?"

"You are." Bad as they were, to hear the bare facts recounted in P. C. Barton's flat Midlands accent made them appear even worse.

He picked up his notebook and resumed writing. He stopped when a ruddy-faced man in a baggy gray suit came in.

"Hello, Chief Inspector," Barton said. "Sorry to call you away. This could be a complicated one. The dead woman is French. Her . . . um . . . her friend here, he's American."

The Chief Inspector nodded indifferently at me and said in a distinct Scottish burr, "My name's Grant. And you are . . .?

"Davis. Jack Davis," I said, putting out my hand. It remained suspended in midair as Grant turned to speak to Barton. They exchanged a few whispered words I couldn't quite make out. Then P. C. Barton looked directly at me, and said, "I'm sorry, sir. Just doing our job." With that he pulled the sheet all the way back to the foot of the bed. Danielle's beautiful lifeless body became an object of official scrutiny. I couldn't bear to watch. I left the room.

Thompson was seated at the dining table. He had discovered the cognac, and had poured two glasses.

"I thought you might need this," he said, holding out one of the glasses. "I know I do."

The door opened. A thin worried-looking man entered, carrying a black bag. "Medical Examiner," he said in a monotone as he walked past us. He closed the bedroom door behind him.

I sipped the cognac and tried, none too coherently, to tell Thompson what I had been up to—my suspicions about the circumstances surrounding Ted's death, about Danielle's unexpected arrival, the help she had given me . . . and about my being attracted to her in spite of my long involvement with another woman I loved, how I was about to make love to Danielle when I discovered she was dead, both of us naked in bed.

"Sorry, old boy, I'm not sure I want to hear this. It's really none of my business. Or at least it wasn't until you rang me, so now I suppose it is. But this seems one hell of a cock-up."

His words were harsh but true. Understated, even. It was a hell of a cock-up, and I knew it. I'd left Danielle alone and in the dark, figuratively if not literally. I hadn't shared my suspicions with her because, my libido notwithstanding, I didn't know whether to trust her. And besides, I somehow thought that my silence would protect her. Instead I had left her vulnerable and exposed. And now she was dead.

"Mr. Davis?" It was the Chief Inspector. "May I have a word with you? Alone, if you please." We stepped into the hall.

"Was the front door locked when you came back?" he asked.

"Yes. And the back door, too."

"Any sign of forced entry—windows or doors?"

"No."

"Does anyone else have a key to the flat?"

"Only the cleaning service."

"Is anything of value missing—jewels, silverware, electronic equipment, anything?"

"No. There are no valuables, really, except the TV and the stereo. And they're both here."

"Was anything overturned or out of place?"

"Nothing I could see."

"Have you or the young woman received any threats?"

"No, none."

"Have you had any suspicious encounters with anyone?"

"No."

"Does she—did she—have a jealous boyfriend or lover?"

"Not that I'm aware of," I answered. "Her only lover, so far as I know, was my late friend Ted Porter."

"Were"—here he hesitated—"you and she lovers?"

"Not really," I answered. "Well, maybe. I mean, I guess you might say we were. Sort of."

Grant's heavy eyelids raised, revealing bloodshot light-blue eyes and a skeptical glint. "How do you mean, exactly?"

"Well, we tried. I mean, I tried. Tried everything. I didn't succeed. Mechanically, if you know what I mean."

He paused. "So you were frustrated? Angry, perhaps?"

"No," I said. "Well, frustrated, yes. I mean, who wouldn't be? And angry too, I guess. Angry at myself. Not at Danielle. Please don't misunderstand my meaning."

Events—innocent events, if you can call them that—were open to interpretations at once more banal and more sinister than any I dared even imagine.

"I must ask that you not go far away," the Inspector said *sotto voce.* "If you don't mind, sir, I'll need your passport. Just a formality, you understand."

I understood only too well. They suspected foul play, I was their only suspect, and they wanted me close at hand for as long as it pleased them. I went to the hall closet and dug my passport out of my coat pocket. I felt my hand tremble as I handed it to him. Memories of a law school seminar in Comparative Legal Systems came flooding back. None of this "rights of the accused" stuff in England. No prohibition on "unreasonable searches and seizures." No Miranda warning. No Bill of Rights, even.

"We'll need to take your fingerprints, sir. If you've no objection."

I knew it didn't matter if I did have an objection, so I submitted. Grant led me into the kitchen where P. C. Barton was waiting with a fingerprinting kit. It was the first time I'd been fingerprinted since I was arrested at an anti-Vietnam war protest at Columbia in 1971. He rolled the thumb of my right hand over an ink blotter, then over a rectangle labelled Right Thumb, repeating for the remaining four fingers of my right and the five fingers of my left hand. Then he gave me two sections of paper towel.

"How did she die?," I asked, trying without much success to wipe the ink from my fingers.

"Too early to say, sir," Inspector Grant said. "The Medical Examiner will do his tests tomorrow. Then, if necessary, he'll order an autopsy. We should know something in two or three days."

Two or three days: it seemed an eternity. I wasn't sure I'd live that long. In the meantime I had a lifetime's work to do.

◄ 13 ►

Shortly before 1 a.m. they took Danielle away on a stainless steel gurney, covered in a sheet. Her clothing, her purse, and suitcase and the bed linens were carried alongside in large plastic bags. By this time the residents of Wycliffe Close were aroused and awake, peering from behind parted curtains and shooting curious and accusing stares at Thompson and me as we watched the ambulance pull away.

"Mr. Davis," a burred Scottish voice addressed me from behind. I turned around and saw Inspector Grant, hands in pockets, shambling toward me. "You might wish to spend the night elsewhere. A hotel, perhaps, or a bed and breakfast. P. C. Barton can help with the arrangements."

"Must I?" I asked. "I mean, is it absolutely necessary?"

"No, not absolutely necessary," Grant said, frowning. He didn't take well to being crossed. "But advisable nonetheless. You won't have access to your bedroom. We've sealed it off until further notice. You're not to go in there under any circumstance, for any reason. Is that understood?"

"Yes," I replied. "Perfectly."

"Come home with me, Davis," Thompson interjected. "It might not be safe here. And in any event this place is freighted with . . . with unpleasant associations. We've a guest room. We'll put you up."

"I'd take your friend up on his offer," Grant chimed in. "For tonight, anyway."

I was tempted. Sorely tempted. But I resisted, repeatedly and firmly. Neither Thompson nor Grant appeared to approve of my stubbornness. Grant grimaced, turned on his heel, and walked over to P. C. Barton's patrol car. The police radio squawked with static and the voices of dispatchers and cops. Grant lit a cigarette, using it to motion in my direction. P. C. Barton shook his head and got into his patrol car, where he sat for a minute or so, making more entries in his notebook. Then he drove away, followed by Grant in an unmarked car.

"One last chance, old boy," Thompson said. "Come stay with us, if only for tonight. Please. You're very welcome. Really."

"Thanks, Martin. I'm grateful. Really, I am. But not tonight."

"As you wish, then. Ring me if you need anything," he said, walking to his car. The blue Vauxhall crept quietly away.

Back inside the flat, I noticed that my suitcase had been moved into the hall. The bedroom door had a blue and white striped plastic ribbon taped over it. Stuck to the door was a posted notice. "Police Investigation Site. Do Not Enter." The door had a tamper-proof metal gadget attached to the handle and jamb. I locked and then barred the outside doors, double locked the windows, and got the large carving knife out of its dark wooden case.

I knew what I had to do. I had to call Grace.

It was just after eight in the evening in New York. But because today was the weekly partners' meeting everyone would be working late. I dialled the country code, then the area code, and then the number. The switchboard was still open.

"Anderson Davis Stein and O'Brien," a perky voice answered. It was Linda, our new receptionist, big bosom, no bra, small brain, and spiky reddish hair done in a topknot that made her look like a less pleasant Woody Woodpecker. She had a tattoo on her ankle and an attitude to match. Linda had been hired over my objections because of Dick O'Brien's insistence and everyone else's knowledge, or at least strong suspicion, that she and Dick were lovers. Worse still, I was genuinely fond of Dick's wife, who looked after the children, the house, and the horses in Connecticut. As a senior partner I had a veto, which a more moral man would have exercised without flinching. But because I was not myself as pure as the Pope in these matters, I demurred. The chattering airhead was hired.

"Hello, Linda. Jack Davis. Could you connect me with Grace Wu, please?" I used her last name deliberately, to introduce a note of decorum into the thought of one to whom all formality was foreign.

"Gracie? Oh, sure. Just a sec." I heard the sound of chewing-gum popping as she connected me with Nate Stein's secretary, and then with Bob Anderson's.

"Try Jack Davis's secretary," I suggested.

Linda emitted a high-pitched high-school giggle. She was thirty-three, going on thirteen.

Finally Grace answered. "Mr. Davis's office. Grace Wu speaking." Ah, dignity. Decorum. A woman who acts her age.

"Grace," I said.

"Jack!," she all but shrieked. "Where are you? I've been trying to raise you for two days. You haven't replied to any of my e-mails. And when I've called your phone just rings and rings, with never an answer. What's wrong?"

"I'm not in Paris, love. I'm in Oxford. I forgot my lap-top. Left it in Paris. So I can't access the Internet. I'm sorry."

"Oh, Jack, you had me worried. I've hardly slept at all."

"What I have to tell you won't help you sleep any better."

"So . . . you already know?," she said.

I was caught off guard. "Know what?"

"About the computer?"

"Computer? What computer?"

"Ted's computer. The Toshiba lap-top that you sent to me. Al had it analyzed at the lab." Al is Alberto Morales, ex-New York City Police detective turned private eye who seems to know everyone and about everything. The lab is the exclusive (and for my money too-expensive) Dietz Laboratories in York, Pennsylvania that would put the FBI lab to shame. "Two things. First, the computer can be traced only so far. The serial number belongs to one of several stolen last December from Nagoya University in Japan. The Japanese police suspect that the thieves had inside information and help, probably from a faculty or staff member. But they can't prove anything. And, what's more, the power pack had definitely been tampered with. Someone had removed the insulating cover on one side, replacing the plastic with metal, which was then repainted with an electric-conductive paint that looked like the original. Then the internal circuit was reversed—rewired—so that instead of reducing the outgoing current, the transformer increased it nearly ten-fold. French current is 220 volts. Ten times 220 equals 2,200 volts. The power pack became, in effect, an electric grenade, ready to kill anyone who touched it and a ground at the same time."

"You said two things. What was the other thing?"

Grace paused. "The girl. This Danielle Dupin."

"Yes, what about her?"

"She packed the computer, right?"

"Right. As a favor."

"Her fingerprints were all over it."

"Well, of course. So what?"

"We had the computer analyzed for prints."

"What? Why?"

"Call it female intuition," Grace said. "Call it what you like—jealousy, even." I felt both flattered and annoyed.

"And?"

She drew a deep breath, exhaling slowly as she spoke. "The prints did not belong to Danielle Dupin. If there *is* a Danielle Dupin. Al ran them through the InterPol files. They belong to someone called—unless of course this, too, is an alias—Jeanne-Marie Masson. No criminal record, but she has a French passport and other official papers, including a surety bond for fifty million francs—she works at a bank in Paris—and so the French police have her prints. The French state bureaucracy never forgets a name, as you know."

I knew that, though I didn't want to believe anything else Grace was saying. But I didn't want to doubt her, either. I felt my world coming unglued.

Who had died in my bed?

"Grace?"

"Yes?"

"This is all news to me. I don't know what to say. There's probably some perfectly innocent explanation. People change their names all the time, for all sorts of reasons," I said without quite believing it. "But something else has happened."

There was a pause. "What else? Jack, you sound awful. What's happened?"

"The girl—Danielle—she's dead. She died here. In my bed. Tonight. While I was away, at dinner at Christ Church. It might be murder. The police suspect me."

Silence. And then a torrent of despair and disbelief. "Mary, Mother of Jesus! Holy Mother of Jesus! Jack!" That was as close to swearing as Grace ever came. Her voice trailed off, her tone incredulous, upset, dismayed. And angry. Very angry.

"I have a lot to tell you, love, and a lot to explain. I hardly know where to begin. And when I've finished you might never want to see me again."

"I'll be the judge of that, Jack."

I came clean. I told Grace everything. How I was attracted to Danielle, how she asked to accompany me to Oxford, how I readily agreed, how we'd ended up in bed, how I'd failed because I was thinking of Grace and feeling guilty, how I'd met with Altmann, how . . .

"Jack," Grace said evenly, "I'm not sure what to say. I've got to think this through. I hate to admit it, but I'm jealous. Yes, I am. But more than that, I'm worried. About you. You're in over your head, Jack. Things are out of control. Please come back home. Please." A pause. "Oxford is close to Heathrow, right?"

"Yes, about an hour away. Why?"

"Because I want you to take a taxi to Heathrow, now, and be on the first plane to New York tomorrow."

I wanted more than anything to do exactly as she said. To go home. To be safe. To be back with the only woman I'd ever loved.

"I can't, Grace."

"Can't—or won't?" She sounded suspicious, hurt, angry.

"Can't. I don't have a passport."

"What? Of course you have a passport! You just . . ."

"No, Grace, listen, please. The police have my passport. They don't want me to leave. They won't let me out of here until they're good and ready. I don't know when that might be. And besides, I'm not ready to leave. I have more business here and back in Paris. For Ted. I owe it to him. I can't come home. Not yet. Not until I have some answers."

A silence, and then the small stifled sobbing sound that came so rarely from Grace's throat. "I know, darling Jack. I know. I'm afraid for you, and I feel so helpless here."

I felt a large lump in my throat. "If it's any comfort, I feel pretty helpless here."

"Cold comfort," Grace said.

◀ 14 ▶

The phone rang. And rang. And rang. I looked at my watch. 11:10. Daylight streamed through the guest bedroom windows. The phone continued to ring in that mildly irritating double-staccato way that English phones do.

"Yes, Hello? Jack Davis."

"My dear Davis, I am most dreadfully sorry. I do owe you an apology for last evening." It was Altmann. "Martin may have told you. I had one of my bouts. Not too bad, fortunately, and I'm well enough now. My only remaining pain resides in the recognition that I abandoned my guest last evening. Do let me make it up to you."

"No need to apologize," I said through a sleepy-sunny, somewhat stunned haze. "But I would like to ask you some more questions, if I may."

"By all means. Fire away." He was as prepared for the day as I was not.

"Not over the phone, if you don't mind. I know you're busy, and I don't like to . . ."

"Why not come to tea this afternoon?"

"Yes, thanks. I will." We agreed to meet at 4:30 at the House and then said good-bye. That was surprisingly easy, I thought. The hard part was that I wasn't sure what questions to put to Sir Jeremiah, or how much, if anything, I should say about what had happened last night. My moral credit rating was at an all-time low with my lover, my erstwhile allies—and certainly with the police.

I tried to go back to sleep, but it was no use. My mind was racing, returning again and again to the events of last evening, which already seemed like a dream. I half expected Danielle to walk through the door, bringing me breakfast.

But Danielle was dead. Doubly dead. The woman I knew as Danielle Dupin was actually somebody else, and both were now dead. And the fault was doubly mine, first for bringing her here to Oxford with me, and then for leaving her alone last night. If only I'd said no, she couldn't come. If only I'd insisted on coming to Oxford alone. If only I'd not gone out last night. The if-onlys kept playing in my head and I couldn't get rid of them.

I got up, made coffee, and stepped into the back garden. I felt the cool and still-dewy grass underfoot and between my toes, and was for a moment a small boy back on the farm in Oklahoma, barefoot and carefree. Of course that is something of a myth that I've created by blocking out the bad memories and exaggerating the good ones. In that sense, I suppose, it's a place that has more in common with the Rogers and Hammerstein musical than with the real Oklahoma of my childhood. But that's okay, because I need that place. That's where my mind returns and takes refuge whenever I'm sad or troubled, as I often am. But I had never been this sad or this troubled before. Death was all around me. And yet—this seems surprising to say—I felt intensely alive in that moment. I too might die. But I was on a quest. A mission. My life, or what was left of it, had a meaning, a point, a purpose.

◄ 15 ►

For the second time in as many days I was back in Sir Jeremiah's rooms. Wisps of steam escaped up the spout of the gleaming silver teapot, being warmed over a candle-lit heater. Beads of silvery sweat enveloped the small pitcher of cold milk.

"Sugar?"

"Yes, thanks."

"One lump or two?"

"One, please."

"Milk?"

"No, thank you."

Sir Jeremiah's large hands contrasted sharply with the delicate china teacup and saucer he handed to me. He offered a plate of cucumber sandwiches sliced into small wedges. Remembering my meal from last night, I declined. I had developed a dislike for cucumbers.

"I've been thinking about your suspicion," he said as he poured a cup for himself. "And I can see why you harbor it. But the more I consider it, the less likely it seems to me that Teddy was murdered. Perhaps the police were right. Teddy's death was an accident. I can imagine several 'scenarios', as they say nowadays. Perhaps curiosity got the better of him and he decided to see what all this commotion over computers was about. He decided to try one on for size, just for a lark, as Teddy would. He didn't know much about their workings, didn't understand the danger that could come from the . . . what do you call that?"

"Power pack."

"Yes, the power pack. He was adept at many things, but Teddy's acquaintance with modern technology was, shall we say, nodding at best. He didn't appreciate the danger; he mishandled the device; and it killed him. Accidents do happen, you know. Ockham suggests that this was an accident."

Ockham? Then I remembered Ockham's Razor—roughly, the principle that, given several plausible explanations of the same event, the simplest is to be preferred.

"Ockham's wrong," I said with a vehemence that surprised us both. "In this instance, dead wrong. Since we spoke yesterday I've learned several new facts. My legal assistant had the computer and the power pack analyzed by a high-powered lab in the States. For one, the serial numbers on the computer and power pack belong to equipment stolen from a university in Japan. For another, the power pack had been tampered with—sabotaged, actually—in such a way that it became a lethal weapon. Someone went to a lot of trouble to kill Ted and to disguise the fact that it was murder." I didn't want to upset Sir Jeremiah by adding that another death, maybe a murder, had followed the first, and that he was at this very moment having tea with the prime suspect.

Sir Jeremiah rose slowly and walked to the window overlooking Tom Quad. He was silent for a long while. Finally he said, "This certainly sheds new light—or perhaps I should say it casts new and darker shadows—on Teddy's death. I had very nearly convinced myself that you were mistaken. Or perhaps I had simply hoped that you were. It's just that I find it so . . . so damnably difficult to believe that anyone would murder our friend. So vital he was." Altmann's large head dropped almost to his chest. "So very vital," he repeated, almost inaudibly.

After a long moment of mutually embarrassing silence, I barely managed to say, "Just because we loved him didn't mean that Ted was universally loved. He had enemies. One of them hated him enough to kill him. I want to find out who that is. That's why I need your help."

Sir Jeremiah turned away from the window and looked directly at me, his face stern and drained of all color.

"My dear Davis, I assure you that I have not even the remotest idea as to who might wish Teddy dead. If I did, believe me, I would tell you—and more especially the Parisian police—at once."

Gathering my courage, I took a deep breath and said, "Remember, Sir Jeremiah, how you used to tell me, 'You already know more than you think you know'—that I knew lots of fragments but that I had not yet connected and put them together in any coherent or patterned way?"

"Yes. I tell all my pupils that. And in most instances it's quite true."

"Well, if you don't mind my saying so, I think you know more than you think you know about the circumstances surrounding Ted's death. You've helped me with a couple of fragments. But I don't yet have enough pieces to put together. All I have so far is an explanation of the abbreviation 'Inst pol' and what appears to be the combination to a safe. I'd like, if I may, to enlist your help in unearthing and piecing together some other fragments."

I sound like a lawyer, I thought.—An inept lawyer. I had a pen to take notes with but no paper to write on.

"May I borrow some note paper?," I asked somewhat sheepishly. "I'd like to take notes on our conversation, if you don't mind."

"Not at all," Altmann said, opening a drawer and handing me several sheets of stationery with the Christ Church logo and letterhead. "I'm happy to help in any way I can. I'm in your hands, my dear Davis, and at your service."

"I'm fishing for fragments here, Sir Jeremiah, so please bear with me." He nodded agreeably, with something that looked like surprise, perhaps even respect, for a strength I was showing but didn't quite feel. "When did you last speak with Ted?"

"Speak with or hear from?"

"Both."

"I last spoke with Teddy some five or six months ago. He was on his way to Paris. We had dinner at my club in London. We haven't spoken since—he didn't like to talk on the telephone, as you know."

I knew only too well.

"But I did receive several letters from him. The most recent arrived about a month ago."

"What did it say?"

"Just that his work was going well. He sounded distinctly chipper. Said that he was happy to be back in Paris. And of course he teased me, as Teddy was wont to do."

"Teased you? In what way?" I couldn't imagine anyone—even Ted—teasing Sir Jeremiah Altmann.

"Would you like to see the letter?"

"If you don't mind, yes."

Sir Jeremiah rummaged through a wooden file box on his writing table. "Ah, here it is," he said, handing a blue airmail envelope to me.

I recognized the handwriting immediately. I pulled a two-page letter out of the envelope. To my dismay it was in French. "Mon cher maître," it began.

"My dear master?"

"Yes, it was Teddy's standard form of address to me. Ironic and teasing at the same time, and yet respectful in its way. You know Teddy."

I did, but we had always communicated in English. I puzzled and mumbled my way through the letter. Thank heaven it was short. *Je suis heureux à retourner à Paris,* "I'm happy to be back in Paris . . . work is going well," something about some archival research at the Bibliothèque Nationale, etc. Then the closing line: *Vos chers amis à la Société de J.-J. envoyient leurs salutations les plus cordiales.* "Your dear friends at the Société de something-or-other send their warmest greetings," I read aloud.

"That's the Société de Jean-Jacques."

"That, I assume, is a professional organization to which you both belong?"

Altmann laughed in the deep chesty way I'd heard only once or twice before. "Hardly. No, it's more of Teddy's teasing, I'm afraid."

If there was a joke here, I wasn't getting it. "So if it isn't a professional society, what is it? I mean, the name itself sounds strange. To use Rousseau's first name only strikes me as awfully familiar, maybe even disrespectful . . ."

"No, not at all. You see, Rousseau regularly refers to himself as Jean-Jacques—and he invited and even encouraged that sense of familiarity among his readers. He was the first celebrity to be known instantly and universally by his first name."

"Oh, you mean like Sting. Or Cher. Or Madonna."

"Who?"

"Never mind. They're modern pop stars."

"I see," he said offhandedly. Clearly Sir Jeremiah was no devotée of popular culture, a phrase which he might well regard as an oxymoron.

"Tell me more," I asked, "about this Jean-Jacques Society."

"Ah, dear me, where to begin? It's certainly not a professional society, as you so politely put it. It's more like a . . . a cult, if that's not too strong a term. It rather resembles some of the Romantic cults whose members worshipped at the shrine of Rousseau in the late eighteenth and well into the nineteenth century. They saw Rousseau as a saint, the noble and selfless savior of the emotions, of feeling, from the acid bath of the Enlightenment, of science, of modernity. On the occasion of various anniversaries they would gather at his tomb on the Isle des Peupliers and later—after the French revolutionary government moved his remains—at the Panthéon in Paris and read aloud from his works and weep copious tears of grief and gratitude, and garland his grave with flowers."

"And that's what this Société de Jean-Jacques does?"

"No, not exactly. At least not so far as I am aware. They resemble the earlier Rousseau cults in that they see him as a saint and savior who showed the way out of the modern world—the world of skepticism, of scientism, of rationalism and unfeeling reason—and back to a purer, more primitive world of authentic emotions, of untutored intuitions, of feelings uncorrupted by reason or rationality or science. But there the resemblance ends. The Société de Jean-Jacques fancies itself as a scholarly society devoted to the study of Rousseau's *oeuvre*."

"Nothing wrong with that, surely?"

"Nothing wrong in the abstract, certainly. But there is *au fond* something rather . . . rather—what was Teddy's word?—something rather nutty, yes, that's it, nutty about the premises from which they proceed."

"And what premises are those?"

"That Rousseau wrote in some sort of secret code to which they alone possess the key. Therefore those not in possession of that key—Teddy and myself, amongst many, many others—haven't a clue as to what Rousseau 'really' meant. Rousseau's real meaning, they say, is encrypted and has to be decoded by the *cognoscenti*. As best I can understand it, this involves knowing—or claiming to know—the significance of certain combinations or juxtapositions of numbers and names and such. All this is in any event really rather fatuous in the face of quite stellar work that's been done by Derathé, Starobinski, Wokler, Riley, Miller, Cranston, and of course Teddy, amongst other modern scholars. But the Société nevertheless insists on its peculiar numerological reading of Rousseau, whom they see as a conduit to *la sagesse antique*—'the ancient wisdom'."

"And that's incorrect?"

"Not incorrect, exactly," Altmann answered. "But debatable. Highly debatable. One could also argue, as Nietzsche does, that Rousseau was 'the first modern man'—the nervous, dyspeptic, self-pitying, endlessly introspective exemplar of modern selfhood. Anxious for the approval of others, yet scornful of those who bestow it and suspicious of those who do not. That, at any rate, is the Rousseau of the *Confessions*. The Rousseau of the *Social Contract* praises the ancient republican virtues of self-denial and service to the public good. The various works of Rousseau are rich enough—or, his critics contend, confused enough—to support these conflicting interpretations, and many others besides."

"So let me see if I understand what you're saying. The Société de Jean-Jacques holds that Rousseau shows the way back to ancient truths. Through some sort of secret trap-door that nobody else knows about . . ."

Sir Jeremiah leaned forward, slapping his knee and smiling broadly. "Very well put. Well put indeed, my dear Davis. A trap-door. Yes. Exactly. I must remember that."

For one brief shining moment I felt like an undergraduate, basking in the glow of his tutor's approval.

Then I remembered. I wasn't an undergraduate. Nor was Sir Jeremiah my tutor. Our business was more urgent, the stakes higher. Very much higher. Like life and death.

"Are there," I asked, "any other noteworthy aspects of the Société—any peculiarities of approach or presentation that I should know about?"

"Nothing serious, so far as substance is concerned. They do of course have their own peculiarity of style, although I doubt . . ."

"Style?," I interrupted. "Prose style? Writing style? What?"

"No, not that," Altmann answered. "I refer to their manner of address."

I had no idea what he meant. Do they, like Quakers, address each other as "thee" and "thou," or what? My confusion obviously registered on my face.

Sir Jeremiah smiled. "Sorry, I should perhaps explain that members of the Société engage in their own unique—and, I must say, somewhat silly—kind of name-calling."

"How do you mean? What kind of names?"

Almost smiling, Sir Jeremiah looked owlishly over the top of his horn-rim spectacles. "One of the more bizarre practices of the Société is that its members take the surnames of Rousseau's friends and allies—the founder and head calls himself Roguin, after Rousseau's faithful friend and protector Daniel Roguin—and they call their critics by the names of Rousseau's real or imagined enemies. I'm told they call me Voltaire, after Rousseau's nemesis and *bête noire.*" He paused, and then chuckled. "It's really rather flattering, now that I think about it."

"And Ted—what do they call Ted?"

"Hume. After the Scottish philosopher David Hume, who tried—unsuccessfully, in the end—to befriend and help Rousseau. Hume brought Rousseau to England to escape persecution and possible imprisonment. He went out of his way to protect and to fête his new friend. But perhaps while in one of his paranoid delusional states Rousseau became convinced that Hume was a *faux ami* who was plotting to destroy him."

"Rousseau was paranoid?"

"Not always or consistently, no, certainly not. He was for the most part lucid, a self-educated genius of the rarest insight—a novelist, composer, playwright, philosopher, political theorist—but he was on occasion quite mad."

"Insane, you mean?"

"That I am not qualified to say. The great Swiss psychiatrist and Rousseau scholar Starobinski concluded that Rousseau was almost certainly insane in his last years, from the mid-1760s until his death in 1778. Of course Rousseau did have real enemies, so his delusions of persecution were not entirely without foundation. Nevertheless—so Starobinski says—Rousseau blew these out of proportion. Many, though not all, of the demons who pursued him were in his own mind. Other scholars, such as Jean Guèhenno, contend that Rousseau's mental illness was at least augmented, if not caused, by his physical problem."

"What physical problem?"

Looking slightly uncomfortable, Altmann paused. "Rousseau, you see, suffered from a . . . a medical condition. From uremic poisoning . . . Do you really want to know about this?"

"Yes, I do. Please go on."

"Very well, then. Rousseau had a problem in passing urine that grew worse as he got older. He wore catheters, which often proved more a hindrance than a help, and had to cover these with a flowing gown and, later, an Armenian caftan. The late Dr. Elosu, in a still-controversial book about Rousseau's illness published in the late 1920s, I believe—*La maladie de Rousseau* was its title—reconstructed Rousseau's medical history in meticulous detail from Rousseau's own letters and diaries and of course his *Confessions*." Was there, I wondered as he spoke, any book that Sir Jeremiah Altmann *hasn't* read? "Dr. Elosu was a physician first, and a self-taught Rousseau scholar only secondarily, both of which are surely to her credit. She concluded that the toxins in Rousseau's blood would from time to time have risen to dangerously high levels, threatening not only his physical but his mental health. It was during these periods that he was at his most paranoid and delusional. He saw plots and plotters, conspiracies and conspirators, everywhere."

"And Rousseau scholars find her explanation convincing?"

"Some do, yes. Others don't. You see, some of Rousseau's admirers were quick to seize on Dr. Elosu's explanation because, they believe, it excuses Rousseau. The 'real' Rousseau, they claim, was kindly, caring, generous to a fault—which is of course Rousseau's own view of himself in the *Confessions*. But on those occasions when he behaved badly—as Rousseau so frequently did—it must be because of his medical condition. On this view Rousseau is granted a sort of posthumous medical absolution for his bad behavior—his pettiness, his paranoia, his suspicions about almost everyone. You can see how very convenient this is for his more uncritical admirers."

"It all sounds somewhat complicated. Where do you stand? With his admirers—or his detractors?"

"With both, I suppose. Although I am not of course a medical doctor I do think there is something to Dr. Elosu's explanation. But I also agree with Starobinski that the exaggerated and all-encompassing excuses that some have extrapolated from—or read into—her findings are entirely unwarranted. Rousseau did on occasion behave very badly. Full stop. No excuses, no extenuations, medical or otherwise. That Rousseau was a genius—and a deeply troubled genius at that—hardly exonerates him for his all-too-human shortcomings. His life, no less than his writings, was full of paradox, not to say contradiction. At his worst he behaved abominably. At his best, however, he was capable of great nobility and generosity of spirit. No doubt some of his worst actions were prompted by the sort of paranoia that uremic poisoning can produce. The problem is, how to tell the one from the other. And on this matter I am agnostic. I simply do not know how to distinguish one bit of bad behavior from another, according to their respective underlying causes. Nor, I think, does anyone else."

"How does—how did—Hume figure in all this?"

"Ah, yes, we were speaking of Hume, weren't we? Hume had a reputation—almost certainly deserved—as the kindest and most genial of men. 'Le bon David,' the French called him. He tried his best to help the beleaguered Rousseau. But Rousseau—perhaps in one of his medically induced paranoid states, perhaps not—came to see his new friend and benefactor in a distinctively unfavorable and unflattering light. Hume, he claimed, was complicit in a massive conspiracy against him. Hume's denials only fueled Rousseau's suspicions. Rousseau left England in a huff. Poor Hume was never forgiven."

"And that's how Ted came to be called Hume—because he's considered suspect, a 'false friend', by the Société?"

"Precisely so."

"But since Rousseau was perhaps deluded in suspecting Hume, doesn't this suggest that the Société is mistaken about Ted?"

"No, not at all. At least, not on their telling. You see, they don't believe that Rousseau really was delusional. They maintain that his problem was purely physical, that it had no psychological consequences, and that the uremic poisoning was in any case brought about by doctors who were themselves part of a massive conspiracy to discredit Rousseau and destroy his reputation. Consequently, anyone whom Rousseau believed to be an enemy actually *was* an enemy—and that includes Hume."

"And so Ted is a latter-day Hume bent on bringing discredit to Rousseau."

"Exactly."

"Who are these people? I mean, where do they come from and where do they get these bizarre ideas?"

"It's a long story, my dear Davis, and I don't claim to know all the details. The Société was organized in the early 1960s by a renegade Gaussian named Merceaux . . ."

"A renegade *what*?"

"Gaussian. A follower—some would say disciple—of the late Professor Léon Gauss of the University of Chicago. Gauss taught that past political thinkers wrote in a kind of code—an Aesopian language of double or multiple meanings—in order to avoid persecution in their own day and to communicate with contemporaries and successors who knew how to read between the lines, as it were. The classics of political theory were written, so to speak, in a kind of invisible ink and their meaning becomes clear only to those who have been specially trained to see through the superficial or obvious meaning to some deeper or esoteric message. It all has to do with numbers and such . . ."

"So then Gauss is the source of Roguin's assertions about the significance of certain numbers in combination with names, and so on?"

"*A* source, yes, to be sure. But not the original one. Gauss himself harks back and is beholden to the cabalistic tradition . . ."

"I'm sorry," I interrupted. "The *what*?"

"The cabalistic tradition. The term comes from the Hebrew *qabbalah*, meaning 'received lore or wisdom'. The original Cabalists—the source of the English word 'cabal'—were mystically minded medieval rabbis who, quite rightly fearing persecution from the Christian authorities, banded together in small secret societies. They read sacred scripture in a way that assumed that ancient authors—also fearing persecution from Philistine, Egyptian, Roman and other repressive pre-Christian authorities—wrote the scriptures in a kind of code. Every passage, every phrase, every word—each letter, even—must therefore be decoded by later readers. And these decodings must themselves be encrypted to keep the unclean from learning or perverting the received wisdom. What Gauss did, essentially, was to extend this way of reading religious texts to interpreting works of political theory."

"Including works by Rousseau?"

"To be sure."

"How does this work? I mean, how do you go about reading Rousseau in this way?"

"I don't read Rousseau in that way, of course, although Gauss tried for a time to persuade me of the merit of his method. He did not succeed, however, because I believe that most authors, most of the time, mean exactly what they say and try—not always successfully—to say exactly what they mean. Gauss and his followers believe otherwise. It's supposedly significant, they say, that Rousseau refers, for instance, to a particular author in a particular footnote of a particular meaning-laden number or series of numbers. For example, the eighth footnote of the *Contrat social* refers to Machiavelli, quoting his *History of Florence*. This, the very first mention of Machiavelli in the *Social Contract*, appears in Book II, Chapter 4; note that the chapter number is twice that of the book number, and the footnote number—8—is twice that of the chapter number; each is an even number, and each a multiple of the others, and in an ascending progression—Book 2, Chapter 4, footnote 8 is the arithmetic series 2-4-8: the numerologist's equivalent, as it were, to the astrologer's ideal of the perfectly straight alignment of the stars and planets. Note next that the first number in the progression, when mulitiplied by the last, yields 16. Now the sixteenth letter of the alphabet is p, which is the first letter in the only noun in the title of Machiavelli's most notorious work, his *Il Principe—The Prince*. So, contrary to what Rousseau actually *says* to mislead the unwary and unwashed multitude, the eighth footnote doesn't 'really' refer to Machiavelli's *Discourses* at all, but to *The Prince*. If you doubt it, you need only look to the next reference to Machiavelli, which occurs in Book II, Chapter 7, footnote 13. Both seven and thirteen are odd numbers, and not in a mathematical series. Moreover—and again significantly—footnote 13 does *not* mention Machiavelli's *Prince*, but refers to his *Discourses*. For the *cognoscenti* this serves as both clue and confirmation that one is in touch with the 'real,' albeit unwritten, text underlying the words on the page. And thereby hangs a tale—much too circuitous and tortuous a tale for my taste, I'm afraid." He paused, pursing his lips and looking bemusedly over the top of his glasses. "Does this make any sense at all?"

"Yes. At least I think so."

"Very well, then. To return to my story: Merceaux was a wealthy young Frenchman who came to Chicago to study with Gauss, apparently because he found this approach attractive. He was quickly acknowledged as one of Gauss's most brilliant pupils, with a promising academic career ahead of him. I do not pretend to know what happened next. All I know is that his doctoral thesis was turned down in 1960 or thereabouts. He was later denounced and disowned by Gauss himself in a more public way before he—that is, Gauss—died in 1972. Reputable Rousseau scholars amongst Gauss's followers were, I believe, in full agreement with their master that Merceaux was brilliant but misguided if not mad. After his dissertation was rejected Merceaux returned to France, changed his name to Roguin, and founded the

Société de Jean-Jacques and served as first editor of its journal, both of which he launched with the aid of a rather considerable inheritance. Although he occupied no academic post, Merceaux/Roguin soon attracted a small but loyal band of followers. The attraction stemmed, I suspect, from a widespread disaffection, in France and elsewhere, with modern technological society, with its *mentalité* of cold calculation, of economic rationality, of spiritless materialism—and the search for an alternative, more authentic way of being in the world. Certainly Roguin was not the first to diagnose the malady—Max Weber had foreseen and despaired of the 'iron cage' of instrumental rationality and the 'cold polar night of icy hardness and darkness' half a century earlier—but Roguin's originality resided in countering the malady with the prospect of a Rousseauian cure. In effect, he founded a secret society whose members thought they had the key to unlock every door—each door being, as it were, opened by a proper reading of a text by Rousseau. It's not so different, I suppose, from some of your American organizations of the period, which originated mostly, I gather, in California—Est, Scientology, that lot—each of which had its own guru and its promise of a route to salvation in this world or the next. And of course the appeal of secret societies, from the Jewish Cabalists to Christian Freemasons and Knights Templar to the present, is something that some people find irresistible. The idea that one is privy to secrets unknown to everyone else is inevitably seductive for certain kinds of people. I am not one of them, so I cannot speak with any authority about these matters."

"Do you know Merceaux—I mean Roguin?"

"No, I've never met him, although I nearly did, once. In 1978 I was in Paris for the commemmoration of the bicentenary of Rousseau's death. It was a very grand affair. There was a reception at the Académie Française. Everyone was there—even Foucault, who was certainly no admirer of the long-departed *philosophe*—and so apparently was Roguin. But when he heard that I had arrived, I was told, he left abruptly and did not reappear all evening, nor the next day, either. He was apparently displeased by my presence, and so we never met." He paused. "The loss was more mine than his," Altmann added graciously.

"Did Ted ever meet Roguin, or have any dealings with the Société?"

"He had infrequent and informal contact with some of them from time to time, I believe, but not with Roguin. Teddy would talk with anyone who was interested in political theory, however bizarre their views. He agreed wholeheartedly with Mill that, in the clash of error with truth, our appreciation of the truth is sharpened. He was interested in errors—in what he regarded as erroneous interpretations—because they might not be so mistaken after all or, more likely, because they bring better interpretations into sharper relief. When we dined at my club—our last dinner together—Teddy told me that the Société constituted a kind of case study of Rousseau cultism, a throwback to the earlier Romantic Rousseau societies that had done so much to create *le Rousseau imaginaire*. He found the Société interesting for much the same reason that a paleontologist finds a fossil-filled rock interesting. And too, Teddy wondered whether the Société might have used part of Merceaux's millions to purchase some of Rousseau's letters and other papers that were believed to exist in private collections or had mysteriously gone missing from libraries in several countries. That suspicion resurfaces from time to time amongst Rousseau scholars; but, so far as I know, it is nothing but an idle speculation that is trotted out more for amusement than for any serious scholarly purpose. Still, in this, as in all other matters, Teddy's curiosity was insatiable."

So, I thought, was the cat's. But it had nine lives and Ted only one.

The early evening skies had grown prematurely dark. Altmann's room was dim with shadows. Outside, rain was falling. Raindrops streaked the leaded glass windows, becoming runny wet prisms refracting tiny rainbows of light from lamps being lit in the quad below.

The tea in my cup was cold.

◄ 16 ►

I had forgotten my umbrella. So I borrowed one from Sir Jeremiah and made my way out of the east gate of Christ Church, into Merton Street, between Oriel and Corpus Christi, turned left into Magpie

Lane, crossed the High and entered Catte Street between the Radcliffe Camera and All Souls, walking past the Bodleian and emerging into Broad Street. The lights of Blackwells bookshop beckoned, and I found myself back inside one of my favorite undergraduate haunts.

Blackwells looks like a small shop but the appearance is deceptive. Walk toward the back of the store and you find a down staircase to your left. The Norrington Room is a vast subterranean chamber on three levels. That's where the philosophy and political theory books are housed. Next to the beautifully restored Duke Humphrey's Library in the Bodleian, this was Ted's and my favorite book-filled room in Oxford.

I descended the stairs and then, turning sharply left, made my way to the politics section. Under the P's I saw multiple copies of several of Ted's books, and wondered if *Rousseau's Ghost* might be published posthumously and put alongside them. Under the R's I found numerous copies of Rousseau's works, in French and English, and almost before I knew it I had purchased—I wasn't sure why—copies of Rousseau's *Confessions*, *The Social Contract and Other Political Writings*, and the first two volumes of Cranston's biography. While the Thames Valley Police kept me in Oxford I would at least have something to read.

I stepped outside. The rain had ceased but the wind had picked up. There was an unseasonable chill in the air. Remembering last night, I shivered more than the temperature warranted. I walked briskly down New College Lane and turned left into the narrow alleyway that led to The Turf, another old haunt. I had to duck to enter the door and, once inside, I couldn't stand up straight without bumping my head on the old wooden ceiling beams. I ordered a pint of bitter and sat in the corner near the fireplace. Not very crowded tonight, I noted. Mostly the locals, a few undergraduates, a tourist or two. The big diesel-exhaust-spewing tour buses from London depart by mid-afternoon, leaving the town relatively free of foreigners until the following morning. Then, like a daily invasion of camera-carrying locusts, they return to take pictures of *homo academicus* in his native habitat and to ask lots of questions, many of them odd, not to say silly. "How do they take pictures with the Radcliffe Camera?"—the Radcliffe Camera being the striking domed annex of the Bodleian Library. I once heard a tourist in the Nuffield College quad say how amazing it is that these centuries-old buildings were in such good repair. In fact,

Nuffield College, built in the 1950s, is among the newer colleges, while New College, new when founded in 1379, is among the oldest.

What an Oxford snob I've become, I mused as I sipped my pint. Less than thirty years ago I had been exactly like many of those tourists, and a good deal less knowledgeable than some. Living here, meeting and getting to know Ted, studying with Sir Jeremiah and other dons, had changed the naïve and unworldly boy from Oklahoma in more ways than I—or he—knew, or probably could know. There's something strange about Oxford. Once you've been here—really here, I mean—you never leave it. Or rather, it never leaves you. It stays with you always, and wherever you go. Now that I was back here physically, I felt myself a returning native, guarding my Turf, protecting my territory. I felt at home here. Welcome. Wanted. Yes, wanted. Even the police didn't want me to leave.

I ordered another pint, a Scotch egg, and paté and toast. The second pint, the food, and the warmth of the wood fire had a soporific effect. I was in no hurry to leave. I picked up my plastic Blackwells bag and examined my purchases. Opening Rousseau's *Confessions*, I turned first to the table of contents. It was singularly uninformative: Under "The First Part" it listed Book One, Book Two, and so on through Book Six. Then under "The Second Part" it likewise listed Books Seven through Twelve. I then turned, as is my habit, to the index. The Penguin Classics paperback edition had none. Since it was a book of some six hundred closely printed pages, I didn't feel quite like tackling it now. Putting aside Rousseau's *Confessions*, I picked up another of my purchases—the first volume of Cranston's handsomely produced and illustrated biography. Once again I scanned the table of contents. It was not, for a beginner, very informative either. Most chapters bore the name of some place—Geneva, Bossey, Annecy, Turin, etc.—where, I surmised, Rousseau must have lived for a time. I turned to the index, my eyes running quickly down the left column and up the right, to see if I recognized anything. It was the "scan and search" technique I'd picked up in law school—the lazy student's method, but useful enough in its way. Budding lawyers, like experienced ones, need to know only a few specific things in a very large ocean of data. You learn to save time by reading selectively, and as little as possible. The best route is always a shortcut. The shortest of such shortcuts is to scan the index. So I scanned the A's, searched the B's, seeing some familiar names—

Aristotle, Bacon, Bayle—followed by the C's and D's—Diderot, Denis, Dijon, Academy of. And then I saw it:

Dupin, C.—seven entries
Dupin, Louise-Marie-Madeline—seven entries
Dupin, Marie-Jeanne—one entry

I almost tore the pages turning to the first entry. I began reading, almost audibly and, I think, mumbling or moaning or making some sort of sorrowful noise. People were looking at me. I felt like a man possessed. Mme. Dupin, I read, was the faithful second wife of one Claude Dupin, who was old enough to be her father. Rousseau fell instantly and deeply in love with the woman he described as "one of the most beautiful women in Paris." He wrote her a love letter. She rebuffed him. He was penitent but persistent. Finally she relented, after her fashion, chastely and cerebrally. Rousseau worshipped her, wanted her, served her with selfless devotion, and basked in her beauty.

At last it was clear. Now I knew why Jeanne-Marie Masson called herself Danielle Dupin. She was one of them. One of the Société de Jean-Jacques. Maybe she had even played a part in Ted's murder.

"*Danielle! No!*," I wailed as I jumped up, hitting my head hard on an overhead beam. It must have sounded like a ripe melon being thumped. The sound was one thing, the feeling another. I saw sharp spikes of light, and felt like I'd been hit on the head with an electrified sledgehammer.

"You all right, mate?," a man asked. The pub was so quiet I could hear myself breathing hard.

"Yes. I'm okay," I heard myself say. The words seemed to come from nowhere and everywhere, through a dense fog of pain. "I have to go," I announced, shoving my books back into the plastic bag.

"But your head's all bloody," the man shouted after me as I walked and then ran outside the pub.

I walked fast, almost at a trot, up the narrow alleyway, along New College Lane, up Parks Road past Wadham College and and then Keble. A warm viscous liquid oozed down my forehead, obscuring the vision in my right eye. It was dark now, I thought, nobody will see me. But everyone seemed to stare, and the harder they stared the faster I walked and the faster the liquid oozed. I didn't have a handkerchief. Not even a Kleenex. I wiped the blood with my sleeve, but still it kept coming. Head wounds, I thought. Bloody head wounds. I giggled giddily at the British double entendre. They always look worse than they are. But halfway back to the flat I felt my knees begin to buckle. My pace slowed. Street lights and automobile headlights had yellow and red halos that merged and diverged by turns. I passed the shops at North Parade, stumbled past Park Town and up to Bardwell Road. Under the bright glare of a mercury vapor street lamp, I saw the blue Vauxhall parked directly in front of what I hoped was its owner's old stone house. I fell to my knees and crawled slowly to the front step.

M.S.P. Thompson, a small engraved brass plate above the doorbell read. I remember pressing the little black button below.

◄ 17 ►

"Ah, good. He's coming round now, I think. Barbara, be a dear and make some tea, will you? And see if there's any more ice in the fridge."

I looked up into a pair of bushy eyebrows.

"You'll live, I think," Thompson said. "Wouldn't you agree, doctor?"

A younger man in a dark three-piece pinstripe suit, late-thirties, tall and broad-shouldered like an Olympic oarsman and with a tangled mass of black brillo-pad hair, nodded. "I think he might just make it," he said. "Still, it was a nasty crack. If the wound weren't hidden by your hair," he said, looking at me, "I'd recommend about a dozen stitches. And if I thought you'd go bald before you grow old and impotent, I'd go ahead and stitch you up. Purely for appearance's sake, you understand, and assuming a normal quantum of male vanity."

"Thompson," I said, trying to sit up, and then thinking better of it, "I am sorry. I always seem to get you involved in my messes."

"Don't upset yourself just yet, old boy. Say hello to Dr. Mansfield, my neighbor, who heard my poor wife screaming and came at once. He's patched you up rather nicely, I'd say."

"Thank you, doctor . . ."

"Mansfield," he said. "Graham Mansfield. You'll have a headache and perhaps some dizziness for a day or two. We'll need to watch for signs of concussion—nausea, sleepiness, disorientation, confusion, memory loss, vomiting—over the next three or four days. You weren't ever completely unconscious, just badly dazed. And your vital signs—pulse rate, pupil dilation and such—seem all right so far. But you'll need to be careful. Get lots of rest. No strenuous physical activity. Keep a cold compress on to reduce the swelling. Change the plaster every few hours until all bleeding stops. Above all, be careful and use common sense." He paused. "If you don't mind telling me, how exactly did you come to crack your noggin?"

"I stood up."

"You stood up? Where?"

"Inside the Turf. The pub just off New College Lane."

"Oh, there," Mansfield said with a chuckle. "Tall men should never go there. Not without a helmet." He paused, laughing at his own witticism. "Well, I'm off to have my dinner. Martin, keep an eye on my patient. And Mr. Davis, do be careful." He handed me his card. "Ring me if you experience any of the symptoms—dizziness, disorientation, vomiting, the lot." He said good-night and let himself out, just as an attractive rosy-cheeked woman carrying a tray came through the door.

"Oh, you're wide awake," she said. "And looking so much better than when I first saw you. How do you feel?"

"Pretty well, considering," I said. "Rigor mortification just about describes my mental state. I'm so sorry to have arrived on your doorstep as I did. I'm told you screamed."

"Yes, silly me. I mean, I didn't know who you were. All I saw was a strange man, bleeding profusely from his head, passed out on my doorstep. Do please forgive me."

In my still dizzy and disoriented state I wondered, Are any people more overly and overtly—and, yes, tiresomely—polite than the English upper-middle class? Always begging pardon, asking forgiveness for real or imagined infractions that don't even register on anyone else's social Richter Scale. An American says, "Please pass the salt." An Englishman of a certain class and age says, "I'm very sorry, but could I possibly trouble you for the salt?" That's more than a matter of degree. It's a yawning chasm of attitude and sensibility.

"Barbara," said Thompson, "permit me to introduce the American I was telling you about. Teddy Porter's friend from New York, the one with the . . . um . . . woman, the . . . um. Mr. Davis."

"Jack. Please call me Jack." I knew it was no use. English people of their class don't use first names, not for new acquaintances anyway. "Mrs. Thompson, I owe you an apology for arriving as I did. I didn't know where else to turn. For the second night in a row. I'm becoming a burden to everyone, including my new friend Martin here."

I could see Thompson wince when I said friend. It was not a term that many Englishmen used lightly. Not as lightly as their American cousins. We weren't friends. He and Ted were friends. Ted and I were friends. Thompson and I were not friends. I was the friend of his friend, full stop. And I was living on my dead friend's line of credit, and sinking ever more deeply into the red.

"I tried washing the bloodstains out of your sleeve and collar, Mr. Davis," the woman said. "But I didn't have much luck, I'm afraid."

It was only then that I noticed that the shirt I was wearing wasn't mine. "Yours?," I asked.

Thompson nodded. "Sorry, old boy, but we weren't about to let you lie on the Louis XV sofa wearing your smock. You looked like a navvy from an abattoir."

"Martin, such language! Please."

"Sorry, my dear. Do have some tea, Davis," he said, starting to pour a cup, and then stopping in midstream. "Or would you prefer whiskey? Some brandy, perhaps?"

"No, thanks, I've had quite enough alcohol this evening."

"It's just that I thought you might . . ." He looked over at his wife. She averted her eyes. Then Thompson looked directly at me. "Brace yourself, old boy. The police rang earlier this evening. Inspector Grant wants to speak with you. Apparently they were looking for you all afternoon and into this evening."

18

My head was still throbbing the next morning as I walked into the new tan brick and glass Thames Valley Police headquarters on

St. Aldates and told the uniformed female receptionist that I was there to see Chief Inspector Grant.

"Your name, sir?"

"Davis. Jack Davis."

"I'll tell him you've arrived," she said as she picked up the black phone and punched in two numbers. "A Mr. Davis is here to see you, Chief Inspector." She paused. "Yes, I'll tell him."

She looked up at me. "If you would just take a seat, sir. The Chief Inspector will see you in a moment."

As I was about to sit down I spied a shock of reddish-orange hair. I walked over to P. C. Barton.

"Hello," I said. "Remember me?"

"Oh, hallo, Mr. . . . Mr. Davis, isn't it?"

"Yes."

"Here to see the Chief Inspector, are you?"

"Yes. I wanted to ask him . . . —but perhaps I can ask you . . ."

"I'm sorry, sir, but I'm not at liberty to tell you anything about an ongoing investigation. Not even about this one."

"No, not about the investigation. About Danielle—about her body, I mean . . . Has her family been told?"

"Yes. Her brother will arrive tomorrow to claim the body."

"Who broke the bad news? I mean, did you? Or did Grant tell them . . ."

"Oh, no, sir. That's not our job, I'm happy to say. We have a woman on staff who handles these matters. As it happens, she also speaks some French. So she told them." He paused. "It can't have been easy."

"No," I agreed, "it can't. I can only imagine . . ."

Just then the receptionist called out. "Mr. Davis. The Chief Inspector will see you now. Down the corridor. Second door to your right."

I thanked the receptionist, said good-bye to Barton, and walked down the narrow hallway. The nameplate on the door read **S.M. Grant Chief Inspector**. I knocked lightly on the large metal door.

"Come in," a gruff voice barked. I opened the door slowly. The office was a mess, even by my sloppy standards.

"Thank you for coming in, Mr. Davis," the Chief Inspector said in his Scottish burr. "Do take a seat." I noticed that his accent had a rough edge. He was a Scotsman, for sure. From Glasgow, I guessed.

Definitely working class. Probably came up the hard way, from some pretty mean streets. A self-made man who did not suffer fools—or criminals—gladly, or at all. A man, I surmised, who had enjoyed many a wee dram in his fifty-odd years. To kill the pain, probably. Small scarlet and blue veins stood out in his pink cheeks and red nose. He was nothing like the Oxford-educated, slightly snobbish, irascible but avuncular, Mozart-loving Inspector Morse, Colin Dexter's fictional creation played by John Thaw on Public Television and who was now every American's idea of the Perfect Oxford Cop. No, this real-life Chief Inspector was an altogether angrier man. A man of many resentments and towering rages. I didn't want to cross him. I removed a pile of papers from the metal folding chair, placed them on the floor, and sat down.

Grant frowned. "What's happened to your head?" It sounded more like an accusation than a question.

"I cracked it on a ceiling beam. In a pub. Your low English ceilings weren't made for tall Americans." I smiled, trying to cut the ice. It didn't work.

"I've a few more questions to ask, following up on our conversation of the evening before last and in the wake of the Medical Examiner's report."

"How did Danielle die? Was there . . ."

"I'll ask the questions, if you don't mind, Mr. Davis." His tone was curt. Correct. Cool to the point of frostiness. "First, some facts," he said, looking across the desk at me. "Your Miss—what did you call her?"

"Dupin. Danielle Dupin."

"Right. Turns out that's not her real name."

"I know," I said. "Her real name is Jeanne-Marie Masson."

"You knew that? Then why in blazes did you tell Constable Barton that her name was Dupin?"

"Because I thought it was. Then. I know better now."

Inspector Grant had flicked on a small tape recorder. He leaned forward, as if speaking more directly into the built-in microphone. "I see. So you misled the Thames Valley Police by giving a name that you knew was an alias?"

"No, I didn't know that then. I found out later. After you'd left. You see, I talked to my legal assistant in New York. She . . ." I saw that Grant was looking at me with great interest. "Could I have a lawyer? Please?"

"Later. If you need one. You also told us that 'Danielle Dupin' had been a student at Pembroke College as recently as a year or two ago."

"Yes, that's right."

"No, I'm afraid that isn't right, Mr. Davis. Pembroke has no record of anyone named Danielle Dupin, or Jeanne-Marie Masson either, enrolled there in the last two years. Or the last five or, for that matter, at any point in the preceding ten years. We even showed her passport photograph around the college in case she had used yet another alias. No one recognized her." He hesitated. "Rather surprising, that. Seeing as how she's . . . she was such a beautiful woman."

On that much, at least, Grant and I agreed. But he wasn't finished yet.

"You knew of course that Mlle. Masson had a serious heart condition?"

"No. I mean, I'm sure she didn't. She's only in her mid-twenties. Too young to have . . ."

"Thirty-one. She wore a Medic-Alert bracelet with a heart symbol on it. And a card we found in her purse contained instructions regarding resuscitation in case of cardiac arrest. You weren't aware of that?"

"No, how could I be? I mean, she never told me anything about any heart condition."

"You didn't notice her bracelet?"

"Danielle, I mean . . . she wore bracelets, earrings, necklaces. Like a Gypsy's. Bright spangly ones that sparkled and jingled. I never noticed what they looked like." As I said this I could almost hear Grace say, "Oh, Jack, don't you ever notice *anything*?"

"And her purse?," Grant continued, his voice rising. "You never noticed the large bright red plastic-coated card she carried in her purse that announced her medical condition and advised about resuscitation? And in six languages, no less, including Japanese. Never noticed that the name on her passport was Jeanne-Marie Masson? You never noticed any of this?"

"Certainly not," I said somewhat self-righteously. "I never went through her purse."

"Apparently you did, Mr. Davis. We found your fingerprints all over her lipstick, her lighter, and cigarette case. You seem to have known the contents of her purse rather well, I'd say."

Then I remembered. "That was only once," I stammered. "I couldn't sleep, and I reverted to an old filthy habit."

Inspector Grant leaned forward, brow furrowed, eyebrows up.

"Smoking, I mean. That filthy habit. I was looking for cigarettes and a light, and I found both. In her purse. Danielle's purse. I didn't look any further."

Grant paused, scowled, and then smiled ever so slightly. Or slyly. "You do seem to have answers for every question, Mr. Davis. You are by profession, I believe, a . . . a . . ." He thumbed through his notes, not altogether convincingly, I thought.

"Lawyer. I'm a lawyer." I might as well have said Professional Paid Liar.

Grant looked up and smiled his most insincere smile. "A lawyer. Yes, that's it. A lawyer. From New York."

"Yes."

Inspector Grant reached inside his jacket pocket and pulled something out. "I believe this is yours," he said, handing me my passport.

"Then I'm free to go? I mean . . . What does this mean?"

"That you're free to go. We can't hold you. You were negligent, but nothing more, so far as I can see. You shouldn't have left your girlfriend alone, given her condition. That's a moral failing, not a crime, more's the pity." He gave me a withering look. "Be thankful you're in the United Kingdom. A land of laws, not of men. If this man had his way we would lock you up for a long time and I'd never lose any sleep at all."

I couldn't account for the vehemence with which Grant had launched this verbal assault which had unaccountably been building throughout the interview.

"Look," I said, hoping to calm these troubled waters, "I know all this looks very bad. And it is. But things aren't at all the way they appear. Not really. You see, I . . ."

Grant stood up. The interview was over.

"Before I go, please tell me what you know. I need to know. Please."

He hesitated, and then, looking into the middle distance at nothing in particular, spoke in the staccato language of policemen everywhere. "Jeanne-Marie Masson, also known as Danielle Dupin, died the evening before last at approximately half past nine, give or take half an hour. You were at that time elsewhere, as more than two-hundred witnesses can attest. There was no blood, no sign of struggle or forced entry. The only apparent abnormality consisted of bruises around her wrists and ankles. The large toes on both feet were badly bruised. Such marks are not uncommon effects of . . . of lovemaking of the kind that you and she had engaged in."

"But we never . . ."

"Mr. Davis," Grant said sternly and disapprovingly, "we weren't born yesterday, you know. We found the four silk cords under the bed, and the Medical Examiner found semen in the vagina and anus and throat of the deceased . . ."

I felt something explode inside my head. "Oh, my God, no," I whimpered. "No!"

Grant was unmoved. "I know that some people get up to that sort of thing. You told me that you"—he referred again to his notebook—"and here I quote your own words, 'tried everything . . . mechanically, if you know what I mean' to make love to the deceased. I know exactly what you meant, but I'm not passing judgment, much as I might wish to. All that is, in any event, beside the point." His pink cheeks were turning red, his nose dark crimson. "The Medical Examiner diagnosed the cause of death as heart failure—massive cardiac arrest as a somewhat delayed result of some rather violent sex-play. The cause of death was so obvious that he didn't need to order an autopsy. Apparently after having had your way with her, you waltzed off to dinner"—he sneered as he spat out the words—"with your fancy friends at Christ Church, leaving the poor woman to die alone and in agony as you enjoyed a meal that's more exquisite than most poor sods can appreciate and more expensive than they could ever afford."

The Chief Inspector's torrent of class anger almost knocked the breath out of my unsuspecting American lungs. I shrank away, as though to ward off the verbal hammer-blows being rained down on me.

"That," he continued, his voice steely and rising with barely suppressed rage, "comes close to criminal negligence but it doesn't quite cross the line, legally speaking. As for myself, I wish it did. But we can't arrest and bind you over for trial on charges of wanton selfishness and sexual recklessness. So, unfortunately and for all practical purposes, this case is closed." Grant opened a desk drawer and looked down into it, at something I couldn't see. A bottle, maybe. He looked up at me with cold blue eyes.

"Mlle. Masson's family is sending someone—her brother, I believe—to claim her body and take it back to Paris. Tomorrow. You might want to be gone by then, if not before." Grant made a motion with his hands, as though sweeping something odious and undesirable out of his office. I left, feeling the kind of pain that I hadn't felt since I was a boy. My head filled with voices unbidden and unwelcome.

"Half-breed," one of the voices sneered.

"Why don't you stay with your own kind?," hissed another.

"Go back to the Reservation. Where you belong."

"Yeah, and stay there. We don't want your kind around here, Chief."

Grant didn't know it, but he and I were a lot alike. We had both suffered slings and arrows. But when Chief Inspector Grant looked at me he saw only an overprivileged, affluent American. A white, or mostly white, American. Which of course I am. Now. But I hadn't always been the polished, well-dressed, reasonably articulate and soft-spoken self-creation that Grant saw standing before him. I shivered, trying to shake off old wounds and ancient insults. Not that concentrating on the present was any help. More recent recollections were hardly less painful.

Just like Paris, I thought as I walked numbly through the main lobby and out of the Thames Valley Police station. Just like Ted's death. I was angry all over again. And puzzled. What had happened? Was Danielle murdered during or after a rape? Had she answered the door, thinking it was me, only to be overpowered by an assailant who then tied her up and raped her? But what rapist brings sex aids—silk cords, no less—to a rape?

So maybe Danielle's death really was accidental. Perhaps she had gone to the Rose and Crown or one of the other local pubs, picked someone up, brought him back to the flat. And then engaged in especially energetic sex during or after which her heart failed. Her lover for the evening would have been frightened, letting himself out and leaving in such a hurry that he forgot his sex toys. But why didn't this kinky coward at least have the decency to call a doctor or an ambulance before disappearing anonymously into the night?

Either scenario would explain several things: why the flat was locked and showed no sign of forced entry; why the sheets were so rumpled and Danielle's hair disheveled; why her pubic hair felt moist to my touch. I shuddered at the memory, still fresh, wiping my left hand on my trouser leg. Then feelings of horror and disgust immediately gave way to guilt. If I hadn't gone out for the evening Danielle would still be alive. If I had been an adequate lover she wouldn't want or need to turn to someone else for sexual satisfaction. Danielle was a sensuous woman. I must have been a terrible disappointment and a source of some frustration. I can understand why she . . .

Wait. What am I saying?, I thought as I walked up St. Aldates toward Carfax Tower. I understand nothing. *Nothing*. Zero. Zip. I'm guessing, imagining the worst, impugning the motives and insulting the memory of a beautiful woman, now dead. I felt confused, conflicted, guilty. Guilty because of what I had—and had not—done. And, yes, guilty because I felt relieved, since I was now off the hook. Someone else—someone whose semen was found in Danielle's body—should be hanging on that hook, suspended by four silken cords. But who?

19

I was packed and ready to leave, waiting for the taxi, when the phone rang.

"Uncle Jack?" It was Jessica.

"Jessica! Dear Jessica. I should have called you before now. But I wanted to see you in person, to wish you a happy birthday and to say how very sorry . . ."

"My birthday wasn't exactly happy." She paused. Then the words tumbled out in a torrent of grief and accusation. "You don't think Daddy's death was an accident, do you?" I was stunned, and struggling for words. "You think Daddy was killed, don't you?"

"What makes you think that?," I said, trying to sound surprised and a little indignant. Had Grace slipped up, I wondered, and said something to tip her off?

"Because you've been gone a long time, Uncle Jack. Too long. Because you didn't call me or, better yet, come to see me, on my birthday. Because Grace is being much too nice and too coy. Because I just received a package from Daddy."

"A package from Ted? What's in it?"

"It was mailed from Paris on the day he died. It includes a letter from Daddy that's . . . that's too cheerful. Way too cheerful, if you know what I mean—like he's trying very hard to convince me that everything's all right when it isn't. And he's included eighteen handwritten pages that seem to have been lifted out of his manuscript. Pages 241b through 241s. I've helped Daddy since I was twelve, when I first learned to type, and he almost never uses inserts, and certainly never one as long as this."

"What does it say?"

"It's about Rousseau's *Institutions politiques*. That's *Political Institutions*, Uncle Jack."

"Yes, thanks, Jessica, that much I know. What else does it say?"

"It says . . . Look, it's complicated. I'm not sure I understand it myself. Let me fax it to you. With Daddy's letter. Do you have a fax number where you can be reached?"

"Yes. At least I think so. Just a minute." I fumbled in my jacket pocket and took out the notes I'd scribbled on Christ Church stationery. The letterhead listed a fax number. I gave it to Jessica. She, unlike Ted, was computer-literate, and owned a lap-top purchased a couple of years ago by her father. She even had her own fax machine, courtesy of Ted. What he wouldn't touch, she was allowed and even encouraged to use. My friend and her father was a man of many parts, not all of which seemed to fit together neatly or even coherently.

"I'm faxing this now, Uncle Jack." I could hear multi-toned beeps, followed by whirring and clicking sounds. "Call me back when you receive it and fill me in on what you've found out. I don't know what that might be, but I suspect this might help."

There was a knock at the door. I told Jessica I had to go and would call as soon as I had something to report. "You're my favorite goddaughter, you know."

"Could that be because I'm your only goddaughter?," she replied, adding: "And Uncle Jack?"

"Yes?"

"You're my favorite godfather. Bye." Jessica was her father's daughter, for sure.

I put on the chain and then opened the door. Through the crack I could see the taxi driver. I slipped him a fiver and sent him happily on his way. Then I called Thompson.

"It's me," I said. "Or maybe it is I. Your American albatross. I need yet another favor from you."

"Davis, is that you?," he said, knowing full well that it was. "How delightful to hear from you again. And so soon." The tone belied the words. I detected a distinct note of sarcasm.

"Only one more favor, and I'll be out of your hair for good. Or at least for the foreseeable future."

"Now that *is* a tempting prospect," Thompson said. He laughed. I took that to be a good sign.

I told him that I was at this very moment receiving a fax on the Christ Church machine and that I needed to retrieve it right away.

"But it's nearly eight o'clock. The college is closed. Can't this wait until morning?"

"I'm afraid not," I said. "I fly to Paris this evening. So time is of the essence. And so is privacy. I don't want anyone else to find this fax. Believe me, it's very important. I wouldn't trouble you if it weren't." I waited for a response. Thompson said nothing. I felt awkward. "You're the Senior Tutor," I added, uncertainly. "So surely you have a key to . . ." I felt like the Ugly American.

"Just a moment," Thompson said at last. He covered the mouthpiece and said something to his wife. The muffled tone suggested indignation and annoyance, but, above all, curiosity. Someday, this would be the stuff of an amusing and oft-told tale. But not now. That present irritation buys future amusement does not make the annoyance of the present moment any less vivid.

"Very well, Davis," he said with the voice of one who does his duty without complaining. "Shall I come round and collect you in twenty minutes?"

I was waiting outside with my bags when the blue Vauxhall careened around the corner and screeched to a stop.

The drafty hall outside the office of the Tutors' Secretary was dark. Thompson fumbled with one key and then another, finally finding the right one and opening the large wooden door. He turned on the light. In the corner the fax machine's small blinking green light signalled a new arrival. I pulled the shiny sheets out of the tray and counted them. A three-page letter from Ted plus eighteen manuscript pages, all handwritten, and none clearly legible. Fax machines don't like fountain pens and the people who write with them. I had some work to do in deciphering the smudged and runny reproduction of Ted's handwriting.

"It's all here. Thanks, Martin. Thank you for bringing me down here to retrieve this. I'm very grateful. And now, if you'd be so kind as to drop me at the station on your way home, I can still catch my plane and you can get back to your dinner, or dessert, or whatever it was I interrupted this evening."

Thompson looked at me in much the same way that Inspector Grant had done earlier in the day. "I don't think so, Davis. I feel myself involved, or should I say complicit, in your recent doings, for good or ill. Perhaps it's presumptuous, but I think I'm entitled to know what's going on. I've grown rather weary of being kept in the dark, thrown a few hints here and there, and left to imagine the worst. I've never been party to anything like this before and, frankly, I don't like it. I don't like it at all. I want the truth. The whole truth as best you know it. You owe me that much, I think."

I did, and I knew it. Thompson had gone out of his way, and more, to help me. And I hadn't reciprocated. I would begin by sharing the contents of the fax message from Jessica.

"You're right. Let's have a look at Ted's letter and the insert from his manuscript. It's a little smeared and runny, so this might take some time."

Thompson looked less stern, more concerned. "Come up to my rooms and let's have a go."

We walked across the darkened and deserted Tom Quad, past the Deanery, around the corner to the library, and up a staircase above the Picture Gallery. Thompson's rooms were less spacious than Altmann's, but brighter. The floor-to-ceiling bookshelves were painted white, the wall-to-wall carpet a light blue. The sofa and coffee table were covered with neat stacks of student examination papers, or "scripts" as Thompson called them. He gathered them up and put them on a desk in the corner.

"Now let's see what we can make of this," Thompson said, putting on a pair of oval reading glasses that made him look fiercely and distinctly donnish. We sat together on the sofa. A gooseneck lamp was pulled down. It shone brightly between us. We began, as best we could, to read.

20

My dearest Jess,

I'm sorry to be so slow in writing to thank you for your letter and the pictures of my No. 1 Girl. They're gorgeous (of course!). You've become a beautiful woman, but don't let it go to your head. And, speaking of your head: your Honors Thesis project sounds exciting—wish I'd thought of it! It might be a *bit* too ambitious, as you've sketched it; but with some more narrowing and focus, the issues will come into clearer view. I wish you were here and we could talk about that, and many other things besides. And now that you're older, I could show you Paris—that is, all the things I couldn't show you last time, when you were at a more tender age and not yet the woman you are now. On second thought, maybe I won't. These French men, young and old, are a predatory lot!

My work here is going well enough, but *Rousseau's Ghost*—do you like that for a title? (be brutally honest!)—has taken an unexpected turn. I've stumbled upon something odd—several odd things, actually, that I *think* I've managed to put together in a plausible, and perhaps even truthful, way. You'll see what I mean in the enclosed excerpt from the initial draft of my manuscript, which I send to you for safekeeping in case something happens (if, say, there's a fire or my apartment is burglarized, as several neighboring apartments have been recently). Please put it in the safety deposit box where your mother and I keep our important papers (your birth certificate foremost among them!). I won't describe here the sources I've used in drafting this part of my manuscript. Let's just say that they have come to me (or I to them) by means that are neither entirely ethical nor irreproachably legal. (About that and other matters I plan to seek advice from your Uncle Jack.) But as soon as I saw them I felt certain that they were too precious to keep under wraps or in private hands, and I acted accordingly. Whether your old man behaved bravely or foolishly remains to be seen.

You asked if I were "dating" anyone. What a question to ask your father! Well, the answer is yes and no. My research assistant is a very able young woman, only a few years older than you, who seems rather fond of me. I'm flattered, of course—she's fetching in the way that only French women can be—but she's a bit on the youngish side. We have dinner occasionally, and even went to the Paris Opera last week. But don't worry, Jess: she's not about to become your big sister/stepmother!

I'm hoping to wrap up my work here by the end of the week, and expect to be back in the States by the 10th (I have to present a paper at Wassenaar on the 9th), and just in time for your birthday. Tell your mother I'll write to her next week when things are a little less hectic than they are now.

Before I close, you'll be amused to learn that your old man now has a computer—one of those lap-dogs like you and your Uncle Jack cart around. No, I didn't buy it—I found it on my doorstep this morning, wrapped in brown paper with only my address on it, but without a return address. Then, when I returned home this afternoon I found a note under my door, from someone saying that his new computer had been delivered to my apartment by mistake and that he would come around to collect it this evening. So much for my brief entry into the world of high tech!

This comes, as always, with hugs and kisses and

love,
Dad

◄ 21 ►

The following narrative is based in roughly equal parts upon previously published sources and on a recently discovered diary that I believe to be authentic. Its authenticity remains to be determined by tests on the age and type of ink, paper (e.g., watermarks), etc. The means by which this has come into my possession I am not, at present, at liberty to disclose. The narrative is, alas, incomplete; several gaps and omissions remain. These can only be filled by conjecture or educated guess, and different scholars will inevitably fill these spaces in their own ways. I have attempted to be sparing in offering my own conjectures, which I have been careful to label as such to indicate their necessarily speculative nature.

In 1745, when Jean-Jacques Rousseau was thirty-three and not yet famous, he met Thérèse Levasseur, a pretty but illiterate woman nearly fourteen years his junior. She worked as a laundry-maid in the Parisian boardinghouse where Rousseau lived, and often took meals with the landlady and her boarders. Rousseau was impressed by her sweetness and modesty. He describes that first meeting in his *Confessions*:

> The first time I saw this girl appear at table I was struck by her modest demeanor and, even more, by her sparkling and sweet expression, the like of which I had never seen before . . . The other diners teased the girl, and I came to her defense . . . I became her ardent champion. I saw that she appreciated my attentions, and her glances, which were enlivened by a gratitude that she dared not speak, became that much more penetrating.
>
> She was very timid, and so was I . . . [T]he girl, having no defender in the house except me, was sorry to see me go out and longed for her protector's return. The rapport of our hearts and the agreement of our dispositions soon yielded the usual result. She thought she saw in me an honorable man [*honnête homme*], and she was not mistaken. I believed that I saw in her a sensitive, simple girl without coquetry; nor was I mistaken either. I swore in advance that I would never abandon her, nor ever marry her.[42]

42. *Confessions, O.C.* 1, pp. 330–1; *C.W.* 5, pp. 277–8.

As they were about to make love for the first time, Thérèse hesitated, resisting his advances. Rousseau initially suspected that she had a venereal disease. When Thérèse understood his suspicion, she wept copiously and confessed her "fault": she had been seduced as an adolescent and was no longer a virgin. "As soon as I understood I gave a joyful shout. 'Virginity!' I cried. What a rare thing to find in Paris, and in a twenty year-old girl! Ah, my Thérèse, I am only too happy to possess you good and healthy. . ."[43]

Thérèse became Rousseau's mistress. "At first," Cranston writes, "Rousseau looked to Thérèse only for sexual gratification, but he soon discovered she could give him a certain tenderness and evoke in him a compassionate attachment, which together transformed pleasure into happiness."[44] He tried to improve her mind—to teach her to read, to count, to tell time, to add, subtract, and make change, to recite the months of the year in order—but all to no avail. "I was wasting my time. Her mind is what Nature made it; cultivation and instruction have no effect on it."[45] Thérèse was also given to saying exactly the opposite of what she meant. Rousseau compiled a dictionary of these malapropisms for the amusement of his friends.

Despite the difference of age, ability, social class, and education, the two lovers were happy enough for a time. Their happiness was clouded only by the meddling of Marie Levasseur, Thérèse's greedy, interfering, and spiteful mother. Then, in December of 1747, a second and darker cloud appeared. Rousseau returned from a trip to find that "As I was growing plump at Chenonceaux my poor Thérèse was doing the same in Paris, albeit in another way."[46] Thérèse was pregnant with their first child. Not wishing to be burdened, Rousseau resolved to pack the infant off to an orphanage:

---

43. *Confessions,* O.C. *1, p. 331;* C.W. *5, p. 278.*
44. Cranston, vol. I, p. 199.
45. *Confessions, O.C.* 1, p. 332; *C.W.* 5, pp. 278–9.
46. *Confessions, O.C.* 1, p. 342; *C.W.* 5, p. 287.

> I readily resolved to take [this step] without the slightest scruple, the only scruples that I had to overcome being Thérèse's, and I had the greatest difficulty in the world in making her adopt this singular means of saving her honor. Her mother, who also feared the fresh embarrassment of a brat, came to my aid; and so Thérèse surrendered.[47]

The newborn infant was given to a midwife, who duly delivered it to the Foundlings' Hospital.

A year later Thérèse became pregnant again. And once again "the same inconvenience was removed by the same method," without "serious thought on my part, and no greater willingness on [Thérèse's]; she complied with a sigh."[48] Three more children were to be born, all abandoned at the foundlings' home over their mother's pitiful wails and powerless objections.

As early as 1751, and doubtless with Mme. Levasseur's help, rumors began to circulate that Rousseau had abandoned his children. In April the outspoken Mme. Francueil (his beloved Mme. Dupin's stepdaughter) asked Rousseau if the rumors were true. Rousseau replied, rather defiantly, that they were. He put a copy of this letter in the diary in which he kept a coded record of his most important secrets. His code is simple to the point of silliness: a = 1, b = 2, c = 3, and so on.[49] Rousseau's encoded copy of the letter of 21 April 1751 begins as follows:[50]

> Oui, Madame, 9:1.9' 12.9.18' 12.5.18' 5.13.6.1.13.18' 1.20.21' 5:13.6.1.13.18' 19.17.14.20.20.5.18

—which, when decoded, reads: "Oui, Madame, j'ai mis mes enfans [sic] aux Enfans Trouvés.—Yes, Madame, I put my children into the Foundlings' Home."

---

47. *Confessions*, *O.C.* 1, p. 344; *C.W.* 5, p. 289.
48. *Confessions*, *O.C.* 1, p. 345.
49. Following the more Latinate eighteenth-century French spelling, the letters j and i are interchangeable, i.e., both are 9; likewise, u and v are 20; w has no number: see Leigh, *Notes critiques*, *Correspondance complète*, vol. II, p. 144.
50. 20 April 1751, *Correspondance Complète*, vol. II, p. 137.

Exactly how—or why—an author as sophisticated as Rousseau believed that this simple code could conceal this, the darkest of his many dark secrets, remains a mystery. As one of his more perceptive biographers observes:

> There is surely no more extraordinary human document than this paper which he carried with him all his life in the notebook into which he had neatly recopied all the important documents regarding his case . . . He believed his code had the power to protect him, as if he were an ostrich hiding its head in the sand. He believed that no one else would be able to understand it. He penned the numbers carefully. What pains he took to cover up the truth! This coded copy contained his secret, a secret which was always burning inside him and that he guarded all his life. Never in his lifetime did he admit the truth, and when questioned, he lied. His admission is to be found only in works published after his death.[51]

Guéhenno's observation is only partially correct. It is true that Rousseau never publicly admitted the truth during his lifetime. The public admission came only in his posthumously published *Confessions*. But he confided his secret to Diderot and Grimm and he confessed in private correspondence, first in the aforementioned letter to Mme. Francueil in 1751 and then, ten years later, to the Duchesse de Luxembourg.

Thinking himself near death—he actually lived another seventeen years—Rousseau in 1761 wrote to the Duchesse:

> There are many things I would wish to say to you before I leave you! But time presses; I must abridge my confession, and confide to your kind heart my final secret. As you know, I have for the last sixteen years lived in the utmost intimacy with the poor girl who shares my home . . . . From this union were born five children, all of whom were sent to the

51. Jean Guéhenno, *Jean-Jacques Rousseau* (Paris: Gallimard, 1952), vol. III, pp. 12–13.

> Foundling Hospital, and with so little foresight for ever recognizing them afterwards, that I have not even recorded the dates of their births. For many years my remorse for that neglect has disturbed my rest, and I shall die without being able to right [this wrong], to the great regret of the mother and myself. All I did was to put in the blanket of the firstborn a mark of which I have kept the copy; he was born, I believe, in the winter of 1746–7 or thereabouts. That is all I can recall. If there were any way to find that child, that would make his loving mother happy; but I hold out no hope of success.[52]

Three years after his letter to the Duchesse, disaster struck. Rousseau's nemesis Voltaire—a great and courageous writer but a malicious and petty gossip—had somehow learned of Rousseau's darkest secret. Never one to keep a secret or stifle a scandal, Voltaire published an anonymous pamphlet, *Les sentiments des citoyens* (1764), in which he spread the rumor that Rousseau had a venereal disease (which was false) and had, moreover, abandoned his five children (which was of course true). Rousseau was livid. He had by now acquired so many real or imagined enemies that he was unable to guess the anonymous author's identity.[53] Rousseau denounced his accuser and denied both accusations. It was in this poisonous atmosphere that he began writing his *Confessions* which, he hoped, would rescue and restore his badly tarnished reputation.

Rousseau's account in the *Confessions* is both curious and contradictory. He begins by saying that the practice of abandoning one's children was not all that unusual in his country.[54] Then he says his children were abandoned in order to save Thérèse's "honor."[55] He subsequently says that he did his children a favor by not raising them in the social circle in which he moved—a circle that included intriguers, aristocrats, conniving schemers,

52. 12 June 1761, *Correspondance Complète*, vol. IX, pp. 14–18.
53. Cranston, vol. III, pp. 105–6, 181–2.
54. *O.C.* 1, pp. 344–5; *C.W.* 5, p. 289.
55. *O.C.*, 1, p. 344; *C.W.* 5, p. 289.

and assorted hangers-on. By leaving his children in the care of ordinary, decent, and unpretentious people he had ensured that they would be brought up to be honest laborers and peasants. These were not the actions of a selfish man but of a virtuous "citizen and father" who saw himself as "a member of Plato's Republic" in which children were raised not by their parents but by the state.[56] Rousseau writes that whilst "the regrets of my heart" tell him that he was wrong to abandon his children, his "reason" informs him that he acted rationally and rightly.[57] How sincere his heart's regrets were remains unclear and, in any case, this apostle of the emotions followed the counsel of his head, not once or twice or thrice, but on five separate occasions. He concludes his account of the quintuple abandonment on a distinctly unapologetic note. "I have promised my confessions, not my justification."[58] And there he leaves it.

Rousseau led his friends, as he leads later readers, to believe that his five children were lost without a trace, their names and fates unknown to either parent. He made no attempt to trace them, nor did he do anything to help anyone else do so. He did not disclose that "number" (or "mark") to the Duchesse de Luxembourg; and in any event fourteen years had passed and, as Cranston observes, "there was nothing that she or anyone else could do to trace the boy; so that the fate of that child, and of the other four born to Rousseau's union with Thérèse, remains a total mystery."[59]

Until now.

Unlike Thérèse, Marie Levasseur, her mother, was literate. Indeed, she could read and write with some facility and served for a time as Rousseau's resident secretary and amanuensis.[60] In what almost certainly appears to be a memoir or diary kept by Mme. Levasseur—possibly for the purpose of blackmailing the now-famous Rousseau, in the event that he abandoned her daugh-

---

56. *O.C.* 1, p. 357; *C.W.* 5, p. 299.
57. *Confessions, O.C.* 1, p. 357; *C.W.* 5, p. 299.
58. *Confessions, O.C.* 1, p. 359; *C.W.* 5, p. 301.
59. Cranston, vol. I, p. 246.
60. Cranston, vol. II, p. 29.

ter (and thereby, indirectly, herself)—she recounted many of the more unsavory episodes in Rousseau's life, several of which are corroborated in his *Confessions*: his numerous affairs and infidelities, his peculiar sexual practices and techniques, and, most notoriously of all, his having abandoned his five children—in short, just the sorts of embarrassing things that the old woman did not believe that anyone, and especially the redoubtable Rousseau, would ever dare confess in public.

But Mme. Levasseur was also privy to information of which Rousseau was unaware. She writes of her efforts to persuade Thérèse to give up her firstborn child, a son that she, without telling Rousseau, had named Pierre-Joseph:

> Thérèse would not listen to reason. She was inconsolable. The nearer the birth, the weepier she became. I told her that she should not risk giving up her meal-ticket only for the dubious pleasure of raising a brat by herself—because, believe me, I did not favor and would not support such a stupid and shortsighted course of action. Finally we persuaded her to turn the child over to Mlle. Gouin [the midwife] to deposit at the orphanage [*Enfants trouvés*]. What a relief I felt! My relief was short-lived, however, for I soon learned from a worried Mlle. Gouin that Thérèse, pretending to be the elder sister of 'the unfortunate 14 year-old mother', was paying infrequent and irregular visits to the orphanage to see the child she called Pierre-Joseph. I was furious, and confronted Thérèse, who was surprised but unrepentant. No, she said—to her own mother's face!—she would never forget her baby, that seeing him made her nipples ache and her milk flow, and a lot of other sentimental nonsense besides. I threatened to tell her master and she dared me to. Her defiant air made me tremble. I resolved never to speak of these matters in his presence.[61]

Much to Mme. Levasseur's regret, Rousseau's wealth did not grow apace with his literary fame. His works were often pirated

61. Levasseur diary, fols. 23–4.

and sold in cheap editions from which Rousseau received no royalties. He complained bitterly, and understandably, about this and about occasions on which his own unscrupulous publishers pocketed royalties that were rightly his. Even so, as a matter of pride and principle, Rousseau refused all offers of gifts and stipends from friends and admirers. He could have been a very wealthy man; but he chose to subsist solely on earnings from his writings and from his lowly labors as a musical copyist—the latter a vocation without modern counterpart. Rousseau did what the printing presses of his day could not do: quill pen in hand, he copied musical notation, note by note, line by line, bar by bar, measure by measure. It was a monkish and medieval trade to which he devoted a great deal of time and for which he received little recompense. His high-mindedness merely irritated Mme. Levasseur, who shared no such scruples. She encouraged and readily accepted all gifts meant for Jean-Jacques, under the table and ostensibly for his benefit, which she then diverted to her own large and rather wayward family. "She grumbled constantly about the policy of frugal living, and encouraged her relations to scrounge what little there was to be scrounged from her daughter's famous lover." And while Rousseau "always refused brusquely any gift from private benefactors," his biographer notes, "Mme. Levasseur furtively proffered, whenever possible, a greedy palm."[62] In exchange she supplied steamy gossip to Rousseau's friends, acquaintances, and hangers-on.[63] And it seems probable that her diary, a dreary compendium of such gossip, was kept in hopes of either (as I noted earlier) blackmailing Rousseau or, in the event of his early death—which he and everyone else expected—of turning a tidy profit by publishing it.

Meanwhile, Rousseau continued to write on a more elevated plane. In the early 1750s he began writing a long, systematic treatise on politics to which he gave the title *Institutions politiques*. As the decade wore on and his health declined, Rousseau became convinced that completion of this work was "beyond my strength."

62. Cranston, vol. II, pp. 1–2.
63. Cranston, vol. II, pp. 41–2, 49–50.

Shortly after excerpting the portion that he titled *Du Contrat social* (1762), the ailing and bedridden Rousseau asked Thérèse to take the larger manuscript outside and burn it. Here Mme. Levasseur picks up the story:

> I saw Thérèse come into the garden carrying, under one arm, a large parcel of papers tied with a string. In her other hand she carried a taper. Has your master written another book?, I asked. Let's hope this one makes some money, I said. Thérèse said this one surely won't make any money because he told me to burn it. She placed the parcel on a pile of dry leaves and twigs and set the leaves alight. I snatched the parcel away before it caught fire but not before it got scorched on one side. I spat into my palm and rubbed the spittle over the edge to stop the smoke. Are you mad?, I said. Anything your lover writes is worth money. Who knows how much longer he'll live? Then where will you be? Answer me that, my girl, I said. I do as I am told, she said. Hah, I said, like visiting your beloved babies behind your master's back? I should have kept my mouth shut, because when I said that a gleam came into Thérèse's eyes and then she smiled and reclaimed the parcel and hugged it to her breast. Thank you, Mama, she said. Only later did I put two and two together. My dim-bulb daughter [*fille stupide*] had hatched a plan. She hid the parcel away, in the cellar, and came back outside with a pile of papers and other scraps and set them atop the smoky pyre so that he, confined to his bed upstairs, might smell something burning. She wrapped the parcel in oilskin and, two days later, took it away. A birthday present, she said, for my Pierre-Joseph.[64]

What happened next we do not know, because several leaves from the Levasseur diary are missing, and others have suffered irreparable damage from water and mildew. Here we must resort to conjectures of the crudest and most obvious kind. It is possible, but unlikely, that Thérèse presented the unfinished manuscript of

64. Levasseur diary, fols. 278–9.

the *Institutions politiques* to her firstborn son; but at the time—1760–61—he would have been about fourteen years old and would hardly have known the value of the manuscript or what to do with it. Another possibility is that Thérèse gave it to someone—a nun at the orphanage, for example—for safekeeping, until Pierre-Joseph left at age sixteen or so to make his way in the world. Or Thérèse might have sold it to someone—a bookseller, most likely—saving the proceeds to give her firstborn son a nest-egg. Or she might have done something else entirely.

In any event the unfinished draft of the *Institutions politiques* seems to have survived, at least for a time and against Rousseau's express wish that it be destroyed. Its survival appears to have been entirely fortuitous—the effect, initially, of Mme. Levasseur's greed and subsequently of Thérèse's desire to provide for her firstborn son. (Whether she expected him to share any profits or proceeds with his four younger siblings, we do not know.) The next legible entry in Mme. Levasseur's diary that appears to refer to this matter is not as clear as one would wish:

> My darling daughter has no head for business. Something that might fetch a good price she sells for next to nothing. She cannot understand it, nor can her son; but they get a few sous for it, and they are happy. She should have entrusted it to me. I know how to turn a profit.[65]

That "something," the "it" that Thérèse and her orphaned firstborn son could not understand and apparently sold for a pittance, was in all likelihood the *Institutions politiques*.

Here the trail grows cold and the scents uncertain. It is possible that booksellers regarded the work as a forgery, and not worth much, if anything; or that it was in such a scattered and incomplete state that its value, both literary and monetary, was doubtful; or that it fell into the hands of a friend or admirer of Rousseau who, familiar with the foreword to *The Social Contract* and recognizing this as "the more extensive work" that should have been "destroyed," hid it away because he had not the heart

65. Levasseur diary, fol. 291.

to destroy it himself. The possibilities are finite, but sufficiently numerous to test even the most fertile imagination.

Has the *Institutions politiques* survived to this day? I have good reason to believe that it has and that I now know where to turn and how to find out. My guess—my hope, if I may say—is that it not only survives, but that it will prove to be of great value to our understanding of Rousseau's political thought. If indeed it does survive, the only recourse open to a responsible scholar is to see that the light of day shines upon it, Rousseau's own wishes to the contrary notwithstanding.[66]

[bold scrawl in lower right corner:]
Hier stehe ich, ich kann nicht anders!

◄22►

"My God," Thompson said, removing his reading glasses and turning off the lamp. "This is the most remarkable thing I've ever laid eyes on. If it weren't so late I'd ring Jeremiah. It's really quite . . . quite unbelievable. And if it had come from anyone besides Teddy Porter I wouldn't believe it. Not for a minute."

---

66. This raises thorny ethical questions which I am unable to answer according to any generally accepted moral principle. I can, however, adduce many particular instances in support of my own view that publication is warranted. Two examples might suffice. Marcus Aurelius's express deathbed wish was that the manuscript of his *Meditations* be destroyed; his faithful lieutenant, who had obeyed every other order to the letter, disobeyed his dying emperor's final command. Franz Kafka, who published only one short story during his lifetime, ordered that his unpublished novels and short stories be destroyed after his death. His literary executor failed to execute this part of the deceased author's will. Who can deny that we are all of us immeasurably richer for these and other acts of disobedience?

I was no political theorist, no student of the subject; but after my informal crash tutorials with Altmann I knew what Thompson meant. "What's that phrase at the end? It's German, isn't it?"

"Yes. Martin Luther's reply when he was ordered to recant and return to the Church: 'Here I stand, I can do no other.' Teddy sounds resolute."

"He always is," I said. "Was, I mean."

"Where—and how—do you suppose Teddy got this diary?"

"I don't know for certain, of course, but I think I have a pretty good idea," I said. "Have you heard of the Société de Jean-Jacques?"

"Do you mean those dotty Frogs who worship at the altar of Rousseau? That lot?"

"One and the same."

"Sure. They're something of a laughingstock among serious students of political theory. They're a bit batty, but fairly harmless, I think. Why?"

"Because I'm not so sure that they're as harmless as everyone seems to believe." I told Thompson what Altmann had told me about the Société—the origins of the organization, their approach to the interpretation of classic texts, especially Rousseau's, their animus against modernity, their adoption of surnames, how their leader called himself Roguin, how they called Altmann "Voltaire" and Ted "Hume." And then I told him about Danielle Dupin, a.k.a. Jeanne-Marie Masson, who had taken her surname from a beautiful woman whom Rousseau had loved. "She was one of them. I think they killed her. And I think they killed Ted. I don't yet know why, or what the connection is. Not yet. But by God I aim to find out."

"Careful, old boy. This is no time for amateur sleuthing. This is police business. Let's tell them what we know and what we suspect and let them take care of it."

I laughed, sounding unexpectedly bitter. "The police don't believe that either death was a murder. The Parisian police think I'm deluded, and the Oxford cops think I'm a pervert." I told him what Inspector Grant had said about the bruises on Danielle's wrists and ankles, about the silk cords, and how he thought I'd used the cords to cause the bruises in the course of kinky sex-play that had led to Danielle's death.

"Good God, man. This is even messier than I'd thought."

"It gets worse," I said, "and even more complicated." I told Thompson about the sabotaged computer power pack that had killed Ted and about the 'heart condition' that had killed Danielle. I told him everything I knew.

"Now I've put you in the picture, Martin. Are you a happier man for knowing what you now know?"

He hesitated. "No, I'm afraid not. But then the Scripture says, 'Know the truth, and the truth shall set ye free'. It doesn't say that the truth will make you happy."

23

Early the next morning Thompson drove me to Heathrow through fog so dense that even the blue Vauxhall hesitated, moving slowly and uncertainly along the M40. The delay, although irritating, proved interesting. I finally got to know something about Martin Thompson the man.

He was, he told me, born in Carlisle, near the Scottish border. His mother was Scots, and one of the few female physicians then practicing in Britain. His father and older brother were career officers in the Royal Navy. Thompson had gone to public, i.e. private, school—to Winchester—on scholarship and did, he said, "reasonably well" at his studies. Which, translated into American English, means that he had excelled. As a teenager Thompson was torn between pursuing a scholarly career and a naval one.

"Fortunately, I didn't have to decide for myself. The decision was made for me—by my tummy and my gut." Thompson told me that being at sea made him violently, almost deathly, ill. "Seasickness scarcely describes it. The ferocity, I mean. But I'll spare you the details." That decision made, Thompson went to Magdalen College, Oxford, "to read P.P.E. and Modern History"—Philosophy, Politics and Economics, and

European History from the fifteenth century to the present—and graduated *summa cum laude* with a Double First in 1967. The following year he went to Christ's College, Cambridge for his doctoral studies. Which explains why our paths never crossed at Oxford. His doctoral thesis was published as "a big boring book," and helped win him a Studentship at Christ Church in 1974. "And there I remain, House-bound, like Prometheus on his rock, with a damaged liver."

"And what," I asked, half in jest, "would you really rather be, if not an Oxford scholar?"

"An officer in the Royal Navy," he said, without a moment's hesitation.

We live, I thought to myself, lives that are made only in part by and for ourselves. The vastly different trajectories of our lives are very largely the product of accident, of luck, of fortune good and bad over which we have little or no control. I felt inexplicably close and almost reached out, to touch Thompson's shoulder. Then I thought better of it. Thompson was no modern touchy-feely type. If he was any "type" at all, he was the type of Englishman who was fast disappearing. The type who had fought the Germans without complaining and then beat them without boasting. The type who would never be caught in public without a tie. Thompson was one of those Englishmen who would wear a jacket and tie even when working in his garden in mid-July.

Clearly uncomfortable talking about himself and his academic accomplishments, Thompson abruptly changed the subject.

Coolly and carefully, he recounted the events of the preceding week, with particular attention to the fax messages we'd deciphered the previous evening.

"One thing's certain," Thompson said at last. "Without corroborating evidence that the Levasseur diary—and, better yet, the *Institutions politiques* itself—actually exists, Teddy will be a laughingstock. The story is *so* strange that no one in the scholarly community will believe it, unless the works in question can actually be produced and examined by others—by experts who can vouch for their authenticity. Without that, the whole thing might as well be a fairy tale."

That possibility, I confessed, had never occurred to me. If Ted told me something, I believed it to be true, period—because it came from a friend I trusted and relied on. Of course the same would not be true of Ted's peers in political theory: they would require more than his word. They would want evidence, proof. Just as in a court of law, dummy, I thought to myself.

So something else, something other than the identity of Ted's killer, was at stake here. Ted's scholarly reputation—a reputation that he valued above life itself—was hanging in the balance and could tip either way.

We arrived at Heathrow Terminal 4 only half an hour before my flight was scheduled to leave. I was certain I'd missed my plane yet again. But I needn't have worried. All flights were delayed, most by four hours or more.

"Before I go, Martin, I want to thank you again for all your help. I don't know when we'll see each other next. When you and Barbara come to New York I'll show you my town." I reached into my jacket pocket. "Here's my card, with my New York address and, on the back, I've written the address and phone number of Ted's apartment in Paris. I'll be there for the next few days, in the unlikely event that you need to get in touch."

"Shall I come in and see you off?," Thompson asked.

"That's kind of you, Martin. But no, thanks. Looks like all the car parks are full anyway. And I'm sure the crowds inside are even worse."

"As you wish, my friend," Thompson said, shaking my hand. "Have a good trip. And Jack—do be careful."

I felt doubly elated. "Thanks, Martin. I intend to."

The blue Vauxhall disappeared into the fog and the traffic.

Inside Terminal 4 the lines were long, the delay interminable. Why do they call this a terminal, I wondered, when there's no end in sight? I joined one of the endless queues. Delays caused by fog. Delays caused by bomb scares and security alerts and baggage checks and computer failures. All the modern amenities. I could almost understand the Société de Jean-Jacques' brief against the modern world.

It was a view that Ted, in his own odd way, had certainly shared. He worried far more than I ever did about the ways in which technology liberates in one direction while enslaving in another. "The whole idea of 'labor-saving machines'," he wrote in a now-famous and oft-reprinted essay, "is a cruel hoax. In the end we work to their requirements, their rules, their rhythms." Even more insidious, in Ted's view, is our penchant for "technofixophilia"—a word of his own coining—"an ugly term for an ugly phenomenon: the love of technical or technological fixes for every ailment, real or imaginary." Ted's point, as best I could understand it, was that this attitude spills over into political and moral reasoning, with regrettable results. "We come to think of all our problems as problems of means, of technique, and not as moral problems of principles and ends. By recasting civic and moral issues as questions of means and technique, we spare ourselves the difficulty of doing hard thinking and making morally difficult choices." The one sin that Ted couldn't forgive was that of trying to make hard things easy. "Hard things are hard. They ought to be. If everything were light we would have no muscles. To build muscles requires weight, resistance, heft. To build minds and morals requires that we recognize difficulties as genuinely difficult, and think and act accordingly. Recognize the weight, get under it, feel it. Lift it if you can. And take responsibility for the result." Ted lived his life that way. And I did not doubt that he had died that way.

I had been feeling the weight—of grief, of guilt, of moral doubt and perplexity—but I felt puny and inadequate, not really up to the task. Not without Ted to talk to. I had always counted on his counsel. In his last days he had counted on, and asked for, mine. And I had arrived too late to offer whatever I had that he might need. Now, belatedly, I was trying to make it up to him. I would do it, or die trying.

"Passport?"

I was at the front of the queue. I fumbled in my jacket pocket and presented my passport to a pudgy, pasty-faced passport control officer. He looked at the picture, then up at me.

"Destination?"

"Paris."

"Next."

Once inside the Secured Area I looked for my flight number on the monitor. Nearly three hours to wait. I found a seat, settled in, opened my briefcase, took out my notes and the faxes, and studied them again to see what was missing, what didn't make sense. Were Ted and Danielle lovers? Danielle said they were. Ted's letter says only that she "seems rather fond of me," and that he feels "flattered." He does say that Danielle is "fetching in the way that only French women can be"—true, but vastly understated—but he hints that she was too young and/or he too old to be lovers. But he doesn't deny it either: "Well, yes and no," he replies equivocally to Jessica's query about "dating." He calls Danielle his "research assistant." But what author dedicates his book to his research assistant? And what professor displays on his desk a framed photograph of his research assistant, and in a sultry pose in a low-cut dress, no less? Ted seems to suggest that he and Danielle were merely professional colleagues and platonic companions who sometimes dined together. Of course the letter *was* written to his daughter. He might wish to spare her feelings—including the distaste she might feel if she learned that her father had a lover who was not much older than she. And anyway, what father tells his children, even his grown children, everything he does?

Ted is hardly more forthcoming about his scholarly labors. He says he's "stumbled upon something odd"—singular—and immediately amends it: "several odd things"—plural—"that I *think* I've managed to pull together . . ." The discovery was apparently altogether unexpected, serendipitous—he's "stumbled" upon, or into, it.

Then there's the Levasseur diary. Ted obviously saw it, handled it, read it, took notes on its contents, quoted from it. In the preface to the excerpt he says that "it came into my possession" and that he expects to have its authenticity determined by means of chemical and other tests on the ink and paper. So, physically, it had to have been in his hands. But where, and how, did he get it? And where is it now? I certainly didn't see it in Ted's apartment. That doesn't mean it isn't there, of course. I had done no systematic search, nor an unsystematic one, for that matter. I made a mental note to myself to scour every inch of his apartment as soon as I returned.

Ted tells his daughter of the "sources I've used in drafting this part of my manuscript." He says "sources"—plural—but the only unpublished source he cites is the Levasseur diary—singular. And, too, he says that these "sources . . . have come to me (or I to them) by means that are neither entirely ethical nor irreproachably legal." So he must either have found or discovered the diary (and at least one other source), or somebody else brought them to him. If the latter, then who? And why? Ted also says that the means used to acquire these sources were not exactly ethical or legal. He doesn't say that they were unethical or illegal, *tout court*, but implies that their moral and legal status was questionable, at best.

On the day he telegraphed me, Ted tells Jessica that he's going to seek my advice "about that and other matters." What kind of advice?

Legal advice? But I don't know anything about French law. And to what "other matters"—plural—was he referring?

And, stranger still, why did Ted send only these eighteen pages out of a 600-plus page manuscript to his daughter for "safekeeping, in case something happens"? Like what? Like a burglary, he says. But what burglar—even an idiosyncratic burglar who specializes in stealing manuscripts—would take only an eighteen-page excerpt, leaving the rest? Even in that highly unlikely event Ted could easily reconstruct the missing portion, unless . . .—unless of course he weren't alive to do so.

Ted was under no illusions; he saw the danger. And the danger had something to do with his "sources": "as soon as I saw them I felt certain that they were too precious to keep under wraps or in private hands, and I acted accordingly." How? By unwrapping them? By removing them from private hands? "Whether I acted bravely or foolishly remains to be seen." Ted did something—I didn't yet know what—to acquire his sources. Something that he knew to be dangerous. And someone had killed him for his trouble.

Then there was that other death. Danielle—I knew that wasn't her real name, but she was still Danielle to me—had died, been murdered and apparently raped, probably because of her connection with Ted. Maybe also because of her link to the Société de Jean-Jacques. Or maybe for something else entirely. Or maybe for no reason at all. The more I thought about it, the less sense it made. The source of the throbbing in my head was more intellectual than physical.

I looked up at the clock. Still more than two hours to go. I closed my briefcase, left my seat, walked around to kill time and stretch my legs, went into the duty free shop, bought a half-litre of Glenmorangie, called Grace and Jessica and left messages on their answering machines, and at last ambled into the airport bookstore. Maybe I needed something to read—something else, I thought, besides what I had in my briefcase. Something distracting. A magazine, maybe. There were magazines for sports enthusiasts, body-building enthusiasts, gardening enthusiasts, sex enthusiasts, none of which greatly interested me at the moment. I looked for, but couldn't find, something for classic car enthusiasts. Or perhaps a murder mystery—what the British call a "thriller"—would do. On second thought, no thanks. The books two aisles over looked a little more interesting, or at least more calming. Books about the arts—opera, music, painting, the theater—would be more likely to lift me up, improve my mind. The books about painting and painters had the most colorful covers and, not surprisingly, the most colorful contents. They were arranged by countries—*The Art of France*, *Classics of Italian Art*, and the like—and, in the case of famous painters, by individuals: *Vincent van Gogh*, *Rembrandt*, *Paul Gauguin*. I picked up the Gauguin book. Color photographs of his paintings were arranged chronologically, with a commentary on each one, describing its connection with a stage in Gauguin's life. The pictures, particularly the later ones, were fascinating, strange, disturbing to look at, hard to draw away from. At £49.50 the book was expensive, but I bought it anyway.

After some searching I found another seat. I opened *Paul Gauguin* and read about how he had become disillusioned with the art of his own time and place—late nineteenth-century France—and began looking for alternative forms and shapes and colors from other cultures and times and places. How he had become fascinated with primitive peoples and cultures untouched by Europe, by civilization so-called, by reason and science. Many of Gauguin's paintings during this period show bare-breasted Polynesian women—natural, unashamed, unselfconscious—and lush leafy jungles. Many had oddly disturbing titles, and none more than *D'où venons-nous? Que sommes-nous? Où allons-nous?*—"Where Do We Come From? What Are We? Where Are We Going?" (oil on burlap, 1897). Gauguin, the commentary noted, wanted to strip off the veneer of civilization, of sophistication, to see what we're really like and who we really are, or once were.

Just like Rousseau, I thought.—Well, well, what do you know? I've made a discovery, a connection. Probably everybody else has too, but at least I did it myself. Did Gauguin himself make such a connection? Did he ever read Rousseau? Or, if not, had he been influenced by anyone who had? Were his later pictures in any way beholden to Rousseau or, more likely perhaps, to *le Rousseau imaginaire*? Ted would know. I'd ask him.

Then I remembered.

Eleven o'clock. Still nearly an hour and a half until my flight leaves. I put my new book in my briefcase, closed the cover and then my eyes, and amidst the hubbub and bustle of the crowded waiting room finally fell into a fitful half-sleep. Rousseau and Gauguin. Rousseau and Gauguin. The two names kept repeating themselves like a mantra, but ever faster and louder. Rousseau-Gauguin. Rousseau-Gauguin. RousseauGauguin. RousseauGauguin. Rousseaugauguin. Rousseau-gauguin.

Roguin! Suddenly I jerked awake, startling those around me. My subconscious, or Grandma Della's dream-world, or whatever it might be, had been busily eliding, punning, compressing, combining two names which, when shortened, yielded one name—that of the man I now knew I was looking for.

24

The flight to Paris, although four hours late, was uneventful. I passed the time by using my scan-and-search method to find out about the original Roguin. Daniel Roguin (1691–1771) was a Swiss who as a young man had served in the Dutch army and later settled in Paris. There he met an obscure newly arrived aspiring writer, a fellow Swiss some twenty years his junior. Roguin recognized the younger man's genius and his goodness, and soon became his friend, confidant, some-time money-lender, occasional refuge, and courageous protector. Cranston describes Roguin as Rousseau's "staunch friend" (I, p. 156), his "loyal friend" (II, p. 174) who assured Rousseau that "I will always happily share with you the little that I have" (I, p. 198). Rousseau himself, upon accepting his friend's offer of Swiss refuge from persecution by the French authorities, wrote of "the pure and intense pleasure of being embraced by the worthy Roguin" (Cranston, II, p. 362). Certainly the difficult and irascible Rousseau had few such friends, and none more faithful or generous. For Roguin, unlike the others, neither asked for nor expected anything in return.

Clearly, the original Roguin was an altogether admirable man, and a fearless and estimable friend. Was the same true, I wondered, of his modern namesake? Somehow I doubted it.

Ted's apartment was as I had left it less than a week ago. It seemed like a lifetime. For Danielle it was. We had left together. Now I returned alone. I remembered her smiling, asking to accompany me. Her girlish delight when I readily, perhaps too readily, agreed. Her hair blowing in the Channel breeze. Our first kiss. How it tasted. I tried to harden myself to these memories that were now so confusing. She was, I told myself, more likely an enemy than a friend. She had lied, used a false name, was almost certainly a member of the Société de Jean-Jacques, was . . . warm. Sweet. Beautiful. Fond of Ted. Kind to me. Or an actress who played her part more skillfully than seemed humanly possible.

I tried to discipline myself, to distract my thoughts. I unpacked my case. Opened a window. Put the kettle on. Made tea. Checked the fridge. Ate cheese with stale crackers for dinner, with dried dates for dessert. I was about to open my duty-free Glenmorangie when I spied a recorked bottle of Château Margaux that I hadn't remembered opening. This was too good to pass up. I poured myself a glass. Took a taste. Too bitter. Took another taste. Diagnosis confirmed: it had in my absence "corked"—exposed to the air, it had turned into a decent, but undrinkable, red wine vinegar. I set the glass aside, and then sorted the mail. Arranged the newspapers in chronological order. Turned on my lap-top. Accessed the Internet. Five messages awaited answers. All from Grace. All in Chokie. Each more pleading and vehement than the last. I felt bad about leaving my lap-top behind. The first message was about the report from the Dietz Lab, the second about Danielle's fingerprints, her real name, and a warning to watch my step, I don't know what I'm getting into. The third: Where was I? Why hadn't I answered? Was I all right? The fourth: "Darling Jack, if you're there, then in God's name please answer." The fifth, dated this morning:

> My dear Jack. Welcome back. Hope you had a good trip. What I really mean to say is, you had me worried like I've never worried before. Ever. Come home soon. I love you. - G.
>
> P.S. Please reply this time?

I started typing. I kept typing. The longest e-mail message I've ever sent. Certainly the slowest—I was writing in Chokie. I told, or tried to tell, Grace everything that had happened since we had talked three days ago. Everything except the four silken cords and Inspector Grant's suspicion, which would require greater care and even lengthier explanation at some later date. All the rest I told in compressed form. About the Société de Jean-Jacques, Ted's letter and manuscript excerpt, the diary. . . Then I remembered: The first thing I was to do upon returning to Ted's apartment was to look for the Levasseur diary. I compressed the rest of the story, confiding my suspicion about Roguin, a.k.a. Merceaux, and concluding, a little too hastily: "I love you, too. - J."

I began searching Ted's apartment. Drawers in the bathroom, bedroom, kitchen. Shelves in the kitchen and pantry. Closets. Compartments. Under the sink. Behind the fridge. Behind the bottles in the large and well-stocked wine rack. Inside the TV and VCR that Ted never turned on. Everywhere. Nothing. If the diary had been here, it was no longer.

Then I remembered the safe or safe-deposit box to which I had the combination that I now knew by heart—right 4, left 20, right 15, left 9, right 13. Perhaps the Levasseur diary was there. But where was there? I hadn't the foggiest idea. The final entry in Ted's small diary—V.D., followed by a phone number—referred to a video dating service in Paris. It was early evening. Perhaps the agency was still open.

Once again I dialed the number. A woman's voice answered, speaking French.

"Hello," I said. "Do you speak English?" She said, in surprisingly good English, that she did. "This," I said, trying to sound more confident than I felt, "is Theodore Porter. Perhaps you remember me."

"Ah, yes, of course," the woman said. "How may I help you?"

"Perhaps you could remind me of our arrangement."

"Arrangement?," she asked.

"Our, er, business—what we agreed to."

"You come in. You make the video tape. You pay for it."

"So the tape is already made?"

"Yes, of course."

"May I pick it up, please?"

"But," she said, sounding very suspicious, "you take it with you. You do not leave it here, on file in our store, as we ask our clients to do. This is no way to meet the women . . ."

"Oh, yes, of course. Now I remember. Sorry to bother you." I said a hasty good-bye and hung up.

Ted had made a tape at a video dating service and then took it away. But why? And where might that tape be now? Maybe it was here in his apartment. Not likely, though: I had already turned the place upside-down and inside-out, looking for the Levasseur diary. My search had yielded neither that diary nor a videotape. The most obvious place to look for a such a tape—the V.C.R. that Ted would never use—was empty. There were no videotapes anywhere.

I felt confused and tired. The sun had not yet set, but already it felt like midnight. I hadn't slept—really slept—in more than a week. Bone weary and dead tired, I barely made it to the bed before sleep overtook me.

25

I looked at my watch but had a hard time reading the blurry dial. 4:35. Too early to wake up. But something seemed wrong. Very wrong. Sunlight streamed through the bedroom window. I heard traffic noise from the street below, the sound of voices in the hallway, music from a radio in the adjoining apartment. Slowly it dawned on me that this wasn't the dawn. It was 4:35 in the afternoon. I was still so sleepy I could hardly keep my eyes open. But I couldn't sleep because I had a splitting headache and a ringing in my ears. And a bitter metallic taste in my mouth. I felt dizzy and nauseous. There was a dried, football-sized reddish-yellow stain on my shirt that matched the one on the bedsheet. A vomit stain. I felt more embarrassed than scared.

From somewhere inside this numb fog a word came to me: Con cussion. All the symptoms were there—dizziness, nausea, the works. I'd been doing too much, moving too fast, not using common sense as Dr. . . . Dr. . . . I fumbled in my pants pocket, pulling out my lucky arrowhead and then the doctor's card. "D.G.H. Mansfield, M.D. Summertown Medical Centre, Oxford OX2 2OD. Tel. 01865 . . ."

That's it, I thought. I'll just phone him. English doctors still make house calls. I'll be okay.

It was only then that I noticed that I was still wearing my street clothes—jacket, shoes, everything. I'd fallen into bed without undressing, which I'd done only once, maybe twice, before, when I was falling-down drunk. But that was nearly thirty years ago, before Ted had taught me how to drink. I hadn't had anything to drink last night, I thought. Then I remembered the wine. But I'd had only a sip or two before noting that it had turned to vinegar. So it must be a concussion. Got to stay awake, I thought, as I squeezed the arrowhead. Got to call Mansfield.

I reached for the phone on the nightstand and with some difficulty dialed 01865 and the number of the Summertown Medical Centre. An electronic musical tone sounded and a recording of a woman's voice said, *Pardon, mais vous devez composer le code du pays avant le numéro nationale et locale*. What in blazes? Since when do they speak French in England? Then I remembered: I wasn't in England anymore.

This is serious, I thought. I'm in a bad way. Worse than I thought. I need help. Where's Danielle? I don't know her phone number or where she lives. I'll look it up in the directory, under D for Dupin. Oops, no, better look under M for Masson. Yes, Masson, Jeanne-Marie, that's her real name. I can remember that, so maybe I'm not in such a bad a way after all. I felt relieved. My relief was short-lived and then gave way to terror: Danielle's dead. Jeanne-Marie Masson is dead. They're both dead. If I can't think straight I'm going to join them.

I knew I had to get help. But I didn't know anybody. Maybe I can ask a neighbor. I forced myself to get out of bed. I staggered like a drunk, trying to navigate toward the bedroom door. What should I say? I need help? Please help me? I tried saying "I need help." My words were horribly slurred. They sounded like "Yuneodel." I squeezed the arrowhead harder, forcing myself to concentrate. "I . . . n . . . need . . . hellpp." That'll do, I thought.

No, that won't do. These people don't speak English, they speak French. Even if they understand a little English, they won't understand mine. Hell, even I have a hard time understanding what I'm saying.

A doctor, I need a doctor. Now. The only doctor I knew was in England. I picked up his card and then the phone. Slowly and deliberately I punched the international access code, 011, the country code, 44, then the Oxford area code, 01865, and then the number on the card.

"Summertown Medical Centre," a Englishwoman's sunny voice answered.

"I . . . nnn . . ."

"Hello? Hello, is anyone there?"

"D . . . Ddotr Mmmnsfud."

"Dr. Mansfield? You wish to speak to Dr. Mansfield?"

"Yyuss."

"I'm afraid he's . . . he's . . . Look, is this some sort of drunken prank? Because if it is . . ."

"Hhllp mu." I squeezed the arrowhead harder. "C . . . con . . . cush . . . un."

"Concussion? You have a concussion?"

"Yuh."

I heard disconnected sounds of commotion at the other end of the phone. The woman's voice said something that seemed to come from a long way off. Then I heard a man's voice close-up.

"Hello, Mansfield here. You have a concussion? Who is this, please?"

"Ddavi."

"Davey?"

"Ddavi."

"David?"

"Ddavi."

"Davis! Where are you? We'll send an ambulance."

"Ppari . . ." I squeezed harder, feeling the sharp point puncture my palm. "Ppaarriss."

"You're in Paris? No, you're not. You're confused. Now get a grip on yourself, man. Think clearly, now: Where are you?"

The edges of my vision became blacker, narrower, until there was only a small circle of light at the center.

From far away I heard a voice. "Hello! Hello, are you there? Hello, Davis?"

The small circle of light reduced to a pinpoint and disappeared into the blackness.

◄26►

An acrid, bitter smell stung my nostrils. I wanted desperately to get away from it, but I couldn't. I shook my head vigorously and tried, unsuccessfully, to sit up. Then I saw a rotund middle-aged man with a gray walrus moustache, peering down at me, waving a vial of some foul-smelling liquid under my nose. He took it away.

"So, now you are back. Very good. We worry about you. You were . . . not so good before."

"Who are you?" I asked the fat man in the light blue tunic. "Where am I? What is this place?" I didn't notice it immediately, but my speech impediment had improved considerably. Nothing else showed improvement; quite the contrary. My whole body ached as though I had the flu, my throat was raw and sore, and a drip tube with a needle was inserted in my left forearm and held in place by several layers of white tape. A cocoon of crisscrossing straps enveloped my body, rendering me immobile.

"I am Dr. Guilloud," the large walrus man said in heavily accented English as he loosened the straps. "This is the Lariboisière Hospital. You are our guest since two days ago."

"Two days!"

"One and a half, to be more precise. You were brought in at 1700 the evening before last."

"Now I remember. With a concussion. I had a concussion."

"This is what your Dr. Mansfield say. But . . ."

"Dr. Mansfield? He's here?"

"No, he telephone to give us your name and the address. He say it is emergency, that you have the concussion and you lose the consciousness."

Mansfield must have phoned Thompson, who told him that I wasn't delusional and that, yes, I really *was* in Paris—and then gave him the address of Ted's apartment. And Mansfield called 15—the French equivalent of 911.

"Good old Mansfield," I rasped. "And good old Martin. So Mansfield told you about my concussion."

"Yes, Monsieur, he tell us this. But he is wrong. You do not have the concussion. You are in the state of severe toxic shock due to the poison. If you have more, or wait longer, then . . . but fortunately, it is not so. We, ah, we pump your stomach and put you on the dialysis to remove the poison . . ."

"Poison? From what? What are you talking about?"

He seemed surprised. "We do not know at first. But we later find it come from the wine."

"Wine? What wine?," I wheezed hoarsely. Then I remembered finding a recorked bottle of Château Margaux on the kitchen counter in Ted's apartment. At the time I didn't remember having opened it, but then I didn't really think about it. It was already open, it seemed a shame to let a good wine go to waste, I poured myself a glass . . .

"The poison," Dr. Guilloud continued, "it is unusual. Is very—how do you say?—old-fashioned. I have read of it in Charrin's *Poisons de l'organisme*, but have not seen it before. Belladonna, it is called in France. Is extract from the root or berry of beautiful bush that belong to *Solancaceae*, genus *Atropa*—what you call 'Deadly Nightshade'—which was popular poison in eighteenth century, before arsenic trioxide become so popular that it is called *le poudre de succession*, the 'inheritance powder', you would say. The belladonna, it work more slowly. First you sleep. Then you die."

I now knew that what I feared really was true. First Ted. Then Danielle. Now me. Almost. And who but a bunch of eighteenth-century weirdos would know about belladonna? Who but the Société de Jean-Jacques?

They had failed this time, by a bird's eyelash, but they weren't likely to fail again. Given their track record, the odds were not in my favor. My first instinct was to check myself out of the hospital and head straight for the airport. To leave my luggage, my lap-top—everything—behind. To go home. To Grace. To New York and safety, strange as that sounds. To everything familiar if not necessarily admirable. Hell, I thought, I'd even be happy to see Linda at the reception desk. I'd hug her. And Dick O'Brien, too. Temptation has never been more tempting.

"Recognize the weight, get under it, feel it. Lift it if you can. And take responsibility for the result." Ted's words came back to haunt me, and I felt ashamed, rebuked by a ghost.

"Dr. Guilloud?"

"Yes?"

"Does this poison—this belladonna—does it do permanent damage? I mean, will I be completely well, or will there be . . . complications?"

"In your case, I think no. You have very little—only a sip or two—of the wine. No more than five cubic centimeters—not so much. The poison, it slow your body functions, including digestion, so much of it is still in your stomach when we pump it. For your dinner you have the crackers and cheese—not good dinner, but very good for absorbing and slowing passage of the poison—so only a little get into your bloodstream. But better than this is that the wine is bad—is almost pure vinegar. And vinegar is best antidote, in early stage, for this poison. You also pump your own stomach," he said, his gelatinous sides and belly beginning to shake with something that looked like laughter.

"I did *what*?"

"You pump your own stomach," he chuckled, "—you vomit. Is very good, is body's way of expelling what is bad." He did an alarmingly accurate pantomime of a man vomiting that could only have come from extensive firsthand experience. "The vomiting, it help you, too. The dialysis we do to clean your blood, it is probably not necessary. Is—how do you say?—is precaution. You will be weak and need to rest. I can prescribe mild sedative if you wish. To help you with the sleep. Otherwise, you are OK."

"But my throat feels raw—like I've got strep or something."

"Of course. Your throat, it is sore from the tube we put into your stomach. But it will be better when you drink the liquid, and not take them in the vein," he said soothingly while removing the bandage from my forearm and then roughly ripping out the hair before swiftly and deftly removing the needle and tightly pressing a gauze pad over the needle mark. The pain in my left arm made me forget that in my throat, if only for a moment. The Arrowhead Effect, minus the cause.

"When can I get out of here, Dr. Guilloud?"

"You stay tonight," he said, pouring two glasses of fizzy mineral water from a plastic bottle on the bedside table. "We look at you, how you say, first thing in the morning. Then, if all is well, you go. *Santé*," he said, loudly clinking the two glasses together before giving me a sip from mine. He then downed his glass in a single gulp, not bothering to suppress the belch that followed.

Good, I thought as my Rabelaisian doctor turned to leave. A minimum of fuss. I'll pay my bill and be gone. And then I can get on with the business at hand.

Or so I thought. The next morning Dr. Guilloud showed up, checked me over, and pronounced me fit. No sooner had he left the room than a plainclothes detective entered, accompanied by a black-uniformed *gendarme*. The gaunt, cadaverous-looking man introduced himself as Inspector Ferrand from the third *arrondissement*. He spoke bluntly and directly, no words wasted. He wanted to know about the wine. Had I intended to commit suicide? Police records, already in the computer, showed that I was despondent, almost manic, over my friend's recent death. Perhaps, he suggested, my despondency had turned to depression and then into a despair so deep that I'd tried to kill myself. Or was someone trying to kill me and, if so, who?

It was Catch-22, a classic case. From my old law school seminar in Comparative Legal Systems I remembered that France, though nominally secular, is in many ways still a devoutly Catholic country. There, as also in some non-Catholic countries, to commit suicide is a crime; to attempt to commit suicide is also a crime. Succeed, and you're guilty, but beyond the reach of human law; fail, and you're guilty—and have to pay the penalty, which is no longer imprisonment, but, in this more enlightened age, confinement in a mental hospital. Émile Zola and Michel Foucault would each in his own way have had a field day with this one, I thought.

No, I assured Ferrand, I had not intended, and would never want, to kill myself.

"Are you then saying, Monsieur, that someone wish to kill you?"

You're damned right someone wish to kill me, I wanted to say. And I have a pretty good idea as to who that might be. But if I tried to explain that members of some renegade Rousseau cult were after me and wanted me dead, they'd lock me up in a French loony bin and throw away the key. Either way, I was going to end up in some rubber-room, and God only knows whether or when or how or by whom I might be sprung.

Then, slowly, like some benign cloud descending, I felt The Calm coming over me. I became inventive.

"Look, Inspector Ferrand," I said in my most confidential tone, putting my right hand on his left shoulder and pulling his face down toward mine. "I have a problem," I whispered. "A—you know—a drinking problem."

"The alcoholisme?," he asked.

"Not so loud," I shushed. "Yes, you're right. I'm an alcoholic. Most of the time, I drink nothing. I never buy wine, whiskey, anything." This was a dangerous game, played for high stakes. I was gambling that he hadn't noticed the bottle of Glenmorangie I'd bought at the duty-free shop at Heathrow. I hoped I had discarded the receipt. "But sometimes," I continued contritely but confidently, "I am weak. Sometimes I see, on the street . . ."

"You pick the bottle from off the street?," Ferrand asked, at once incredulous and comprehending.

"Sometimes, yes. Sometimes. I am ashamed to say so, but, yes, I do this." Even as I spoke my words seemed to be badly translated from English into French, and back again. Could I pull this off?, I wondered. The Calm was still with me.

Ferrand shook his head. "This is sad, I am sad for you. But this bottle you find—where do you find it? The one with the strange poison that almost kill you?"

My senses were still operating in slow motion but now I had to think fast. "Two streets down. In a trash-can at the corner of Rue Clauzel and . . . I can't remember the cross-street."

"Avenue Kléber?," Ferrand asked.

Yes, that's it, I started to say. Then I thought better of it. This could be a trap. I didn't know the names of the cross streets. Answer in the affirmative, and I might catch myself in my own lie. "Maybe. Maybe not. I can't remember. But take me there, and I can show you."

Ferrand frowned. "No need, Monsieur. We know the general vicinity." He turned to the uniformed officer and spoke to him in French. He said something to the effect that a homicidal maniac was out there, attempting to poison winos like our American here, and that announcements and warnings should be posted and broadcast immediately. The *gendarme* left in a hurry.

"You should take more care," Ferrand said reprovingly. "You should seek help for this . . . this problem with the alcohol."

"I know," I said. "I've learned my lesson. The hard way."

Ferrand stood up and shook my hand.

I thanked Ferrand sincerely, because he was doing his duty and he meant well and I'd played Br'er Rabbit to his Fox. If I felt guilt, I'd deal with it later. I had other, more pressing things to think about.

27

Ted's apartment looked more menacing than I'd remembered it. Someone could come and go as they pleased, probably with the aid of a key, and they apparently knew the place pretty well. I considered checking into a hotel, but then thought better of it. If I'm going to meet this "person or persons unknown," my chances are better here than elsewhere. My more jargon-prone junior partners would probably call this a "pro-active stance." But, for safety's sake, I bolted the door.

I searched through the large two-volume Paris telephone directory under R, for Roguin, and under M, for Merceaux. I found one Roguin, G., and two Merceaux, B. and R. I seriously considered phoning all three and shouting, in English, "Look, Roguin, I'm alive, I'm angry, and I'm waiting for you. You know where to find me." Two of the three—or, quite possibly, all three—would doubtless be very confused. But suppose I did manage to contact the real Roguin? He would come, all right, in his own time, in his own way, and probably with strong and well-armed assistants. I would be no match for them. And this time they would almost certainly succeed. One option out the window.

Then I picked up the large commercial directory, looking under S, for Société de Jean-Jacques, and found lots of sociétés but not the one I was looking for. Next I searched under J, for Jean-Jacques, Société de. Nothing there, either. How, I wondered, had Ted managed to contact them?

I was pacing Ted's apartment, angry and apprehensive, hands in my jacket pockets, fidgeting, fiddling with my arrowhead, when I felt something small and familiar.

The initials and addresses in Ted's little diary that I had previously thought unimportant and run-of-the-mill looked much more interesting at second glance. One looked especially intriguing: "SJJ 44 R St Lazare."

My first impulse was to take a taxi to 44 Rue Saint Lazare, ring the doorbell or, better yet, walk in, announce my presence, and challenge anyone and everyone there to . . . to what? A duel? A fistfight? This is stupid, I thought. Really stupid. Think. You're one-quarter Cherokee. Think like your ancestors. Do something smart. Indian-style.

Nothing came. Apparently the other three-quarters—Scots, Welsh, and German—were in charge and dominant, but also lethargic and unimaginative. Forget this ancestor stuff, I thought. Think for yourself. Like your life depended on it.

I wanted to devise a plan, preferably a clever one. But all I had were some hunches, a few half-educated guesses, some gut feelings. And not much more.

The first thing I had to remember is that Roguin, or whoever had tried to poison me, would think me safely dead. In a few days' time the neighbors would smell something suspicious and call the police, who would force the door and discover my decomposing corpse. An autopsy would show that I'd been poisoned. They would find the wine glass and the bottle, both laced with ample amounts of belladonna, and both with my fingerprints all over them. Parisian police records would show that I was upset, unhinged, almost manic. Deeply depressed over my friend's death, I had taken my own life. Case closed. Again.

My would-be murderer's mistaken belief was my only edge. Not an ace, maybe, but at least a card. Somehow I would have to play it wisely and make it work in my favor.

I also needed to check out 44 Rue Saint Lazare, to see where it was, what it looked like, get the lay of the land. Ted's copy of *Paris A–Z* showed it to be between here and the Seine, to the southwest, and within easy reach. I could take a taxi, cruise past, check it out. Or I could be a pedestrian, sauntering on the other side of the street, preferably at some busy hour. Did Roguin and company know what I looked like? Maybe. Probably. I would have to operate on the assumption that they did. In any case my height made me conspicuous, so speed and stealth were all-important. It should be a speedy pass.

That's it, I thought: I'll run past 44 Rue Saint Lazare, pretending to be a jogger. Joggers were now everywhere, all over the world, even in Paris. So common that no one really even notices them. Present but invisible. Invisible presences.

I'd brought with me a pair of running shoes, no longer used for running but for walking. Among Ted's clothes, now systematically sorted into bundles by Danielle, was a pair of blue sweat pants and a gray sweat shirt. Both were a little small for me, but they'd do. From a street vendor on the Rue La Bruyère I bought a pair of cheap sunglasses and an American-style baseball cap. Less than half a mile away was the Rue Saint Lazare. I began running. Well, jogging, actually, and at a fairly leisurely pace. I didn't want to tax my newly cleansed blood *too* much. Besides, it was a sunny Monday morning, shortly before noon. My mission was serious but I was in *Paris*, after all. I should at least take some time to savor my surroundings. Throughout my life, everyone who has ever cared about me—Grace and Ted especially—said that I worried too much; that life was short, and I should savor it; and so, I thought, I shall, starting now. I had come close to death, but didn't cross over. The new, more relaxed Me gets born this bright Monday morning. In Paris. Gay Paris—gay in both the older and the newer senses—the City of Lights and lovers.

The main boulevards and side streets were jammed with buses and trucks and cars that barely moved, and motor scooters, mopeds and bicycles that moved much faster as they dodged in and around the traffic. Pedestrians walked at a leisurely and unhurried pace, pausing to talk or to look in department store windows at the *haute couture* knockoffs draped around bald, bored, emaciated-looking mannequins. From sidewalk cafés came pungent smells of onion soup, dark roasted coffee, and freshly baked bread. And, of course, the ever-present smell of cigarette smoke, a cloud of which came from two very thin male joggers who had been running ahead of me before suddenly and unaccountably stopping for a smoke.

I hadn't jogged since I'd injured my Achilles tendon two years ago. It felt better than I'd expected it to. Picking up my pace as I jogged down the Rue Pigalle, I turned left onto the Rue Blanche, and right onto the Rue Saint Lazare. I was breathing heavily as I approached no. 44. What I saw when I got there made me breathe even harder.

Banque Merceaux was inscribed on a large bronze plaque on the massive granite exterior of no. 44. The New Me felt a sickly, sinking sensation. Not unlike that experienced by the Old Me. But worse. Much worse.

◄28►

As soon as I veered off the Rue Saint Lazare and turned the corner at the Rue du Havre, I stopped running and rested my sweaty back against the cool stone façade of the Lycée Condorcet. What am I going to do now?, I asked myself. I'm up against a brick wall—a granite wall, actually—and at a dead end. There's no way I can sneak into a bank, of all places, and . . . what? Case the joint? Find and then try to open a safe—a large walk-in vault, maybe—to which I might, repeat *might*, have the combination? And then identify and snatch . . . what? The Levasseur diary? The *Institutions politiques* itself? Had Ted done that? Or tried to? If so, how had he managed? They certainly knew what he looked like. They probably know what I look like. In any event there would be video surveillance cameras taping me, from the first moment I walked through the front door. I couldn't even get inside without giving up the only card I had, or thought I had—my would-be killer's belief that I was safely dead. Give that up and the game would be lost, along with my life. I'd almost lost it once. I didn't relish the thought of losing it again, this time for real. And for keeps.

The walk back to Ted's apartment seemed to take forever. My feet felt leaden, as though clad in concrete boots. My shoulders sagged. My tall frame felt a foot shorter. I was stymied. Stuck. Only seconds left in the game, and my team was down twenty points. Hell, a hundred points. There was no way to recover. Might as well give up and throw in the towel. I'd made as good a try as I could, and it wasn't good enough. Time to go home, I thought as I trudged slowly up the stairs.

I turned on my lap-top and accessed the Internet. I was going to send a short message to Grace, saying that I was coming home shortly, safe but empty-handed. The "message waiting" line at the top of the screen read "New Mail. Press CTRL-ENTER to clear." I pressed the CTRL and ENTER keys and found a message from Grace that had arrived while I was out jogging. It was written in evident haste and apparently in anger. But not in Chokie.

> Dearest,
> Went to yr apt. early this a.m. (Mon.) to water yr plants, pick up mail, check ans. machine, etc., for first time since last Wed. Found phone message from a Dr. 'Gee-you' (hard g) from a Paris hospital, La-something-or-other, saying that you had been brought in, were very ill, but were expected to recover. He left the phone no. of hospital, which I called immediately. Said you'd checked out on Sat. Jack, dearest, WHAT THE HELL IS GOING ON over there? I've had it. Since you're not coming here, I'm going there. Lv JFK @ 11:05 this a.m., arr. 10:15 p.m. Meet you @ Ted's apt by midnight. Be there. - G.

Grace's dander was up. She was hellbent and determined. There would be—could be—no stopping her now. She was already at the airport, about to board. Very soon she'd be over the Atlantic, heading east.

The apartment was almost as much a mess as I was. I began cleaning, straightening, dusting, changing the sheets and pillowcases. I went to the laundromat, bought freshly baked baguettes from the *boulangerie* next door, walnut cheesecake from the *pâtisserie* down the street, and smoked ham from the *charcuterie* around the corner. From the *épicerie* I got red grapes and two ripe Cavaillon melons, a fragrant soft cheese from Burgundy, *pâté de foie gras* from Provence, and two bottles of Château de Beaupré. Grace would not subsist happily, as I had, on old cheese, canned soups, and other scraps and leftovers. In a city known for its fine food and great restaurants, she would insist on eating well.

The more I thought about Grace's impending arrival, the stranger it seemed. How, I wondered, had she managed to get away from Paul, her husband? What had she told him? "Going to Paris. Be back soon."?

What would she say to my partners at Anderson Davis? "I'm off to Paris to be with Jack. Oh, and in case you didn't know, we've been lovers for a long time." And what would we do, once she was here?

I felt myself smile for the first time in a long while. I mean, what *else* would we do?

29

The candles on the dining table were lit, the Château de Beaupré open and breathing, the two sparkling glasses catching the candlelight. Nearly midnight. Why wasn't she here? I paced and fidgeted. Was my shave close enough? My hair needs cutting, I thought. Why does hair grow in my ears now, when it never did before? My palms are sweaty. Why do I have these dark pouches under my eyes? My eyes are a bit bloodshot. Maybe I need . . .

A knock at the door. I felt as nervous as a teenager on a first date. The door opened. Standing in the doorway Grace looked small but never more beautiful, in the dark green silk dress we'd bought together last month. We said nothing. I touched her face, wrapped my arms around her tiny waist, feeling, as I always did, large and awkward in her petite presence. We kissed, tentatively at first, and then fervently. I felt warm, wanted, loved. She reached up, running her fingers softly but firmly over my scalp—"Jack Davis' second and more sensitive erogenous zone," she once called it—and through my hair.

"Jack, what's this?" Her fingers had stopped on the scab that had formed over my head wound.

"It's nothing, really. Just a scab." She pulled my head down and turned on a lamp for a closer look.

"Good Lord, this looks serious. You should see a doctor."

"I did see a doctor. It's okay. It looks worse than it is. I bumped my head in a pub in Oxford. You know me. Always bumping into something. Anyway, it's all right now."

"But darling, why didn't you tell me? I thought you said you'd told me everything that had happened."

"Everything important," I said. "This wasn't important." Not as important, I thought, as something else I hadn't told her. The tale of the four silk cords could be related later. But not now. Especially not now.

"What other unimportant things haven't you told me?"

I swallowed hard. "I can't remember. Must be the bump on my head," I joked. "Amnesia. Can't remember a thing. Except," I said, no longer joking, "I love you."

Grace smiled and touched my face. "And I love you, Jack. I didn't know how much before. But now I do. Ever since you left I've been beside myself with worry. I was so afraid that something was going to happen to you. That you . . . you might . . . And I just couldn't bear the thought of losing you. It scared me, Jack. Like I've never been scared before."

I wasn't sure if she meant losing me to death or to Danielle, or to both, but I thought it better not to ask. I poured two glasses of the Château de Beaupré and handed one to Grace.

"Cheers, my love," I said. "Here's to you."

"Here's to us," she said, touching her glass to mine.

We each took a sip, and smiled. Then I felt my smile fade. "Grace?"

"Yes?"

"There's something I've been wanting to ask you. Maybe now's not the time . . ."

"Ask me what?"

"About Paul. I assume he knows you're here. What did you tell him?"

"Of course he knows where I am. I wouldn't just leave without letting him know where I was going."

"But what did you say?"

Grace frowned and took in a deep breath, exhaling slowly as she spoke. "He knew I was worried about something. Last Friday he finally asked. I told him the truth—that I was worried about you. Then I couldn't hold back any longer. One truth led to another. I told him about us. I'm not sure he was completely surprised. It was almost as though he expected it. Then I told him I was thinking of coming to Paris to see you. To be with you. He was hurt. Angry. We quarreled all weekend. He said if I went, don't bother to come back because he won't be there. Then, early Monday morning—shortly before 6:00—I stopped by your apartment to water your plants and pick up your mail. And the sun was just coming up and I thought of all the stolen afternoons and early evenings we'd spent together and how it would be so nice to stay all night, every night, and wake up in your arms in the morning and watch the sun come up. And I wanted that, Jack. Wanted it so badly that my body ached with missing you. I tried to distract myself by listening to your phone messages. Then I heard the message from Dr. Guilloud about your being in the hospital, and suddenly I knew what I had to do. I called Air France and made a reservation on the first available flight. Then I called the office and left a message on the machine saying that I was taking a week off for a personal emergency. I went straight home and packed my bag and took a taxi to JFK. And now here I am, with you."

I still couldn't quite believe it. "Sounds like you've burned some bridges."

"All the way down to the waterline, my love. And Jack?" She sounded both worried and eager.

"Yes, love?"

"I've got some other news to tell you."

"What news?"

"I've been seeing a lawyer."

I was taken aback. "'Seeing' in what sense?" She looked puzzled. "I mean, seeing as in dating, or seeing as in consulting?"

Grace burst out laughing. "Seeing as in consulting, of course. The only lawyer I've been 'seeing' in the other sense is you. And I haven't been seeing nearly enough of you. In the dating, not the consulting, sense."

"So this lawyer you're seeing—consulting—is he a . . . a divorce lawyer?" My hopes had begun to rise.

"No," she said. My hopes fell fast. "Not exactly," she added. They stopped falling.

"How do you mean, 'not exactly'?"

"He's a canon lawyer. A Church lawyer. There just might—and I repeat *might*—be a chance to have my marriage annulled."

"After . . . how many years has it been? But your marriage has . . . it's been consummated. Sexually, I mean. You've had . . ." My face was flushing and I felt unaccountably embarrassed.

"Yes, darling Jack. You're right. Right on all counts. None of which matters very much, in the end, from the Church's perspective."

"I'm sorry. I'm not Catholic. I'm a badly lapsed Baptist. And a very confused one. You've told me for years that you couldn't get a divorce. And now you're saying you can get an *annulment*?"

"Yes."

"On what grounds?" I must have sounded more like an officious lawyer than an ardent lover. But I wasn't quite believing what I was hearing, and this is the way lawyers pinch themselves.

Grace opened her slim black briefcase. It contained two large books. One was a black leather-bound Bible; the other a thick tan paperback volume I didn't recognize. "On these grounds," she said, pulling out the tan paperback. "The new—the 1994—*Catechism of the Catholic Church* continues the Church's teaching on divorce. Divorce is still forbidden, except for adultry and other egregious violations. Which Paul, so far as I know, isn't guilty of . . . although I am. He could divorce me, if he wanted—which he says he doesn't—but I can't divorce him, even though I wish I could. Ironic, isn't it? But consistent, too. That's my Church. Straitjacket, body bag and cuddly warm down comforter all at the same time. Inspiration and irritation in equal measure."

"So what does the new *Catechism* say? About annulment, I mean?"

"It expands and extends the grounds for the dissolution of marriage. Not a lot, but a little, anyway. I think—and the canon lawyer agrees—that there's a way out. A trap-door or escape hatch that I'm entitled to use."

"Any porthole in a storm?," I quipped, warming to what seemed to be imminent.

"I'm not joking, Jack. This is serious business for me, if not for you. You might be lapsed from your faith, but I'm not from mine. I still love my Church. And, foolish though I might be, I still love you." She shot a searingly affectionate look at me. "Hence my problem."

"Our problem," I said. "I'm sorry, love. I would never make light of the Church or your attachment to it. I know how much it means to you. It's just that I'm . . . I don't know. Maybe I'm envious. Or maybe I'm just pig-ignorant about the things that matter most. There's a lot I don't know, as I'll be the first to admit. But I do know that I love you. That much I know for certain. And if there's any way—any way at all—that you and I can be together, then I'm all for it. Hell or high water, I'll take it."

"Hell I can do without," Grace said with a slight flicker of a smile. "I'm not so sure I can do without you. Much as my better self might wish otherwise."

"And what does your better self tell you?"

"That there is a way out of my marriage that is legal, legitimate and just, and that I can live with." Grace opened the thick tan book to the midway point, and began to read. "Here, under the heading of 'Matrimonial consent,' section 1626, it says, 'The Church holds the exchange of consent between the spouses to be the indispensable element that "makes the marriage." If consent is lacking there is no marriage.' And then, in section 1628, it says that 'The consent must be an act of the will of each of the contracting parties, free of coercion or grave external fear. No human power can substitute for this consent. If this freedom is lacking the marriage is invalid'."

"By these lights, Jack—by my Church's own lights—my marriage is invalid. I married Paul to please my father. It was out of love and respect for, and not a little fear of, my father, may God rest his soul, that I married. He never hit me, never abused me. Physically, anyway. But verbally . . . his words were weapons. Weapons as sharp as that arrowhead you used to carry, that could cut me to the quick and down to the bone of my being."

From my pocket I pulled my arrowhead and handed it to Grace. She stroked the cracked crystalline triangle between her thumb and fingers. "And now that he's gone he's no longer a threat. He's still a presence, if you know what I mean. But not a threat. I'm not afraid anymore. Father meant well. Paul is a decent man, and I've never denied it." Tears began to gather in Grace's dark almond eyes. "But I don't love him. I never have. I care for him. I wish him well. He deserves to be happy. But I can't bring him that happiness. Not now. Not ever." She put her arms around my waist and hugged me hard. "And so here I am, with you. Actions *versus* words, and all those clichés. I'm here. With you."

I held her close and wished the moment would never end. But, inevitably and predictably, it did. Not that that was a bad thing. Grace was tired after her trip, a little jet-lagged, but energized too. She seemed ten years younger, happier, more carefree than she'd ever been in New York. We snuggled close and talked into the night about all sorts of things. Some serious—Jessica, especially—and some less so.

"Your concierge is a piece of work, isn't she?," Grace asked, almost laughing.

"Yes, and that's putting it mildly. She's something of an old racist, I think. Did she give you trouble? About being Asian, I mean?"

"No, not about being Asian. She asked if I were Japanese. 'Etes-vous Japonaise, Madame?,' she asked. It wasn't exactly a friendly question. And when I answered, 'Non, je suis Chinoise-Américaine. Pourquoi?', she looked relieved and loosened up. 'De rien,' she said, with that slightly repulsive gap-toothed smile of hers. Then, as she waved me up the stairs, she told me to give you her best regards. She rather fancies you, I think."

We both laughed at that.

It was late, the end of a long day. We went to sleep happy, knowing that we would wake in each other's arms and watch the sun come up.

◄30►

The dawn sky was a dull slate gray. Grace was still asleep. I tried to get out of bed without waking her.

"Jack?," she whispered hoarsely, almost inaudibly.

"Yes, love?"

"Why were you in the hospital? I kept waiting for you to tell me, but you never did. What was this illness?"

It wasn't really an illness, I started to say, but a concussion. I wanted to lie, to invent something plausible. Maybe something associated with physical and emotional exhaustion. Chronic fatigue. Pneumonia. A lie to protect Grace from the truth. From the threat that she too might face if we stayed in Paris much longer. But because I didn't want our new beginning to get off to a false start I came clean. I told her the truth.

"Someone tried to kill me, to poison me. They didn't succeed. Obviously."

Grace's face grew as gray as the skies outside. "My God, Jack. My God. What's happening? Who would *do* this? And *why*?"

It wasn't the best way to start the day, but I told Grace what I knew, or suspected, amplifying what I told her in my long e-mail message and what I'd learned since, and about the Banque Merceaux. She was silent. Then, trying to sound cheerier than I felt, I said, "Let's leave this apartment and check into a hotel. We'll have a proper honeymoon in Paris. Eat well. Drink well. Live it up. Make love. And then get the hell out of here."

"Honeymoons come after weddings. We're not married, Jack."

The wind left my sails.

"Not yet, anyway," Grace added.

My limp sails filled again. And then they emptied abruptly.

"Where exactly is this Banque Merceaux?," Grace asked, sitting up in bed, the satin sheet sliding away to reveal her small perfectly formed breasts. "They might know you, but they don't know me from Eve. I think maybe I should go check it out."

Grace had that gleam in her eye that I called The Look. I knew exactly what she had in mind. "No, love, please no. These people aren't fooling around. They're dangerous. They killed Ted, and then Danielle, and they almost killed me. Please don't even think about getting involved in this mess."

"But Jack, I already am. We are. We might as well see it through. In for a penny, in for a pound. And don't forget the most important thing."

"What's that?"

"Ted. He was my friend, too. I loved him almost as much as you did. You took risks to find out who killed him. You tried your best. Now it's my turn." She hugged her knees to her breasts, like a little girl contemplating an adventure.

Grace looked fragile, vulnerable. I wanted to protect her. I felt torn between love for my dead friend and love for my dearest living friend and, I now hoped, future wife.

"What, exactly," I asked warily, "do you have in mind?"

"I was thinking about maybe renting a safe-deposit box at the Banque Merceaux. That would get me inside the building and, I'd guess, in the general vicinity of the vault. Close enough to check things out."

Close enough to get into serious trouble, I thought, as Grace threw back the sheet and got out of bed. She was wearing only a tiny gold ankle bracelet. My eyes followed as her slim, beautifully proportioned, compact body moved lithely across the floor and disappeared into the bathroom.

Grace came into the kitchen just as I was pouring my second cup of coffee. She wore a dark blue linen jacket and matching skirt, a gray silk blouse, and the faux-ivory cameo necklace I'd given her last Christmas. All of which I wanted to remove, one by one, except for the necklace, and take her back to bed. She must have read my mind, or, more likely, my eyes.

"I know what you're thinking, Jack. I'm thinking the same thing myself. But business before pleasure. Pour a cup for me, my love, and then show me how to find the Banque Merceaux."

We spread the fold-out map from *Paris A–Z* on the table. I showed Grace where we were, and where the Rue Saint Lazare was, making a pencil mark on both, and drawing a jagged line along the streets connecting them. "Take this with you," I said.

"No, I'd rather not. I don't want to look like a tourist. I want to look like I know what I'm doing, even if I don't. Draw me a map of this little section here," she said, pointing to the small area of the map that I'd marked with my pencil, and handing me the small black notebook she always carried. On the first blank page I sketched my own serviceable if not very well-drawn map.

"Now," she said, "write the combination on the back."

"Grace, you're not going to . . ."

"No, of course not. But just in case. For future reference. And Jack?"

"Yes, love?"

"I need one other thing."

"What?"

"A shopping bag. Preferably a large one."

"You're going shopping?"

"No, silly. I want to *look* like I've been shopping. So I won't call attention to myself. Have you seen any of these Parisian women without at least one—and usually more—shopping bags?"

"I hadn't really noticed," I said as I pulled a large shiny green paper shopping bag from the hall closet.

"I figured as much," Grace said, rolling her eyes and stuffing a white sweater into the shopping bag.

We walked together as far as the Rue de Châteaudin.

"Better not come any closer, Jack. I can find my way from here. I'll meet you back at the apartment in about an hour. Two, at most. Keep the door bolted, and don't open it unless you hear three fast knocks, a delay, and then two more. That's our signal." She blew a kiss in my direction and turned to go.

"How's your French?," I asked as she walked away.

"Better than yours," she said, looking back over her shoulder and smiling.

◄31►

It had been more than two hours since Grace and I had said good-bye, and there was still no sign of her. What if we'd been followed? Or seen together? Maybe she was at this very moment a captive, tied down with four silken cords. Tortured. Or already dead. Why did I let her go through with this? I should have said no. No, I should have said nothing—not a word about the Banque Merceaux, about my suspicions, or any of the rest of it. It was all my fault, from the beginning to this terrible end. I would never, ever forgive myself, I thought, reaching into my pocket and wrapping my fingers tightly around the arrowhead.

There were three fast knocks on the door, a delay, followed by two more. I unbolted the door. Grace shot past me like a greyhound. She looked excited, scared, almost stricken.

"Bolt the door, Jack. Now, quickly, please." She was breathing hard. "These were kind of heavy," she said, turning around and holding up the shiny shopping bag.

"My God, Grace, you didn't . . ."

"I did, and here they are. At least I think so. Here," she said, putting the bag on the table and removing the contents. Under the white sweater were three magenta-colored boxes, one large—about twelve by sixteen inches, by six inches deep—and two almost half that size. "I wasn't sure which was which. I was in a hurry, so I grabbed them all."

I opened the large box. The contents smelled old and musty. It didn't have a title page, but it looked like a manuscript of six, maybe seven-hundred carefully handwritten pages. The paper was brown and cracked. In places, the ink had run and words were illegible. Some corners were broken off. The pages felt powdery to the touch. Then I noticed that one side—the right side—was slightly charred, dark gray, almost black.

"Jesus Christ, Grace, this is it—the *Institutions politiques*."

"How do you know?"

"I just know, believe me. I'll tell you later. Now maybe you'll tell me how you . . . No, on second thought, tell me while we pack. We've got to get out of here. Now."

"And go to a hotel?"

"Go to the goddamned airport. And right away. There's no time to lose. Not a minute." Now I was breathing hard. "Did anybody see you? Follow you?"

"I don't think so. No, I'm pretty sure no one did."

We started packing. I didn't open the other boxes. One of them, I guessed, contained the Levasseur diary. I wasn't even able to guess what the other might contain. But I didn't have time to try to figure it out. I'd leave that to the experts back in the States. For now, all I could think about was leaving. And the faster, the better.

We threw our clothes willy-nilly into the largest suitcase. I took one of Ted's carry-on cases out of the hall closet, put the large magenta box inside, surrounded by socks and underwear, and closed it gently. I wrapped my raincoat around the two smaller boxes and put them into my own cloth-sided suitcase. Both, I hoped, were compact enough to carry on board the plane. The last thing I wanted was the airline losing luggage containing Rousseau's *Institutions politiques*, which had already cost the lives of an old friend and a new one. My throat was tight, my adrenalin level rising rapidly.

"How," I asked Grace in an almost soprano stage whisper across the room, "did you get these things?"

"I went into the bank and asked about renting *un coffre-fort*, a safe-deposit box. '*Gros ou petit*'?, I was asked. Turns out there are two sizes, the larger being about the size of a small trunk or suitcase; the smaller ones about the size of a shoebox. They're housed in two different rooms near the back of the bank. I figured if the Société de Jean-Jacques was using a box to store old folio-sized manuscripts, they would have to use the larger ones. So I asked for *un gros coffre-fort*, filled out a form, and was given the key to the room and a number and combination for my box. And get this, Jack: As I was being taken to the back room we walked down a long corridor, first passing, on the right, the room where the smaller boxes are kept. Then, just before we got to the other room, there was a large polished wooden door to the left. A brass plate on the door said, '**78. Privé. N'entrez Pas.**' 'Le président de la banque?,' I asked. 'Non, c'est une société savante pour les études Rousseauistes', I was told. 'Vous connaissez, Rousseau le philosophe'. Then I was led a little farther down the hall to the room where the larger boxes are housed, tried my key and went inside. Unfortunately there was an old man there who took the longest time. He was looking at something—I couldn't see what—but I waited and waited, pretending to look at something in my box. Finally, after nearly an hour, he left. I had a hunch. I went over to box 78 and tried the combination you'd written down. And, Jack—it worked! Like a charm. Opened right up. There were three boxes and some file folders inside. I scooped the boxes into my shopping bag, closed the drawer, and got out as fast as I could. I wanted to run back down the hall, past suite 78, through the lobby, and out into the street. But I didn't. I took my time, looking cool and casual and a little haughty, as so many of these Parisian women do, just like I owned the bank."

"Were there video cameras?"

"Yes, of course, all over . . ."

"No, in the safe-deposit box room—were there cameras in there?"

"Yes, one. But I don't think it was working."

"Oh? Why not?"

"Because the other cameras had a little red light under the lens. You know, to show that they're on? Well, this one didn't have a red light. So I assume it wasn't working."

"Yes, Grace, but what if it was?"

"Relax, Jack. Don't hyperventilate. If these cameras are like the ones in American banks, they merely record what they see, on videotape, on a two to four second digital delay. It makes bank videos look like silent movies, with a kind of jerky, Charlie Chaplin look. But don't worry. The video cameras don't broadcast live to humans watching monitors in some central control room. Of course, the banks don't want you to know that. But in reality the tapes are pulled and played only after the fact, after there's been a bank robbery . . ."

"Like the bank robbery you just pulled," I said incredulously.

"Yes," Grace said, smiling as she pulled the thigh portion of a pair of her pantyhose over her head. "Like the one I just pulled. Call me Bugsy Wu." She pretended to spray the room with bullets from an imaginary machine gun.

"How do you know all this stuff—about bank security systems and such?"

Grace frowned through the mask. "From Paul. It's his business, remember?"

Then I did remember. Her husband Paul owned a commercial security service specializing in everything from electronic alarm systems to guard dogs. Strangely, I felt better, less frantic. I stopped stuffing clothes into my suitcase and walked over to Grace, peeling the pantyhose back from her face just far enough to expose her lips. I kissed her.

"Who is this masked woman, armed and dangerous?," I asked.

"She's got arms, all right," Grace said, removing the pantyhose mask and dropping it to the floor, the first of a trail of garments, hers and mine mingling. Showing strength far beyond her size, my diminutive lover began pushing me backwards toward the bed. "And breasts and buttocks, too. And legs. To wrap around you and crush you if you try to resist. Don't cross me, see? 'Cause I'll waste ya, see?" Her Jimmy Cagney impression wasn't impressive, but her intentions were clear. I got the point.

It was the strangest sensation. We were both on a drug-free high in the aftermath, and as a result of, a highly illegal act. Finally I understood what Ted must have meant about using "means that were neither entirely ethical nor irreproachably legal." Had he done the same thing some three weeks earlier? Had he acted alone? Or had he had a partner in crime? I lost my train of thought as my strong-willed lover, now wearing only a faux-ivory cameo necklace, covered me with kisses and caresses.

Our lovemaking was always good, and often more than that. But this broke beyond the usual boundaries to—I'm not sure what words to use. And in any case modesty and a due sense of decorum forbids my saying more. *Privé. N'entrez pas.*

32

Through a groggy post-coital haze a question came to me. "Grace?" No answer. "Grace?"

She stirred like a drunk in a stupor. "Yes?," she replied, rolling toward me.

"You said you filled out a form at the bank. To rent the safe-deposit box."

"Yes." She rolled away from me and covered her head with a pillow. "Why?," a muffled voice asked.

"What name and address did you use?"

A silence. Then, slowly, she pulled the pillow away. "My name—they asked for an i.d.—and this address. It's the only address in Paris I know."

I felt like I'd been shocked by an electric eel. Or by a computer power pack.

"Good God, Grace, our first instincts were right. We've got to get out of here. Now. I mean immediately. It's been . . ."—I looked at my watch—"about four hours since you took that stuff. If they've discovered it missing, they'll look at the videotapes. But, tapes or no, they'll ask what safe-deposit box renters—especially new or first-time renters—came in today. And they'll find the form with your name—and, what's worse, this address—on it. And they'll be on us like flies on shit—excuse my French."

Grace sat bolt upright. "My God, Jack, you're right. I wasn't thinking."

"No, darling, you were thinking hard and straight. You had a lot on your mind. You did a truly fine job on . . . on everything else."

"Except for that," Grace said. "Damn! If only . . ."

Grace was always harder on herself than anybody else ever was, or could be.

"It's all right," I said, trying to sound more soothing than I felt. "Everything's probably okay. Most likely they haven't missed anything yet. But we do need to get out of here right away. We're pretty much packed and ready to go. All that remains is to call for a taxi. No, on second thought, let's get out of here and take our chances out on the street."

Grace was already up, pulling on a pair of jeans and a jumper. In ten minutes we were ready to go. I unbolted the door and turned around to pick up the suitcases and my lap-top.

Suddenly, the door flew open and I was kicked hard from behind and fell over a suitcase. When I turned around and looked up my worst fears were confirmed.

33

"Miss Wu, I believe." A trim, tanned man in his early sixties addressed Grace in an American midwestern accent. He had large sad eyes and a long gallic nose set in a deeply lined face, a flowing white mane, a well-trimmed goatee, and wore a dark gray pinstripe suit with a white turtleneck. "You have several things that belong to me, I believe. I must ask you to return them at once."

He was accompanied by two men. One, as tall as I but much heavier and more muscular, had his hand over Grace's mouth. Her eyes were wide with terror; I don't doubt that mine were too. The other man, who looked to be in his late twenties, was of medium build, and extraordinarily handsome. He looked familiar, but I couldn't quite place the face.

"Coindet," the older man said, motioning to the handsome one. "Les valises, s'il vous plaît." He opened our suitcases roughly.

"Voilà!," Coindet said triumphantly as he extracted the magenta boxes. The older man with the ample white mane nodded approvingly.

"Merceaux," I implored, "it's not her fault. Let her go. She has nothing to do with this."

"Oh?," he said incredulously. "You even know my name. Or think you do. My name, sir, is Roguin. And who," he sniffed, "might you be?"

"Davis. Jack Davis. I'm responsible. She has nothing to do with this."

"So, Mr. Davis," he said, his voice dripping sarcasm, "that was really you on the surveillance tape, much shorter—and may I say much prettier—in a woman's dress and looking fetchingly feminine and, how shall I say, distinctly non-occidental?"

In my terror and confusion I'd forgotten about the surveillance cameras. This was not going well.

"Look," I said, "I put her up to this. She did it for me—because of me."

Despite having her mouth covered by Goliath's hand, Grace was shaking her head in vigorous disagreement. I wanted her to stop, to nod in agreement, but she would not.

"Obviously, the lady disagrees," Roguin said, almost pleasantly. "Turk"—he addressed Goliath—"Permettez à madam de s'exprimer." The man-machine let Grace go. "You must forgive Turk. He does not know his own strength. I hope you are not hurt. Bruises do so ill-become a lady."

"I'm no lady," Grace replied curtly, "and I'll wager none of you is a gentleman, either. We're thieves, yes. We—no, I—took the manuscripts. But at least we're not murderers. We never killed anybody."

Roguin seemed taken aback. Probably, I thought, because he had not expected so small a woman to have such a large mouth. My spirits, already way down, sank even lower. Now they'll kill us for sure.

"But Madame," he said, "surely you are not suggesting that I or my associates would stoop to murder. Murder is the prerogative of criminals and the state. I assure you that we are neither."

"What about Ted, then?," Grace demanded.

"You accuse me of that?" Roguin seemed genuinely insulted. Of course he—or more probably Turk—had killed Ted, and then murdered and raped Danielle. Now he was denying it as though insulted by the accusation. "I learned of Hume's . . . of Professor Porter's death the day after it happened. It was in all the papers. But it was not murder. It was an accident."

Accident, indeed. Only a real psychopath, I thought, can lie with such sincerity and conviction. As Grandma Della would say of a calculating and cold-blooded liar, butter wouldn't melt in his mouth.

"And what," I asked, emboldened by Grace's courage, "about Danielle Dupin? I suppose you had nothing to do with her death, either."

There was an ominous, heavy silence. I heard breathing and, I thought, the low muted thud of heartbeats.

"My sister," the handsome one said at last in slightly accented English, "she die of the heart attack. At least this is what I am told when I travel to Oxford last week to reclaim her body and bring her back to our parents. But Jeanne-Marie, I mean Danielle, she never have the heart condition. She was healthy as . . . as—what animal do you say?"

"A horse," I said distractedly, automatically. As he spoke I kept having flashbacks, thinking of—no, actually picturing—Danielle. He had her accent, her mannerisms, and a masculine version of her extraordinary beauty. He had her gray-green eyes, her olive skin, her curly brown hair cut short. I couldn't take my eyes off him, even to look at Grace.

"Yes, healthy as the horse," he continued. "She was never ill. Never. Not for one day. But the policeman, the Inspector Grant, he say she wear the bracelet and carry the card that say she have the heart condition. This is lie. Someone leave these things with her body. I am thinking at first that it is you, since she die in your apartment. But the inspector, he say she die when you are away, and that many people see you somewhere else. For you, this is good. I would kill you myself if you kill my sister. This I would do even though she side with Hume and betray our Société. Now I do not know what to think. All I know is that someone kill her. Then, when she is dead, they rape her." His voice began to break. "My father, who is physician, he order a, how do you say, a independent autopsy. It show this. It show her heart stop because it beat too fast. There is," he said, his eyes glistening, "much adrian . . ."

"Adrenalin," Roguin interjected, "to bring on violent cardiac arhythmia. Unmetabolized traces were still in her blood and in the subcutaneous tissue where she was injected. She was apparently given massive injections of adrenalin, in her scalp and under the nails of her big toes, where the needle marks wouldn't show, except as bruises. For this Danielle was tied down . . ." Roguin's face was ashen. If he was acting, he was doing a superb job of it. "What you and the English police saw was the serene aftermath of a very violent death. There were," he continued calmly but with evident difficulty, "perhaps three killers. Or at least three men were present at Danielle's death. Traces of semen from three different males were found in three orifices. In the vaginal and anal cavities. And in her throat. Apparently Danielle—or Danielle's body—was raped after she had died. The English Medical Examiner's report also noted the presence of semen. But, believing the death an accident, he didn't perform an autopsy. Nor did he do the DNA tests that showed the semen came from three genetically different sources. The English police prejudged the case and misinterpreted the evidence. They were remiss in almost every respect."

I could have said the same about the Parisian police investigation into Ted's death. But I didn't. I was too overcome by the enormity of the horror.

"You see," Roguin said in what seemed like a *non sequitur* and in complete contrast with the clinically detached description that had gone before, "beauty is important. Supremely important. In a human being beauty is fleeting, as youth and life are fleeting. It is all the more important for that. For human beauty is not like that of a statue or a painting or a piece of music. It is of the moment. Danielle was of the moment. Supremely beautiful and then gone, like *le papillon*."

It was Roguin's first lapse into French.

For once and at last I did not need to comb my memory for the translation. Not a beautiful word in English, but beautiful in French, *le papillon* denoted something both beautiful and exquisitely ephemeral. Unbidden images of butterflies flitted across the screen of memory, from the fields of my grandparents' farm before the pesticides wiped out the butterflies that flitted by day and the fireflies that flickered by night. Superimposed upon this old memory was a newer one, of Danielle with the wings of an angel. Or a butterfly. Yes, that's it, a butterfly. She was anything but virtuous and monochromatic, like an angel, but earthy and multicolored, like . . .

"Nevertheless," Roguin's recomposed voice resumed, breaking my reverie, "Danielle was a traitor. Now she is dead. And we are here and alive. And you," he said, his eyes darting from me to Grace and back again, "are thieves." It was as though someone else were speaking, quite distinct from the benign, almost avuncular voice that had welled with sorrow and some difficulty through the larynx and vocal cords of our captor. Which, I wondered, was the real Roguin? Or was I now seeing the more relentless and merciless Merceaux?

"We are thieves, yes," Grace repeated. "As God is my witness, I confess it. But before God my conscience is clear. Before a French court my conscience will count for nothing. So, go ahead. Phone the police. The telephone's in the study."

Smart move, I thought. We'd surely fare better at the hands of the Parisian police than we would in the clutches of Roguin and his henchmen.

"Very clever, Miss Wu," Roguin replied evenly. "But I won't be calling the police. And I won't be pressing charges. I've recovered what you stole from me . . ."

"Why not call the police?" I interrupted, hoping to reinforce Grace's inspired suggestion. "After all, we did take the . . ."

"Mr. Davis," Roguin glowered. "I'd rather not involve the police, if"—he shot a withering glance at Grace before meeting my gaze—"you and Miss Wu don't mind."

"But we're thieves," Grace interjected. "We deserve to be tried and punished."

"Oh, please, Br'er Fox," Roguin purred in a perfect American southern accent, "whatever you do, don't throw me into 'dat 'dere briar patch. You see," he continued coldly, "I know your American tricks. Much as I would like to see you punished, I shall not leave that task to the police and prisons of my country."

"And why not?" Grace goaded.

"Because I do not wish any publicity regarding the whereabouts, or even the existence, of the *Institutions politiques.* It is bad enough that you and your late friend knew of it." I didn't like the way he used the past tense of know. "But to involve the police and the press would be unwise. Worst of all, curators from the Bibliothèque Nationale would have their curiosity aroused. They would insist on seeing this manuscript, to test its authenticity. And then, in the name of the French state and for the sake of that chimera they call 'French culture', they would confiscate it—to make it available to the prying eyes of so-called scholars who will once again attack Jean-Jacques, this time for writing something that he himself ordered destroyed." Roguin's furrowed face had metamorphosed into a sculpted steel mask, from which a metallic voice emanated. “This I will not do, *ever*, under any circumstances. I trust that I make myself clear.”

As Roguin’s visage hardened, Grace’s seemed to soften. Then, almost sweetly, she said, “Our dear friend Ted died—was killed—apparently for doing what we did. He, too, took the Rousseau manuscript . . .”

“Oh, but he didn’t,” Roguin interrupted, the mask metamorphosing back into a mobile face wearing a look of almost childlike wonder and surprise. “He could have, of course, but he didn’t. He did, however, take the Levasseur diary, which he then . . .”

“Wait a minute,” I said, hearing the incredulity in my own voice. “Ted *didn’t* take the *Institutions politiques*?”

“No,” Roguin said. “And that is the curious thing. He took only the Levasseur diary, leaving in its place a—how do you say?—a video tape. To trade the one for the other is an insult, a slap in my face. To have passed over the *Institutions politiques* is a slap in the Master’s face.”

“In Rousseau’s face, you mean?”

“Of course. But at the same time I am relieved that he—unlike you—did not remove the Master’s manuscript from the vault which protects it not only from thieves but from the extremes of moisture and dryness which will destroy it. Which is why we must,” he said, motioning to Turk, “return it and the diary at once.”

“Wait,” I said, “I mean, *arrêtez-vous*.” Turk grimaced and then stopped. “What’s on this videotape that Ted left in place of the Levasseur diary?”

“This I do not know,” Roguin replied. “I have not seen it. I do not have a—how do you call it?—a video machine. The bank guards, they have one; but I do not. Nor do I have a television. These things do not interest me. But even so I would not view this video display.”

“And why not?,” I asked, even as I remembered Sir Jeremiah’s account of the Société’s hostility to modern technology.

“Because,” Roguin replied, “it is an insult. He takes my manuscript and leaves a videotape. A videotape! And worse, the tape has a label saying that it is from a video dating service—as though I were some silly girl to be wooed and won by these means! What is this, if not an insult?”

“You won’t know until you’ve seen the tape,” Grace said. “If it’s insulting or in any way offensive, give me a match—or, better yet, a hammer—and I’ll destroy it myself.”

For the first time Roguin looked perplexed.

"Look," I said in my most measured tones, "Ted—Hume—shared so much of your antipathy to modern technology. To use a phone was for him an irritation, and a fax a real pain. To make this videotape must have been an ordeal. He was trying desperately to reach you, to catch your attention, to say something important. We won't know what until we've seen that tape."

Roguin frowned and then turned to Turk and asked, in French, if the tape still existed. Turk nodded affirmatively. Then go get it, Roguin said, and bring it back here immediately. And take the manuscripts back to the vault. Now go. Turk left at once.

I could see Grace's body relax. To have been in the grip of that gorilla had obviously been a nightmare, and I immediately embraced her. Then I turned toward Roguin.

"How," I asked, "did you get the Levasseur diary back?"

"Without taking it from Ted," Grace interjected, "and then killing him to avenge the theft."

Roguin winced and then shook his white mane. "Hume returned it," he said. Seeing the puzzlement on my face he added, "Not in person, of course. He dropped it into the exterior night-deposit safe at the bank, two days after he stole it. It was wrapped in brown paper, marked 'private', with my former name on it."

The mention of his old name prompted another question. "I know why you are called Roguin," I said, "and why Ted was called Hume." Roguin seemed surprised that I knew the nomenclature. "But I don't know where Mr. Coindet gets his name, or why Mr. Turk is called Turk."

"Then obviously you know little," Roguin replied, "about the life of Jean-Jacques. François Coindet was, as you Americans might say, a 'groupie'. He was an ambitious, star-struck young Swiss bank-clerk who became a hanger-on in Rousseau's household. He ran errands for the Master, and traded inside information and gossip for favors from others who were eager to know of Jean-Jacques' comings and goings. And as for Turk, he was of course Rousseau's most faithful and constant companion."

It was my turn to be surprised. I pictured a large Turkish man wearing a fez. "More faithful and constant than Roguin?," I asked.

"In his way, yes. You see, Turk was Rousseau's dog."

Instinctively I smiled.

"Before you betray your ignorance by laughing," Roguin said, frowning, "let me add that Turk was what every dog should be—loving, loyal to his master, a menace to his master's enemies. When Turk died, Jean-Jacques was inconsolable. He wept uncontrollably, for days on end. He received letters of condolence from friends and admirers, including members of the French nobility, all attesting to and remembering Turk's canine virtues."

"Virtues," I queried, barely suppressing a smile, "in a dog? How can that be?"

A pained look crossed Roguin's lined face. "Mr. Davis," he said, "I cannot begin to compensate for your years of miseducation. But on pain of embarrassing us both, let me merely remind you that the English word 'virtue', like the French *vertue*, comes from the Latin *virtus*, which is a rather bad translation of the Greek σρετε, which means something like 'role-related specific excellence.' So the *aretē* of a soldier is courage, that of a racehorse its speed, and the *aretē* of a guard-dog its loyalty to its master and its ferocity to his master's foes. Homer describes Odysseus' dog Argos as having canine *aretē*. You might recall the final proof of this in the conclusion to the *Odyssey*. When Odysseus returns to his homeland disguised as a beggar, no one—not his wife Penelope, nor his son Telemachus—recognizes him. But the faithful Argos does. His master having returned at last, the old dog—neglected, unwashed, left to lie on a dung-heap—leaps for joy and then, his duty done, he dies. That is canine *aretē*—doggy virtue, if you like. Rousseau's Turk had it in full measure. And so does my Turk. He would tear the limbs off anyone who dared threaten me."

I took the point. Not that I was thinking of threatening Roguin, who was proving to be even more intriguing than I had expected. Could he actually be innocent of the murders of Ted and Danielle—and of trying to kill me? If so, my best—in fact my only—hypothesis was down the drain and into the Parisian sewers.

Turk returned with a pink plastic case. He offered it to Roguin, who frowned and refused to take it, saying, "Je ne sais rien de l'opération de cette machine infernale." He motioned to Turk to give it to me.

The pink case bore the Vidéo Date logo, which looked like a modern or abstract depiction of a flower and then, looked at differently and more closely, of a couple copulating. I walked across the room and turned on the television set and VCR that Ted never used, opened the pink plastic case and removed the cassette. The black plastic cassette was marked only with the initials T.J.M.P., a six-digit number, and the Vidéo Date address and telephone number. I slipped the cassette into the VCR and pressed the play button.

The television screen showed an array of colors, followed by numbers in a circle and a ticking sound as the numbers ran backward from 10 to 1. The screen faded to black and the volume increased markedly as loud throbbing music, dominated by a bass drum and other percussion instruments, picked up tempo. Scenes of lovers holding hands as they walked along the Seine, stealing kisses, embracing each other's backsides, and generally looking lascivious as the throbbing intensified and the come-hither voice of a female narrator pouted, "Pourquoi la vie seule, la vie triste?" She whispered sultrily that "le monde merveilleux de l'amour" could be yours. The throbbing intensified to a fever pitch and I pressed the fast-forward button on the remote control. A blurred collage of images included bare breasts and buttocks, a hand moving up a thigh. Had Ted actually seen this, I wondered? Somehow I doubted it.

Then, suddenly, Ted, moving fast and gesticulating wildly like Charlie Chaplin, appeared on the screen. I hit the rewind button and brought the tape back to Ted's first appearance. I pressed the play button. And there he was, leaning forward, looking straight into the camera, and speaking in the precise and persuasive way that seemed uniquely Ted's.

> My dear Roguin [he began], I do apologize for appearing before you in this rather distasteful fashion. And I do hope that you will forgive my speaking to you in English. I do so only because your English is so much better than my French. But most of all I hope that you will forgive me for taking Mme. Levasseur's diary from your vault. Rest assured, my dear Roguin, I have not stolen it. I have merely borrowed it to make a larger and more important point. Quite simply, that

> point is this: If I, a rank amateur in matters criminal, could break your code and take the Levasseur diary, then, believe me, my friend, I could certainly have taken the *Institutions politiques* as well. And don't think I wasn't tempted! I have never faced a greater temptation. But the larger point is that if I could take these things, then so could someone else. They are, if I may put it this way, unsafe in your safe.

Ted looked tired and drawn and, for him, uncharacteristically rumpled in his brown corduroy jacket and black turtleneck. But his eyes were clear and his gaze concentrated. As I saw my old friend I could feel a large lump welling up in my throat. I looked over at Grace. Her eyes were wet and red. I turned my eyes back to the screen.

> The threat of theft [Ted continued] is not merely an abstract one. You apparently believe that no one save yourself and select members of the Société know of the existence of the *Institutions politiques.* Please believe me when I tell you that you are mistaken. And please believe me when I say that I did not divulge your secret. Rather, the reverse is true. I learned of it by a rather circuitous route. As I'm sure you know, some of the best scholarly work on the history of Western political thought is now being done in the East—in Japan. The Japanese are avid and affluent collectors of letters, manuscripts, first editions, and even entire libraries. The universities are honest, but some private collectors are not so scrupulous. Works that are not for sale, or for which the price is very high, are sometimes stolen. To make a long story short, your secret is out: some pretty shady Japanese characters have apparently learned of the existence of Rousseau's *Institutions politiques.* This I heard from my old friend Professor Yukio Sugiura of Nagoya University, who had in turn inferred it from an exchange he had with his former colleague Reiji Yamomoto. You might know of ex-Professor Yamamoto, who was last year fired from the faculty of Nagoya for trafficking in stolen manuscripts and works of art. It seems that Yamamoto had been told—almost certainly by an informant inside the Société de Jean-Jacques—of the existence, if not the precise where-

abouts, of the *Institutions politiques*, and asked Professor Sugiura if he could confirm this—Sugiura being an expert on Rousseau, as you know, and Yamamoto an amateur and dilettante who uses his and others' knowledge for nefarious purposes. Sugiura told him that he for one was convinced that the manuscript had been burned, just as Rousseau himself tells us. But, upon hearing this, Yamamoto merely smiled and went away. My old friend began to worry that Yamamoto might actually be onto something, and so he contacted me and told me what he knew and what he suspected. He suspected that Yamamoto was merely the front man, as he had been previously, for wealthy collectors in Japan, Singapore, and Hong Kong, who have a peculiar fondness for rare manuscripts. This is scarcely surprising, since their value increases with age and some—including, I daresay, the *Institutions politiques*—can command prices at auction in the tens of millions of dollars and the hundreds of millions of francs. My friend Sugiura suspected that, as before, Yamamoto was working with the *boryokudan*, the Japanese mafia, but this time on the biggest prize of all. When I asked Sugiura what he wanted me to do about it, he said that I should make discreet inquiries here in Paris. Since I am well-acquainted with the standard sources and archives in Paris, Neuchâtel and Geneva, and know that they contain nothing of interest in this regard, I thought immediately of approaching you and the Société de Jean-Jacques. As you no doubt know, rumors have long circulated that the Société might have in its possession several unpublished and heretofore unknown items from Rousseau's *oeuvre*—although no one ever dared believe that the *Institutions politiques* might be among them. I tried several times, always unsuccessfully, to contact you. I was not entirely surprised to be rebuffed—I know you call me "Hume," and why—but in the course of my unsuccessful entreaties I did manage to meet one of your members, Mlle. Dupin. I did not so much meet her as remember her from a conference several years earlier. Perhaps "remember" is the wrong word, since one can hardly remember someone whom one finds unforgettable. In the course of our conversation I decided to take a chance, to confide my concerns to Danielle.

To my great surprise and relief, she was receptive. It seems that she, too, was worried that your secret could not be kept forever and that the manuscripts—the *Institutions politiques* in particular—should be put in a safer place. I agreed, and added that the only real safeguard lay in publishing them. She said that you would never agree to that. Danielle also said that it would be difficult, if not impossible, to convince you of the danger of leaving these manuscripts in your vault. And that, my dear Roguin, was my reason for hatching my plan to take the Levasseur diary but leave the *Institutions politiques* behind. I could conceive of no other way of convincing you that the secret was out, the manuscripts insecure, and the danger of theft both palpable and imminent. It was, to use a current American expression, a rather rude wake-up call. I should add, as an aside, that Danielle did not give me the combination to your safe. I asked, yes; but she refused, saying that she would never divulge your and the Société's most significant secret. She told me only that it was a five-digit combination that she carried with her always and that I knew enough about Rousseau to figure out the rest. She was right. It didn't take long to crack your code, because it is Rousseau's own exceedingly simple and—may I say with all due respect to him and to you—very silly system. All I had to do was to find a name, term, or title with five letters in it and that was in some sense significant to Rousseau. When I asked Danielle if my first choice—'Émile'—was correct, she replied with a question: "Am I carrying with me a copy of *Émile*?" Clearly, she was not. Then, all at once, it came to me. The five-letter word is 'Dupin': right 4 (= d), left 20 (= u), right 15 (= p), left 9 (= i), right 13 (= n). And this is the combination to box number 78, which is of course the year of Rousseau's death. This isn't exactly rocket science, as my daughter would say. It is *so* simple and so obvious as to be downright dangerous. Almost anyone could figure it out in an afternoon. Now if an amateur cryptologist as inept as I could crack your code and steal the Levasseur diary, I could also have taken the *Institutions politiques*—and so, my dear Roguin, could someone else with motives more, how shall I say, more impure than mine. I strongly suspect that our Mr.

> Yamamoto is, at this very moment, planning to do what I could have done, but with disastrous and possibly deadly results. I do not exaggerate when I say deadly. I just learned, two days ago, that my dear friend Sugiura has died under rather mysterious circumstances. He fell—or more probably was pushed—from the *Hikari shinkansen*, the Osaka-to-Tokyo 'bullet train'. To do this, someone with considerable knowledge of electronics had first to disable and then override the computer-controlled electronic device that keeps the doors shut while the train is in motion. My guess is that Yamamoto's backers and associates don't want anyone who might point the finger of suspicion in their direction to be alive to do so. The *boryokudan* are clever assassins and vicious killers who have a reputation for enjoying their work, some of their murders even culminating in ritual necrophilia. They are an exceedingly nasty lot. I don't know if they know about Danielle and me, though I suspect they do. Not wanting to take any chances, I've persuaded Danielle to leave Paris for a few days. Since she knows the location of and combination to your vault, and since the *boryokudan* will stop at nothing, her life could be in danger. So, my dear Roguin, could yours. And so, of course, could mine. I have seen the same Japanese tourist—a man in his mid-thirties with a camera around his neck—several times over the last two days. He doesn't appear to be following me; he merely seems to show up wherever I happen to be—including the Vidéo Date store in whose soundproof booth I am making this tape for your viewing displeasure.

Then I remembered: I had seen a Japanese tourist—probably the same one—several times. The first time was on the Channel ferry, taking Danielle's and my picture as we kissed. Then again in Oxford, at the Godstowe Lock in Port Meadow, on the day Danielle died. But I had paid no attention because Japanese tourists, like joggers, are now everywhere. Present but invisible. Invisible presences. I recalled the concierge rattling on about the *menace Japonaise*, which I'd simply brushed aside as the lunatic rantings of a racist. But then there was also her exchange with Grace, in which she was relieved to learn that Grace wasn't Japanese but Chinese-American. The old woman must have seen something—I didn't know what—which I hadn't recognized because her French was fast and my mind too slow to comprehend and too quick to judge. Older and previously disconnected pieces were falling rapidly into place, making me dizzy with new knowledge.

> The man with the camera also appeared [Ted continued] at the post office where this morning I sent a telegram to my old friend Jack Davis, asking him to join me in Paris. Jack is the finest and most honorable man I've ever met, and a brilliant lawyer who knows everything there is to know about contracts, copyright laws, patent protection, and"—a brief flicker of distaste crossed Ted's face—"intellectual property rights. He is also absolutely reliable and utterly discreet. I can assure you that your secret is safe with him. I intend to ask him to draw up an agreement—an ironclad contract with every safeguard and no holes or exceptions—whereby you allow the *Institutions politiques* to be placed in an archive of your choosing, securely sealed and unopened for, say, fifty years. After that time scholars will be allowed to examine and possibly publish its contents. Profits from publication will go to the Société or any charity of your choosing. My reason for proposing a fifty-year moratorium is quite simply this: by then—if the actuarial tables are at all reliable—you and I will both be dead. I shall therefore be unable to profit in any way from having discovered your secret. This will, I hope, convince you that my motives are purely and simply scholarly, and not in any way self-serving. I do hope that you will agree to remove the *Institutions politiques* from your vault posthaste and put it in a safer place, for its sake and yours. My friend Jack Davis should arrive shortly to draft an agreement to this effect. Time is very short. I am hopeful that we can move quickly to . . .

Here Ted was interrupted by a voice off-camera saying, in French, that his five minutes were up and that they must end the tape. The last words on the tape were Ted's.

"Un moment. J'ai besoin de . . ."

The screen went dark. The throbbing music returned. The female narrator said that if you would like to meet this "homme charmant," then phone or visit Vidéo Date and ask for file number . . .

I hit the off button.

Roguin, chin in hands and completely motionless, continued to stare at the blank screen. He looked a thousand miles away. Turk stood impassively behind him, arms folded. Coindet fidgeted nervously. Silent tears streamed down Grace's face.

Coindet spoke first. "Look, we have no way to know if this is real. It sound to me like the, how do you say?, the fairies' tale . . ."

"Silence," Roguin said softly, returning from his reverie. "This gives me much to think about. Perhaps I have misjudged Hu . . . Professor Porter."

A long, almost prayerful silence fell upon the room.

"Roguin," I began tentatively, "what Ted says makes a lot of sense. Or so it seems to me. But now that Ted is dead, his plan for a fifty-year moratorium seems moot. He can in no way profit from the publication of the *Institutions politiques*. So why not go public with it? Publish it and be done with it. And avoid the risk that someone will steal it and it'll be lost forever. As Ted said, the threat of theft is imminent. And so is the threat of death. It now seems certain that the *boryokudan* tried to force Ted to reveal the whereabouts of the *Institutions politiques*. They didn't succeed, and they killed him—they would have killed him even if he had revealed your secret. Then they followed Danielle and me to Oxford. It's entirely possible, even probable, that the man with the camera forced Danielle to reveal the location of, and the combination for, the vault that holds the *Institutions politiques* before he . . ."—I could feel my voice thicken and begin to break—"and his henchmen killed and then raped her. At any rate, you should assume that they know how to get their hands on Rousseau's manuscript. It's in great danger—and so are you. So are we all. They came after me because I suspected foul play and wasn't giving up the chase. If it weren't for a lucky accident, I'd have been their third—no, fourth—victim. My 'suicide' was perfectly staged, except for one thing: they didn't bother to taste the Château Margaux before lacing it with poison. If they had, they would have noticed that it had corked and turned to vinegar. So please, I implore you, take Ted's advice. Now. Don't wait until it's too late. Publish it. Put it in a public archive where . . ."

Roguin looked up and slowly shook his white mane.

"Obviously you understand nothing," he said, more in resignation than anger. "I am not at liberty to publish the *Institutions politiques*. Or to make it available to the public."

"But of course you are. You own . . ."

"I do *not* own it, Mr. Davis. It is merely in my possession, for safekeeping."

"Well, if you don't own it, who does?"

A look of incomprehension crossed Roguin's furrowed face. "It is not mine. It is the Master's. The manuscript belongs to Jean-Jacques. It was stolen from him. By Thérèse. She was disobedient. She should have burned it, as she was told to do. Bad deeds have distant and unforeseeable consequences. If Thérèse had done as she was told, Professor Porter and Danielle would still be alive. His intellect and her beauty would still grace the world."

"Then," Grace interjected, "why don't you do what Thérèse didn't do? Why not obey Rousseau's command, at long last, and burn this manuscript that has caused so much misery?"

"Because," Roguin replied, "I cannot bring myself to do it. Perhaps I should do so. Perhaps I do not because of *akrasia*."

Because you're crazy?, I started to say, until Grace's gaze stopped me. "It's Greek," she whispered. "Weakness of the will."

"But to have something in the Master's own hand," Roguin continued, "is . . . it is indescribable. For many years I have thought that having the *Institutions politiques* in my possession, but keeping it a secret, was complying with the spirit of Jean-Jacques' wish. But now I am not so sure."

For the first time Roguin looked old and vulnerable. Grace walked over and touched his shoulder. Turk looked suspiciously at her. His eyes narrowed, his large body stiffened as though preparing to pounce.

"Ça va, Turk, d'accord. Ça ne fait rien," Roguin said gently. He turned to Grace. "You see, my secret is no longer a secret. I cannot . . ."

"I know," Grace said soothingly, resting her hand on Roguin's shoulder. "But you must recognize that you now have two choices.

And only two, I'm afraid. One is to burn the *Institutions politiques*, as Rousseau wished. The other is to publish it, as Ted suggested, either now or at some future date. But there will be danger—and maybe more death—until you do one or the other."

Roguin's head was bowed as if in prayer. He stared at the floor. After a long silence he looked up and said, "You are right. Your friend and Danielle, they are right. I am wrong. What is that English expression?"

"Better late than never?," I ventured.

"No," Roguin said, looking levelly at me. "There's no fool like an old fool." He patted Grace's hand, and stood up. "There is surely no place more secure than a Swiss vault . . ."

"A Swiss bank vault—perfect. What an inspired idea," I said.

Roguin shot me a withering look. "No, not a Swiss bank vault. Certainly not. Never. The Swiss banks and bankers disgraced themselves during the War by accepting gold and other valuables that they knew had been stolen from the Jews by the Germans. And after the War they kept for themselves the funds deposited by Jews who perished in the Holocaust. I shall never do business with them. Never."

The recent revelations about Swiss banks had slipped my mind entirely. Of course Roguin was right, and I felt foolish and ashamed. Grace saw my embarrassment.

"What Jack—Mr. Davis—is trying to ask is, who else besides the Swiss banks would have a vault secure enough to store the *Institutions politiques*?"

"Why, the Bibliothèque Publique et Universitaire in Geneva, of course," Roguin replied as though the answer were obvious. "I shall make arrangements to deposit the *Institutions politiques* and several other items, including Mme. Levasseur's diary, in their vault. I shall take them there myself." He turned to Turk and said, in French, something about preparing the car for the trip to Switzerland.

Turk nodded.

"Is this wise?," Coindet asked, breaking his long silence. "If you do this, the Master's enemies—Voltaire and everyone else—will distort the true meaning of the *Institutions politiques*. To make it available to his enemies is disservice. He would not approve, I think."

"Do you wish me to burn it, then?," Roguin asked.

"No," Coindet replied with a look of surprise and dismay. "I say that we keep it. But change box number and combination in vault."

"That's naïve," Grace said coolly. "It's only a matter of time until someone else discovers your secret. If they don't know it already. The cat's out of the bag."

Coindet looked puzzled. "What is this cat?"

"C'est une expression Americaine," Roguin chuckled. It was the first time a smile had crossed his face. As much from relief as amusement, Grace laughed, and so did I. Coindet looked offended, almost angry. Turk remained his stolid self.

"Please do not be angry with me, Coindet," Roguin said, serious once again. "When I was as young as you, I too believed my reading of Rousseau to be the only real or true one. As I have grown older I have become less certain. Although I still believe mine to be the better, perhaps even the truer, interpretation, I am no longer so sure that others are always entirely wrong. And now, because, thanks to you"—he nodded at Grace and me—"I finally understand why Professor Porter acted as he did, I no longer believe him an enemy. If he were still alive he might even become a friend. And if I am wrong about Hume, I could also be wrong about Voltaire and others whose views differ from ours. I have learned a great deal this afternoon." He paused and, looking at Grace, smiled slightly. "Who says you can't teach an old dog new tricks?" He was obviously proud of his mastery of idiomatic English.

Coindet's handsome visage suddenly turned ugly. "You talk of dogs and cats like some silly old man," he shouted, shaking his fist. "You are old fool. The Société, it is finished." Turk moved menacingly toward Coindet. He had, I thought, probably understood Coindet's tone of voice and body language rather than his words.

"Non, Turk, arrêtez-vous," Roguin said sternly. Turk stopped in his tracks and glowered at Coindet.

"For five years you treat me like the child. You give me the name I hate. Coindet was unworthy. I am not. You trust Danielle with combination to vault. But you don't trust me. You always humiliate me, old man. I do not accept this any more." Then he spoke quickly in French I couldn't understand, save for the words 'Danielle' and 'verité', pointed angrily at Grace, then turned on his heels and left abruptly, slamming the door behind him.

The aura of anger he left behind was almost palpable. No one spoke. Finally Roguin broke the silence.

"Forgive him. He is still young. Impetuous. He will cool his anger and come back."

I looked at Grace. Her eyes said, "No, he won't be back. Ever." She's surely right, I thought.

Roguin seemed surprisingly unshaken, even convivial. "Tomorrow we go to Geneva. I would be honored if you would accompany me. As my guests. Turk will drive. My chef will pack a picnic luncheon. With the best breads and cheeses. And of course"—he smiled again—"the wines. I shall select them myself. From my own cellar. Please say you will come."

It sounded almost irresistible. I happily and perhaps too readily accepted Roguin's invitation, and agreed to be picked up at 4:30 a.m. Roguin was by his own description the earliest of early birds. He apologized for the early hour, and assured us that this would allow us to avoid the notorious Parisian rush hour that began before 6:00 a.m. and continued through the day until mid-evening.

Roguin shook my hand. "Thanks to you," he said, "I now know what to do. It is for the best." He turned to Grace, this time holding both her hands in his. "I look forward to seeing you in the morning, my dear. Rest well tonight. Tomorrow we go to Geneva." He kissed Grace on both cheeks.

In light of what had happened over the last three hours, the invitation seemed like a miracle—a complete and utter reversal of everything I'd believed and feared. Best of all, Ted's fondest hopes were about to be realized. It all seemed to be too good to be true.

It was.

36

"Well, that was easy," I said as I closed the door after Roguin and Turk.

"Yes, too easy. Something's not right," Grace said. She looked troubled. Her unease unsettled me.

"What's not right?"

"I can't quite put my finger on it. But it doesn't compute. Call it woman's intuition. Or my suspicious nature. Maybe I've lived in New York too long. Or maybe I just don't expect sad stories to have happy endings."

"What," I asked, "was Coindet saying in French as he left?"

"That's part of what bothers me," she said. "He said that Roguin was an old fool who would always fall for a pretty face—he mentioned Danielle's and mine—and that he was moved more by beauty than by truth."

"Oh, is that all?," I interrupted. "That's hardly the worst of crimes. If it's a crime at all. I'm rather inclined to agree with Roguin." Then I caught myself. Coindet referred not only to Grace but to Danielle. Better get out of this one, fast. "At least where your pretty face is concerned," I added, nuzzling my beaky nose against her flatter one.

"Nice try, Jack. I'm not so easily fooled." I must have looked embarrassed. Grace touched my face. "But I'm not angry, either. Danielle must have been something else, at least in the looks department. She was obviously gorgeous. The two men I've loved most agree about that. And they both have exquisite taste." She shook her head. "That beautiful woman, and one of those lovely men. Both dead. So sad to think about what might have been. If they had lived, Ted might have found happiness with a woman he really loved and who really loved him. At long last. Lord knows he needed and deserved it."

Amen, I thought. "But something's still bothering you. Is it Coindet? What else did he say that I couldn't understand?"

She paused and frowned. "Actually he mentioned three pretty faces: Danielle's, mine—and his own. I think Coindet is jealous, as only a jilted lover can be jealous. And I think Roguin is an equal-opportunity appreciator of human beauty, if you get my drift."

I was taken aback. "He's bisexual, you mean?"

"Maybe. Maybe not. I'm not sure. But one thing's certain: if we don't get some sleep, we'll feel like living death tomorrow. Let's go to bed, Jack. It's late."

37

When the alarm sounded at 3:30 I was already awake. Grace's worries were infectious and I'd caught them. I lay awake all night as my bedmate slept a deep and untroubled sleep. How does she do it?, I wondered. She had the uncanny and, for me, unnerving ability to say her nightly prayers and then set all worries aside at will. I, on the other hand, took my troubles to bed and wrestled with them through the long and sleepless night, after which I would rise exhausted and haggard.

"Grace? Wake up. It's 3:30. Time to rise and shine."

"Five more minutes," a muffled voice mumbled into the pillow. I got up, ground the dark aromatic coffee beans in the Moulinex, boiled a kettle of water, poured it over the freshly ground coffee in the vacuum pot, let it steep for three minutes, and pushed the plunger down. I poured a cup of steaming black coffee and took it in to Grace.

"Your five minutes are up, my love. More like ten minutes, actually. Here, drink this." She opened one eye, then the other, stifled a yawn, and smiled a sleepy smile. "Today's the big day," I said, sounding brighter than I felt. "The *Institutions politiques* goes to Geneva, accompanied by us, to be deposited in the Bibliothèque Publique et Universitaire. Ted's last wish gets granted, and we get to go home with our heads held high. I have a feeling that everything's going to work out okay," I said, omitting to mention the worries that had kept me awake all night.

"I hope you're right," Grace said, sitting up and sipping her coffee. She leaned forward as I placed a large pillow behind her back. "Thanks, love. You're already up and about. So why don't you shower first?"

I was washing my hair under a cascade of hot water when I felt Grace step in beside me. She soaped my back and, moving her hands in a firm but gentle circular motion, travelled slowly downward to my buttocks and then my legs and back up between my thighs. I felt myself rising to the occasion.

"Is that a pistol you're packing, mister, or are you just happy to see me?" We both laughed at that old line from Mae West.

"I'm happy to see you. Obviously."

"Well, you'll have to express your happiness some other time. It's already after four and we aren't even dressed."

"So what was that all about, then?," I asked in mock irritation.

"Just testing your reflexes, my love. They're in fine working order, I'd say."

"Not bad for an old man, then?"

"Not bad even for a young man."

For a moment I wished we weren't going to Geneva. Then I remembered Ted. The shock of stepping out of the steamy shower and onto the slippery cold white tile floor had a distinctly deflationary effect.

We had just finished dressing when we heard a hard rapping sound. I unbolted the door, leaving the chain on, and opened it. Through the crack I could see Turk, resplendent in a gray chauffeur's uniform and carrying a peaked cap under his arm.

"C'est moi," he grunted. "Monsieur Roguin attend."

"Un moment, s'il vous plaît," I replied, closing the door and removing the chain before reopening it. "Entrez-vous."

"Non," he said flatly. He loomed motionless just outside the door, like a large granite statue in a Parisian park.

Grace grabbed her purse and I the small suitcase we'd packed the night before. Turk said nothing as he led the way downstairs and out onto the Rue Clauzel.

My eyes took a few seconds to adjust to the change from the brightly lit hallway. The pre-dawn street was dark and foggy. There was a damp chill in the air. What I saw under the streetlight surprised me. It was a large dark green Marmon V-16 seven-passenger limousine from, I guessed, the late 1920s or early 1930s, with wire-spoke wheels and outsize white sidewall tires. I had seen pictures of this most classic of classic cars, but this was the first time I had actually seen one.

What I saw when Turk opened the door surprised me even more.

38

"Coindet," I heard Grace say, scarcely concealing the surprise in her voice.

"Good morning," he said pleasantly, as though nothing noteworthy had happened the night before. "I am pleased you could join us." Grace turned around, looking quickly and quizzically at me before climbing into the cavernous Marmon. Roguin reached over and took her hand as she scooted across the plush leather seat facing the one on which he and Coindet sat. I got in and sat down beside Grace as Turk closed the door behind me. The car smelled of leather and wood polish, of strong freshly brewed coffee and unsmoked cigars. On the floor between us were a wicker picnic hamper and a wooden chest with oiled leather straps and brass hinges and hasps with locks. I didn't need to ask what it contained.

"Café?," Roguin asked Grace as he poured steaming coffee from an elaborately engraved brass samovar.

"Yes, thank you."

"Black or white?"

"Black, please."

"Sugar?"

"No, thank you."

The Marmon's large and powerful engine purred as Roguin poured coffee for me and, proffering an open wooden humidor, asked if I would care for a cigar. They were aged Havanas from Castro's Cuba and even at this too-early hour I was tempted, but I declined. Grace's look showed that I'd made the right decision. She didn't tolerate tobacco smoke or those who produced it.

The old Marmon picked up speed as we drove through the nearly empty dawn-streaked streets, along the Avenue Daumesnil, past the Zoological Park in the Bois de Vincennes, across the Marne, and into the drab eastern suburbs. By the time the sun came up we were well out of Paris, heading toward Burgundy and beyond, bound for Switzerland.

On his own turf Roguin was the perfect host. So I hoped my question wouldn't offend him.

"How," I asked tentatively, "do you reconcile your and the Société's aversion to modern technology? Surely this splendid machine in which we are riding is a masterpiece of modern technology. The seven-passenger Marmon is perhaps the only car ever to surpass the old Rolls-Royce Silver Ghost. It's got a V-16 engine with an aluminum block, duplex down-draft manifold, four-wheel independent suspension, hydraulic brakes, and . . ."

"I see you know your automobiles, Mr. Davis. I'm impressed. But you are mistaken."

"About what?"

"You are mistaken in viewing my old Marmon as a piece of modern technology. It isn't. You see, what is 'modern' about modern technology is its ugliness, its soullessness, its complete lack of character, of distinction, of individuality. Modern automobiles are mass produced. Each one is like the last. My dear old Marmon is one of a kind. Unique. Different in subtle but significant ways from all other Marmons. Handcrafted by skilled artisans who knew what they were doing and loved doing it. The seats on which we sit were cut and stitched by hand by tailors skilled at their craft. The instruments in the teak dashboard—which, incidentally, was handcrafted by a cabinetmaker—were made by watchmakers in Switzerland and Germany. And this is only the interior of my Marmon! The chassis, the engine, the body—these were handcrafted, and no less carefully, by blacksmiths and machinists who sculpted and molded the metal like the artists they were. So, no, Mr. Davis, we are not entombed in a soulless machine, mass produced by robots and slave-laborers. We ride instead in a beautiful work of art created by men whose labor liberated them, making them both free and dignified."

I stood corrected. Ted and Roguin, I thought, would have agreed about this, and a great deal more. They weren't Luddites or knee-jerk technophobes, but lovers of craftsmanship and, above all, of beauty. And speaking of beauty, I noticed that Coindet looked even more handsome this morning. He wore a white silk shirt with a black cravat, topped by a tan jacket. Roguin, dressed as before in a gray pinstripe suit with a white turtleneck, seemed to enjoy gazing at Coindet—when, that is, he wasn't gazing appreciatively at Grace. So, yes, I thought, Grace was probably right about Roguin's somewhat catholic sexual proclivities.

The old Marmon hummed and purred by turns, as Turk went through the gears. Roguin's moods seemed similarly modulated, sometimes subdued, sometimes expansive, moving in some strange harmony with the rhythms of this old car. He told stories—of his childhood, as the reclusive lone offspring of wealthy parents, left in the care of successive wet-nurses, nannies, and governesses, and later of a live-in tutor. Except for occasional weekend afternoons spent with cousins, he was kept away from other children. The only other child around the Merceaux estate was the chauffer's son, some ten years younger, who followed him everywhere. He was so attached and attentive to the young Merceaux that he acquired the nickname *le chiot*, "the puppy." As he grew ever larger and stronger, the chauffeur's squat fireplug of a son acquired another sobriquet, *le bouledogue*, "The Bulldog." While the young Merceaux exercised his mind, the younger Bulldog exercised his body. But the bright colors of childhood were soon darkened.

"It was the period of the Nazi occupation. The worst in my country's long history of very bad periods. The Germans marched into Paris on my sixth birthday. I remember it because my mother and her father—my Grandfather Guisan—were crying at my birthday party. The Germans, I thought, must be the most evil people in the world, if they could make my mother and grandfather cry. And then one evening, only two or three weeks later, I got out of bed and crept downstairs because I heard laughter and music." Roguin's face grew pale with painful memory. "Peering through the bannister rail, I saw below my mother and father entertaining a large group of German officers, including a contingent of black-uniformed S.S. officers. I must have made a sudden move or a gasp, because one of them looked straight up at me and smiled a cold, thin-lipped smile and said with a voice that immediately silenced the conversation and the music, 'It appears that we have a spy in our midst.' And everyone else looked up at me and laughed and applauded the S.S. man's cleverness. I fled upstairs, terrified, and hid under my bed. Now they will execute me, I thought. But why are my parents entertaining my executioners? I did not have the words for it then, although I do now: without knowing it, they were simply following the counsel of Hobbes and putting themselves under the new Sovereign. They bent to the prevailing political winds. When Vichy was sovereign, they went along; when Vichy was overthrown and General De Gaulle returned triumphant, they became staunch Gaullists. It was to that early experience that I now trace my aversion to Hobbes—and also, I am afraid, to my own parents—and my attraction to Rousseau, Hobbes' most ardent and articulate critic. But of course I was then a child, and I thought and acted as a child. I did not reason; I withdrew from a world I did not understand and from parents whom I both loved and loathed. I retreated into my own very private and safely apolitical world."

The cloistered and bookish Merceaux lived as an active participant in his own world of childhood fantasy. His companions were the "noble Greeks and Romans" of *Plutarch's Lives*, along with King Arthur and Lancelot, Don Quixote, Rob Roy, Robinson Crusoe, Ivanhoe, The Count of Monte Cristo, Swiss Family Robinson, the Three Musketeers, and other romantic figures of the fiction of an earlier age.

"So much better than television," he said with understatement more English than French. He told of his subsequent move into the *lycée*, of his hopes of gaining his loved and loathed parents' favorable attention by finishing at the top of the grueling *baccalauréat* examination at age sixteen. Nothing worked. His parents praised him in passing, but generally ignored him, favoring instead the glittering company of wealthy friends from the higher echelons of post-war French society. They were more often in Monte Carlo than at their estate with their lonely only son, whom they regarded as something of an oddity—bright, but too brooding and bookish to be a social asset. Then, in the mid-1950s, before the idea or the phrase had become fashionable, the young Merceaux dropped out. Taking the late French philosopher Simone Weil as his model, he, like her, held a series of factory jobs. Including, he said, a stint as a worker on a Renault assembly line.

So, I thought, he really does know whereof he speaks. At least when he talks about cars and how they are made.

Then two things happened to change his life. He read the works of Rousseau. Not just the major works, but *everything*, even the most obscure and least well-regarded. He found in Rousseau the voice of a prophet, the Jeremiah of the modern age, thundering against its pretenses and excesses, and calling for a return to a purer and simpler way of life.

"I cannot begin to tell you how Jean-Jacques spoke to me—to my heart, my innermost feelings. It was almost as though the words were arrows, each sharper than the last, penetrating ever more deeply into my heart. I felt myself dying and being born anew, with a better heart and a clearer vision. I saw the idea of progress for what it really is—an illusion, a myth, a sham, a cloak to cover the corrupt and shoddy and superficial from the eternal and unchanging standards of beauty, of truth, of goodness. The only antidote to sham-learning, to shoddiness in thought and living, was the recovery of real wisdom—the enduring wisdom of the ancients. And Jean-Jacques was the last of the moderns to know that—to hold the key—to even remember that there were secrets to unlock."

Then came Merceaux's second revelation. At age twenty he heard of an American professor—a German-Jewish emigré teaching at the University of Chicago—who apparently agreed with him. Who had constructed a deeply learned case against the superficiality and philistinism of the modern world. Who had much to teach the young Merceaux. Within the month he had left for Chicago, his departure devastating to his faithful Bulldog. Three months later Merceaux was the most active and articulate member of Gauss's seminar. He seemed somehow much older than his twenty years, and his self-taught erudition and show of wisdom did not go unnoticed by his new master. He, for his part, came to see Gauss as the attentive father he never had. He became a member of the master's inner circle. Like many an immigrant, he felt himself reborn in the New World. An Adam who had shed European dress for the swaddling clothes of an infant. And, like a baby, he learned the language of his elders. A meticulous mimic, Merceaux soon developed an American midwestern—more specifically, a Chicago—accent. Sounding more American than his American counterparts, he seemed well on his way to a brilliant American or even perhaps a European academic career when something strange happened. He did or said something—he didn't know what—to offend his mentor. It was, he thought, something slight—some minor point of disagreement on the meaning of a particular passage in a text of Rousseau—that triggered an exaggerated reaction. The proud and prickly professor did not tolerate correction or disagreement from anyone, and from his pupils in particular. And, what was so much worse, the emphatic rejection by his newly adopted surrogate father was far more painful and intense than the indifference he had suffered at the hands of his French father. After that, nothing he did or said would heal the breach. His dissertation on Rousseau's critique of Enlightenment was rejected, its author disowned and sent back to France to lick his wounds like some outcast cur, welcomed only by his faithful Bulldog. He felt, he said, like "a lone wolf howling in vain against an indifferent moon."

He became a recluse, rereading Rousseau by day and, somewhat dramatically, dressed in a dark cape and black silk scarf, haunting the streets and boulevards of Paris after dark to observe and record the darkest daily atrocities of the modern world. "I had become the spy that the S.S. officer had detected two decades before." From behind his silken veil he spied the child prostitutes, the pornographers, the drugs, the senseless random violence, the thousand lesser varieties of vice and its allures that suffuse the air of Paris and Chicago and other cities. And from these metropolitan centers the sickness radiates outward, invading the hinterland, so that no place is left untouched by the infecting hand. We live, he concluded, in the midst of a sickness so widely shared that we don't recognize it for what it is—the modern Plague, borne not of rats and mice but of men. Not always or even necessarily evil men, but unthinking men, dying and killing by turns as they go through the motions of living the unexamined life.

My God, I thought as I listened, this sounds *so* much like some of the things Ted used to say, it's almost spooky.

The young Merceaux was accompanied on his nocturnal ramblings by his faithful Bulldog. One evening a gang of street toughs set upon Merceaux and were quickly routed, their heads opened and bones broken by the ferocious fourteen-year-old Bulldog. " 'My dear Bulldog,' I told him then, 'I now give you the name you deserve—that of Jean-Jacques' most faithful friend.' And that is how Turk got his name." Soon thereafter, and in that same spirit, Merceaux christened himself Roguin and organized the Société de Jean-Jacques. He gathered around him other idealists, sickened by the corruption and materialism of the modern age, and together they looked to Rousseau for a corrective and a cure.

"But," Roguin continued with a wan self-deprecating smile, "I was young. And idealistic. And, yes, probably foolish. I have come in my old age to have a certain sympathy with my dear Don Quixote, who lived in an imaginary past populated by books about noble knights who worshipped worthy damsels from afar and tilted at windmills that he mistook for dragons, much to the amusement of his contemporaries. He was an oddity in his time, as I am in mine. We do not choose the age in which we live. Nor do we choose our foes. These things are given to us by a malevolent god."

I saw Grace wince. Her jaw tightened. This was not the God she knew and worshipped. I thought I should say something before she did.

"If God—your god, I mean—is malevolent, then why obey him? Why not defy such a god?"

Roguin smiled benignly. "I am of course speaking metaphorically, Mr. Davis. But I take your point. A malevolent god would not deserve our allegiance. But by the same token we would be foolish to ignore his power. He is god, after all. He exacts vengeance against those who defy him."

"His vengeance consisting of—what? Of hell-fire?" I was thinking of the angry and vengeful God of my own Oklahoma Baptist upbringing.

Roguin smiled and shook his white mane. "Hardly, no. That would be too obvious. A truly malevolent god would punish in truly malevolent ways."

"Such as?"

"Such as letting one live amidst the hell of the modern world without being able to do anything about it. And then making that life attractive in material and other ways. A hell with swimming pools and beautiful women and good wine, as it were."

Grace and Coindet frowned in unison.

"And so the question," Roguin continued, "comes down to this: do you live comfortably or uncomfortably in this high-fashion hell? Do you resist? Or do you go shopping? The choice is yours to make. But, either way, the end result is the same. I long ago chose to resist. And what has it produced? So far as I can see, it has produced nothing. Nothing, that is, except two corpses."

Roguin fell silent. Coindet put a reassuring hand on his knee, and then abruptly withdrew it.

◄ 39 ►

The rising sun and our ever-increasing distance from Paris seemed to have a therapeutic effect. Roguin was recovering from his rather gloomy reflections by opening an excellent cognac and adding ample amounts to our second cups of coffee. For me it produced a distinctly odd sensation. I felt at once alert and ever so slightly drunk.

Grace, by contrast, had drunk all her first cup of black coffee and had refused the offer of a heavily spiked second cup. Stone-cold sober and alert, she would, as always, be the last to lose any semblance of control. In the midst of the general gaiety she spoke.

"Monsieur Roguin," she began.

"Please call me Daniel," Roguin interrupted with a hospitable smile.

"Very well, then. Daniel. You haven't volunteered the information, so perhaps you don't want us to know."

"Know what, my dear?"

"How you came to acquire Rousseau's *Institutions politiques*. Was it—forgive my bluntness—bought or stolen?"

Roguin looked surprised and somewhat pained. "Neither."

"If you'd rather not say, then . . ."

"Not at all. It's quite an amusing story, really. My mother's father—my Grandfather Guisan—was an avid collector of first editions of books by Balzac, Victor Hugo, and many other, and earlier, French writers. He even had an early edition of Fénelon's *Télémaque*, as well as works by La Bruyère, Dumas, Renan, and a lovely leather-bound first edition of Tocqueville's *Democratie en Amerique*, which I particularly prize. Dear old Grandfather Guisan's bibliophilia might be more accurately described as bibliomania. No one, as my mother said, ever saw Grandfather actually *read* any of the books he collected. He collected eagerly, madly, indiscriminately. He was, as you would say, a pack rat. He had a better eye for first editions than for manuscripts, which he also collected, although in a most unsystematic and careless fashion. Any manuscript that looked old and musty he would buy. By the time of his death, shortly after I had returned from your country,

Grandfather's collection had completely taken over two large rooms of his château. The stacks of books and manuscripts were wall-to-wall and waist-high. He had no catalogue—not even a list—of his helter-skelter library. He claimed to know where every item was, where it had come from, how much he had paid for it. But he never wrote anything down. The collection was chaotic—a 'mess', as you might say. In his will Grandfather did me the dubious favor of leaving his entire collection to me, because I was as bookish as he and the only member of my family who would appreciate what he had acquired. I was both grateful to Grandfather and, I am now sorry to say, slightly irritated by his bequest. I spent several months sorting and shelving and cataloguing, trying—not entirely successfully—to bring some order out of this chaos I had inherited. Then one day, near the bottom of a stack of papers so old and musty that I considered fumigating—or even burning—them, I came across a curious item. It was either an unfinished manuscript or a large fragment from a finished one. The manuscript was not continuous; pages and even entire chapters were clearly missing. It was obviously very old, and looked like it had survived a fire. I also noticed another odd feature. The manuscript pages were bordered by straight red lines two or three centimeters from the edge. The red ink had faded, of course, and the lines were hardly visible. But their purpose was quite clearly to mark off a slightly smaller page within the larger one. All the neatly penned words and sentences were contained within this smaller area. So much for the curious appearance of the manuscript. As for its contents, they were even more curious. The topic was morals and politics, analyzed historically and institutionally. There were short histories and somewhat longer critical analyses of the constitutions, that is, the fundamental structure, the laws, the institutions, of several republics—chiefly Sparta, Rome, Venice, and Geneva—in the manner of Machiavelli's *Discourses*. The longest of these was a very critical discussion of *Venezia serenissima*. The much-vaunted 'supremely serene Republic of Venice,' the author claimed, was very largely a myth created and carefully maintained by the hereditary aristocracy and the powerful banking and shipping interests to legitimize their behind-the-scenes domination of that city-state. From a republican-*political* perspective, the author argued, the vaunted 'serenity' of Venice was the serenity of the grave. And in that grave was buried the liberty of the people. But the people had bought the myth that theirs was a free republic; and so although they thought they were free, they were actually in chains."

" 'Man is born free, and yet everywhere he is in chains'?," Grace chimed in. Even I recognized that line from the opening of *The Social Contract.*

"Exactly. The paradoxes, the striking turns of phrase that characterize Rousseau's two *Discourses*, and of course *The Social Contract*, are much in evidence throughout this old manuscript." Roguin reached down and patted the oak trunk with the leather straps and shiny hasps and hinges. "I was by then quite familiar with Rousseau's writings, including his *Confessions*; so I dared not even hope that I had in my possession the *Institutions politiques* which, Jean-Jacques assured us, no longer existed."

"So what," I asked, "did you think you had?"

"A fragment of a manuscript from some self-styled Rousseauian—some writer who admired and tried to imitate Jean-Jacques. Or perhaps a forger."

"What convinced you otherwise?," Grace asked.

"Several things. The least of these was the handwriting which, swirl for swirl and loop for loop, matched the Master's perfectly, as can be seen from his original manuscripts at Neuchâtel, Geneva, Paris, and London. But of course any talented forger can do as much, and so this is hardly a decisive test. A better test of plausibility, though not of authenticity, consists of chemical analysis on the ink and paper. These showed the paper to be roughly three-hundred years old, give or take half a century. Much as I detested the idea, I also hired a content analyst to do a computerized word-frequency analysis of a partial typescript. After comparing this with works known to be Rousseau's, he concluded that the passages in typescript were almost certainly written by Rousseau. But what finally convinced me had nothing to do with the handwriting, or the age of the paper, or anything that modern technological means or methods might establish." He paused, seeming from somewhere deep within to savor the moment. "In the end it was the style, the flavor, the . . . the Master's mood and manner, the qualities of mind and spirit that cannot be reproduced on the page, by even the cleverest of forgers or imitators, in Jean-Jacques' day or ours. This anonymous author would have to have had a lifetime of thinking and being like Jean-Jacques—which is to say, he would have to *be* Jean-Jacques. And only one person who has been Jean-Jacques, has ever lived. As he says at the beginning of the *Confessions*, "Je ne suis fait comme aucun de ceux que j'ai vus; j'ose croire n'être fait comme aucun de ceux qui existent."

"I am not made like anyone I have seen; I dare to believe that I am not made like anyone who exists," Grace chimed in helpfully, looking in my direction and smiling slyly.

"Yes," Roguin continued, "it is impossible—logically impossible—to duplicate or imitate what is truly unique. Little by little I became convinced that I had in my possession the Master's *magnum opus*, or what was left of it after he had taken the *Contrat social* from it. If you look at both works as parts of the same jigsaw puzzle, they do fit together. *The Social Contract* is as abstract and ahistorical as the rest of the *Political Institutions* is concrete and historical. Each completes and complements the other. The fit is almost perfect."

"Almost perfect?," I asked, sounding more skeptical than I meant to.

"Yes, almost; but not quite. Nor is this surprising. The *Political Institutions* was not a finished work but a sizeable portion of a larger work that was never completed. After Jean-Jacques took *The Social Contract* from that fragment, he made changes—adding, subtracting, polishing—so that the smaller work would stand on its own."

"Adding what, for example?," I asked.

"Several things—the most notable of which was the chapter on the civil religion, which appears at the end of *The Social Contract*. There is no counterpart to that chapter in the *Institutions politiques*, or in the earlier drafts of the *Contrat social*, for that matter. It was added after the manuscript went to press in 1761, and was later revised. That controversial chapter got Jean-Jacques into hot water from the authorities in Paris and Geneva, and remains to this day a matter of intense scholarly controversy. So, no, the fit between the two works is far from perfect. But it's close. Very close. Too close to be coincidence."

"All right," Grace said. "You've told us how you came to own Rousseau's . . ."

"Oh, no," Roguin interjected. "I do not *own* the *Institutions politiques*. As I said yesterday, it is only in my possession. Owning and possessing are not the same thing. Owning is a moral and legal relationship of *droit*, or 'right', as Jean-Jacques says. Possessing is merely a physical fact. If a thief steals my wallet he possesses it, to be sure; but he does not *own* it. I still own it, although I no longer possess it. With ideas it is different. Ideas cannot be owned. They are public property, as it were; once they are published—made public—they belong to no one, not even their authors or originators. A book can be copyrighted, but not the ideas it contains. The ideas in *The Social Contract* originate with, but do not 'belong' to, Jean-Jacques; they were not 'property' that he 'owned' but gifts that he gave to his readers. They are, as Thucydides says of his *History*, κτη^μα´ τε ε's αιει, 'a *possession* for all time'—a public possession, not the private property of this or that individual."

Hmm, I thought, as I remembered Ted's arguments against the "obscene oxymoron" of "intellectual property." I wonder what would happen if I tried out *that* line of argument with my clients? I'd be fired in a New York minute. And then the firm would grant me medical leave and refer me to a good therapist.

"I stand corrected," Grace said. "So how did your grandfather come to *possess* this manuscript? Where did *he* get it?"

"That I do not know," Roguin replied. "As I said before, he kept no receipts, no lists, no paperwork of any kind. Sometimes, though very rarely, I would find a bookseller's mark or receipt in a book. One he bought in Riga, in Latvia; another from Berlin, before the War. But most of his books—and all of the manuscripts—were without any indication of their origins. Grandfather Guisan kept all his records in his head. And now they are gone. Forever."

"Did the Levasseur diary also come from your grandfather's collection?," I asked.

Roguin smiled. "No, I bought that one myself. From a manuscript dealer in Amsterdam. Six years ago. He seemed not to know manuscripts, and had no idea what he was offering for sale. He was interested, I think, in selling something else." Roguin looked expectantly at our uncomprehending faces. "Drugs. He was selling drugs. Manuscripts were, as you would say, a 'front' for his real business, which was not about memory but about its obliteration. Someone—an addict who stole to support his habit, perhaps—had traded this old diary for drugs. Not hashish but hard drugs. Heroin. Or opium. Or cocaine, perhaps. I paid the dealer's full asking price, which surprised him as much as it pleased me. The ratty and mildewed old manuscript was a bargain. Its contents finally corroborated my belief that that other old manuscript in my possession was indeed Jean-Jacques'. Mean old Mother Levasseur's story of its survival supplied the explanation that had long eluded me, right down to the scorch marks." Roguin gave a sly gallic wink, and we all laughed. All, that is, except Coindet, who seemed strangely glum and apprehensive.

Grace held out her coffee cup. "May I have more coffee, please?"

Roguin nodded agreeably and poured steaming black coffee from the brass samovar.

Then Grace surprised me. "May I have a splash—just a small splash—of cognac?"

"But of course," Roguin said, smiling and pouring more than a splash of cognac into her cup.

Grace took a sip. And then another. Then she looked up at Roguin and said, "You, like Rousseau, are an admirer of the ancient wisdom and a student of the classics. The works of Plato in particular, yes?"

Roguin nodded affirmatively and pleasantly, even as his eyes narrowed. So, I think, did mine. She had what I have come to call The Look—quizzical, sly, and somewhat "leading," in lawyer lingo. What in blazes, I wondered, is Grace up to?

"I'm no expert," Grace continued, "but I've always been curious about one of Plato's dialogues."

"And which one would that be, my dear?"

"Plato's *Symposium*. I remember reading it as an undergraduate at Berkeley, in Professor Pitkin's class. I wasn't keen to read it at first, because I knew—or thought I knew—what a 'symposium' was. Namely, a dry academic discussion of some esoteric topic."

"Yes," Roguin interrupted, "that is a common mistake among the ignorant. Do go on."

"Well, she explained that 'symposium', in Greek, actually means 'drinking party'. So Socrates and his friends get together, drink a lot of wine, and get looped."

"Looped?," Coindet asked.

"Un peu gris," Roguin answered in his most avuncular tone. Coindet nodded knowingly.

"And the topic of this symposium, this drinking party," Grace continued, "is love. What it is, its several varieties, how we know it when we experience it, and how to distinguish true love from various counterfeit feelings that purport to be love but actually aren't. Such as sheer physical attraction or lust, and the like."

Roguin was leaning forward, his eyes fixed on Grace. He was attentive, impressed, curious above all.

"Anyway," Grace went on, "this increasingly drunken dialogue—in which many profound and true things are said: *in vino veritas*, as the Romans later put it—is suddenly interrupted . . ."

"Ah, yes, and famously so, by Alcibiades," Roguin interjected.

"Yes, by the beautiful Alcibiades, the handsomest man in Athens, maybe in all of Attica. Accompanied by flute-girls, no less. And drunk as a skunk."

"Drunk as a . . .?," Coindet asked.

Before Roguin could answer, Grace said, "Skunk. De plus en plus gris. Comprenez?"

"Ah, oui, I mean, yes," Coindet replied.

"As I was about to say," Grace continued, "the drunken Alcibiades crashes"—she looked sharply but not unkindly at Coindet—"interrupts this drinking party. He is amusing, annoying, but, above all, he wants to be heard on the topic of the evening. He is, he says, proud of his beauty. Everyone tells him how handsome he is. He thinks, or once thought, that he should be admired and loved by—and therefore able to sleep with—anyone he fancies. He fancied Socrates. The squat, bald, fat, fifty-something Socrates. Not because the older man was handsome, but because his head contained such marvelous things—so much wisdom—and that this somehow more than made up for what Socrates lacked in the looks department."

Coindet seemed about to say something. Grace glowered at him and he remained silent.

"But Socrates," she continued, "was unimpressed. He agreed to lie through the night with his handsome young friend. The two lay naked under a blanket. But Socrates did nothing. First conversation, then sleep. No sex. Alcibiades was by turns perplexed, offended, outraged. How could this ugly old man refuse the advances of a handsome young admirer? Socrates even made light of Alcibiades' beauty. How could—how *dare*—he poke fun at the attribute of which Alcibiades was proudest?"

Uh, oh, I thought. *Now* I remember the story of Plato's *Symposium*. And, unless I'm very much mistaken, Grace is trying to draw or suggest some sort of parallel between Alcibiades and Coindet. And maybe even between Socrates and Roguin. Between wisdom and beauty. If so, she's setting the stage for trouble. Big trouble. But why? I wanted to take her aside and ask. Or, better yet, beg her to stop. But that of course was impossible. I felt helpless as Grace's monologue continued. I tried to distract myself by listening to the quietly powerful thrumming of the Marmon's sixteen cylinders. I turned around and, on the other side of the glass partition, saw the back of Turk's head, which seemed to be joined directly to his torso without benefit of neck. As Grandpa would say, Turk could give ugly a bad name.

I looked out at the Burgundy countryside. The sea-wave folds of the hills of the Massif Central and the Côte d'Or were covered from horizon to horizon by vineyards, the verdant expanse interrupted only occasionally by the chalk white contrast of a farmhouse or winery or church spire. Then, as though having spent their force in showing off all this luxuriant fertility, the large green waves of this earthy inland sea slowly splayed out, losing themselves in the flat and calm lowlands of the upper Saône Valley.

The beauty outside, and the cognac inside, made me feel almost dizzy. God, I thought, I'm feeling a little too tipsy for comfort. I need relief. Air. And, above all, a pee. Up ahead I could see but not yet read a road sign. As we drew nearer I read, "Dijon 12 km." Good, I thought. We can stop soon. All this coffee, not to mention the cognac, is rapidly reaching my bladder. I turned around and saw Coindet, looking a little puzzled, and Roguin beaming solicitously.

"And what, my dear, do you not understand about Plato's *Symposium*? You seem to know it quite well."

Of course she knows it quite well, I wanted to say. Grace had graduated *summa cum laude* from Berkeley with a double major in Political Science and Classics. Even Ted used to be impressed by her grasp of Greek and Latin and her knowledge of classical texts and authors—Plato in particular.

"Thank you," Grace replied with a shy, slightly sly and perhaps not altogether sincere smile. "My question, Monsieur Roguin—I mean, Daniel—is this: The dialogue is about love and beauty—and the love of the beautiful—but Plato dismisses physical beauty and sexual attraction as something superficial, ephemeral, transient. I could never understand why such deeply ingrained human instincts are dismissed out of hand, and the love of truth and wisdom—philosophy, in short—is deemed the truest and purest love. I gather you would disagree with Plato on this point. Or do I misunderstand your—and, I believe, Rousseau's—emphasis on the importance of human beauty, even for philosophers?"

So that's it, I thought. Grace is trying to ensnare Roguin in a web of her own weaving, with Plato as the bait. But why?

Another question was pressing even more insistently. When would we stop so that I could go? I felt like a first-grader in Mrs. McMains' class, my bladder bursting but me afraid to ask. Afraid of what? Of humiliation, mainly. Of calling attention to myself. Of being laughed at. Of sticking out like a sore thumb, or rather—let's drop the euphemism—like a tiny engorged penis, the small frail dam against the flood about to be unleashed by the overflow of large Lake Bladder. In one way or another, the oldest and most primitive fears involve water and fire, two archetypal opposites that somehow seem to run deeper than all the others. They never really leave us. Too bad, I thought. I wish that the water could extinguish the fire, which would in turn evaporate the water, each fear thereby cancelling the other. But life doesn't work that way.

Turk had turned off before reaching Dijon, where I had hoped to find relief. On a meandering back road we crossed the River Saône and then the eastern reaches of the Saône Valley, heading southeast into the foothills of the Jura Mountains.

The road was rising steeply now. Gorges on one side and then the other grew deeper, and greens gave way to browns and grays as the landscape became rocky and more sparsely vegetated. We were somewhere between Dijon and Geneva, rising to meet the Jura. There was almost no traffic on this scenic mountain road. We approached and then passed a dozen or so cyclists who, their sinewy legs pumping furiously, inched slowly up the steep road. They looked lean and fit, as though readying themselves for the Tour de France. The only other car I could see was a black buglike speck far behind us. Around me, oddly and countrapuntally, the strange mobile seminar on Plato's *Symposium* continued.

"Ah, now I think I see what troubles you," Roguin was saying. "You hold that there is a contradiction between what Plato believes about beauty, and what Jean-Jacques and I believe." Grace nodded, more querulously than affirmatively. "But it is entirely consistent, you see," Roguin continued, his body animated and his voice rising. "Plato does not deny the power of human beauty or, indeed, of sexual attraction. Not at all. He merely puts these in their proper place in relation to philosophy, that is, the love of wisdom. This love is erotic—that is, life-affirming—but it is not sexual. One can contemplate and appreciate truth—and, yes, beauty—but one can hardly have sex with them, that is, with ideas or ideals. To be sure, one can have sex with someone who is beautiful—who exhibits the quality of beauty—but that is only our poor and fumbling human way of attempting to capture and partake of the beautiful. But of course it cannot succeed. Beauty—human beauty—is fleeting and transitory. It can be appreciated but never captured. To try to capture and hold it sexually is futile and leads only to loss and disappointment."

"But," Grace added, "Rousseau was himself a sensual man. A very sexual being, I believe . . ."

"Yes, of course. He was a man, a biological being with a body and therefore with natural drives and urges that needed an outlet. He found what he needed, as men will do, in a succession of lovers and mistresses. Among the first was the exotic and voluptuous Venetian courtesan Zulietta. She not yet twenty, he not much older; she was experienced far beyond her years and he a young and inexperienced Swiss Calvinist newly arrived in Venice. He was smitten and disgusted simultaneously. The tension between sexual desire and moral aversion marked Jean-Jacques' love-life. Or should I say his sex life? But, of all the women, there was one in particular . . ." A look of distaste crossed Roguin's lived-in face. "Thérèse was, to put it crudely, Jean-Jacques' chamber pot. She served his sexual needs. But," he continued with a slight smile, "his relationship with Mme. Dupin was altogether different. Deeply loving but entirely chaste. He knew he could never possess her sexually. He loved her for her great beauty alone."

Coindet was clearly agitated. He seemed in agony as he looked in one direction and then another. His handsome features were so distorted that he became almost ugly. I could hardly bear to look at him. Roguin, gazing intently at Grace, seemed not to notice this transformation. Grace was taking it all in, and seemed to know exactly the effect all this was having on poor Coindet. Embarrassed, I looked between and beyond the two men, to the road as it disappeared behind us.

The black speck that I had seen in the distance now loomed larger. It was a black Toyota 4-Runner sport utility wagon. Its windshield was so darkly tinted that it too looked black.

◄ 40 ►

Coindet continued to squirm. My bladder was so full I felt like doing some squirming of my own. "If your brain were as small as your bladder," Ted once quipped as we were kayaking in Lake Superior, "your I.Q. would be in the single digits." We'd had to go ashore on one of the Apostle Islands so that I could relieve myself. I smiled at the memory. But, truth to tell, Ted's quip was funny only if one's need wasn't urgent. Mine was then, and even more so now. I needed relief, and soon. Rousseau had had trouble passing urine; I was having trouble holding mine in. Either condition can make you crazy. I looked behind me, to the road ahead, and saw two signs on a single post. "Vue scènique," said the one on top. An arrow pointed to the right. The lower sign said "Frontière Suisse. 2 Km."

I tapped on the glass behind Turk's head. He turned slightly. "Turk, arrêtez la bas, à la vue scènique, s'il vous plaît." Turk seemed at first to ignore me. Then he pulled down a flexible metal speaking-tube and spoke into it. His hoarse voice boomed inside the passenger compartment, asking Roguin for permission to stop.

"Oui, Turk, d'accord," Roguin said into his speaking-tube. "Et préparez le pique-nique. Nous allons dîner ici." Turk nodded and downshifted. The Marmon slowed smoothly, gradually, easing off the pavement and onto the gravel pullout, and came to a stop. Turk walked around and opened the doors. Grace got out first, then Roguin and Coindet, and finally me. I stretched and smelled the thin dry mountain air.

The view was stunning. We were on a ridge line running roughly north to south in the Jura Mountain range along the Swiss border.

The higher peaks were swathed in white. Below them stretched the icy gray fingers of glaciers and, lower still, the quicksilver streamers of tumbling waterfalls. Immediately ahead there loomed a precipitous drop into a deep alpine valley, at the bottom of which a small silver ribbon of river ran its winding course.

But the natural beauty of this place was no match for the natural urge I was feeling. I hastily excused myself and went in search of a private place. I spied a steep rocky path that led from the gravel parking area up a craggy incline. I followed it up to the top and turned around, just in time to see the string of cyclists cresting the summit and coasting quickly past the parking area, hands high in the air in the posture of triumph. Below me I saw Roguin, his left hand lightly touching the small of Grace's back, right arm raised and sweeping in an arc as he pointed out some distant peak. Turk had set up a small folding table at the edge of the parking area and had covered it with a blue-checkered tablecloth that threatened to blow away in the updraft until he weighted it down with the picnic hamper and two bottles of wine. Wines from Roguin's own cellar; so they're bound to be *extraordinaire*, I thought as I turned and then disappeared behind a large boulder. Out of sight of the others I unzipped my fly. The relief so long sought was instantaneous. I took a deep breath and let it out slowly.

Then, seemingly out of nowhere, a thought came to me. I had seen the cyclists pass in an accelerating downhill blur. But I hadn't seen the black Toyota. I tried to dismiss it, to put it out of my head, but the thought wouldn't leave. Okay, maybe like Rousseau, retaining your urine for too long has made you paranoid. But follow your instincts, Cherokee-style, I thought as I circled around the massive boulder behind which I had taken refuge. Feeling a little foolish, I crouched low as I approached the road. As I peered over a small rocky outcrop the breath froze in my lungs.

There, below me, pulled off the highway just before and out of sight of the turnoff, was the black Toyota. Three men were getting out. One of them I recognized immediately. But this time the "Japanese tourist" didn't have a camera. He had a black long-barreled pistol. One of his compatriots carried a shorter silver-barreled pistol. The third was loading shells into a pump-action shotgun. I could hear the snick-snick and then the click as he pulled the pump to put the first of several shells into the chamber.

My first instinct was to run like crazy back to the parking area, bundle everyone into the Marmon, and get the hell out of there. But there wasn't time. The three gunmen had already started walking and were about to disappear around the corner.

"Oh dear God, please God, help me now," I said, scarcely noticing that I was on my knees with hands together. Then The Calm came. Everything shifted into slow motion. I scrambled as quietly as I could manage down the incline to the road. Please God, if you exist, let the keys be in the Toyota. I'll drive it at top speed around the corner, surprising—and, I hoped, hitting and disabling—two, or possibly all three, of the gunmen. As I reached the road I crouched low, moving behind the Toyota and along the left side. I opened the driver's door, felt—and then looked—for the key in the ignition switch. Nothing. I looked in the map compartment on the door, and then atop the dash. Then under the driver's seat and in the compartment between the bucket seats. And then in the red plastic tool box. It contained only needle-nose pliers, screwdrivers, wire-cutters, and assorted switches, wires, connectors, and other electrical gear. I looked in the back seat. Still nothing. No key anywhere. One good plan—hell, my only plan—down the drain.

What to do now? The Calm was still with me. I scrambled back up the incline, making my way around the large boulder, and then dropping down on all fours as I approached the parking area. Below I saw, lined up alongside the Marmon, Roguin, Coindet, Grace, and Turk. Except for Coindet, all were facing in my direction with their hands up and behind their heads. All three gunmen had their backs to me. Coindet was talking angrily and animatedly to Roguin, but I couldn't make out what he was saying. I crawled closer. The sound of sliding rocks and pebbles—not to mention my own heartbeat—seemed deafening, but no one else seemed to hear. The wind was in my favor. An updraft from the valley below carried sound more easily in my direction than the other way around. Thank God for that, I whispered to no one in particular as I stroked the sharp edges of my arrowhead. I crawled even closer until I caught Coindet in mid-sentence.

". . . no other way to avenge the humiliation, old man. You tell me how handsome I am, how you love me for my beauty. You say this to my sister also. When at last you let me lie with you, nothing happen.

Nothing. Danielle, she say same thing happen with her. She take your name—Daniel become Danielle—because she love you. She lie with you. Again you do nothing. *Nothing*! You mislead my sister. You mislead me. You are sadist."

Roguin shook his white mane in vigorous disagreement. "No," he said imploringly, "I am a lover of beauty. I love your beauty, I love Danielle's beauty, I love all . . ."

"*Silence*!," Coindet shouted, shoving Roguin hard against the car. The old man crumpled. Then something even stranger happened. Coindet moved away from the others and toward the gunmen. They seemed to know him, and he to be unthreatened by them. Then Coindet, speaking French, said something to the cameraman-turned-gunman, pointing up the hill in my direction. Although I couldn't quite hear, his gestures showed what he was saying: There's another one of them. He's up there somewhere. Go find him. The cameraman said something in Japanese to the man with the shotgun, who started walking in my direction. Then, when he found the path, he followed it up to and behind the boulder. He didn't see me. Yet. But I had only seconds before he did. With my right hand I picked up a rock about the size of a baseball. My left went automatically into my pocket and grasped the arrowhead.

Down below, the ex-cameraman waved his pistol impatiently, signalling Grace and the others to step aside. He handed his pistol to Coindet and reached inside the passenger compartment.

Suddenly Grace shouted. "Coindet! For the love of God, think! Think, man. Who killed your sister? Not Jack. You know that. Who *else* could it be? You'll know the answer if only you *think*." She paused, and then shouted, "Think, man. *Think*!"

The ex-cameraman, leaning forward and reaching deep inside the car, was pulling the heavy wooden chest toward him. Suddenly, upon hearing Grace's words—he understood English, or maybe he merely sensed their tone—he stopped, withdrew his torso, and stood up. He turned toward Grace, paused for an instant, and then hit her, hard, across her face, knocking her into the passenger compartment. All I could see was her foot, and it wasn't moving. I almost jumped out of my hiding place.

Then it happened. Fast. So fast I wouldn't now be able to remember it if The Calm hadn't still been with me. The cameraman turned toward

Coindet, who seemed at last to have recognized the skeins of causal connectedness, of real responsibility for his sister's murder and rape. Three men. Three orifices. Suddenly, with a rapid pop-pop-pop, Coindet fired his pistol three times into the cameraman's chest. I jumped up and threw my baseball-rock at the second gunman, barely grazing his left shoulder. Immediately he swung around, pointing his pistol up at me with both hands and taking unsteady aim as I dodged from side to side. All at once Turk was airborne, like a large gray steeplechaser, landing heavily on the second gunman. The third, hearing the shots, ran from behind the boulder and down toward the parking area. When he saw me, still standing and exposed like I've never been exposed before, he raised the barrel. It rose slowly, almost comically. I spread-eagled my body and floated downward to the rocky earth below. A bright flash, followed by an explosion. The sound echoed again and again from a thousand rock-faces. Pellets zinged and zipped over my head, ricocheting off the rocks around me. I felt a hard blow and then a sharp stinging and burning sensation in my left shoulder. I heard the pump-action snick-snick sound as he walked toward me. Then he turned to his right. Below he saw Coindet, pistol still in hand but slack at his side, standing over the dead cameraman. Turk had thoroughly throttled the other gunman. For the second time I saw the shotgun barrel being raised. But not in my direction.

"Coindet!," I shouted.

He looked up at me blankly as the shotgun blast opened his chest, turning his white silk shirt into bright red shreds. As he fell backward his pistol discharged its fourth shot, striking sparks from the underside of the Marmon.

One gunman to go. But I had nothing, no weapon . . . No weapon? But I did have one. Small, sharp, and primitive, but a weapon nonetheless. Pulling the arrowhead from my pocket I ran in slow motion toward the remaining gunman. For the third time I saw the barrel being raised. At me. Point-blank. I ran slowly, so slowly, as in a bad dream, toward the still-smoking barrel. I heard the snick-snick of the pump. Then the click of the trigger. Then nothing.

Am I dead?, I wondered. They say you don't hear the shot that kills you. But then, how would they know that? My slow-motion reveries ended abruptly as I collided with the large man, barely moving him. His gun had jammed. With a scream that came from God knows where and all the force I could summon I brought my right hand down on his face, gouging his left eye with my arrowhead. "This is for Ted and Danielle, you goddamned . . ." Blood and thick milky eyeball fluid ejaculated from the now-blinded eye. For one small fraction of a second I looked into the Cyclops' single eye, which radiated an intense and inhuman hatred of what it saw. With a gutteral roar he knocked me to my knees and raised the shotgun high over his head like a Samurai sword. Suddenly Turk blindsided him with all the force of a Forty-Niner offensive lineman and he went down hard. As Turk's huge fists rained their fierce blows, I heard the sickening sound of bones breaking beneath the flesh. His fists seemed hardly human appendages. They were paired pile-drivers, steam-driven and relentless in their ferocity. Gasping, gargling sounds came from the one-eyed gunman's thick throat, and snotty bloody bubbles from his mouth and nose. With a kind of detached horror I watched a small wet spot on his crotch grow larger as Turk continued to pummel the motionless man.

"Non, Turk, c'est fini," I said gently, pocketing my arrowhead. "Il est mort." His duty done, the human attack-dog stopped as suddenly as he had begun.

Grace. Where's Grace? As I stumbled down the hill my shoulder felt on fire, bleeding and burning at the same time. Then, all at once, I forgot my pain. The Marmon had begun to roll downhill, leaving a trail of oily black liquid in its wake. Brake fluid. Coindet's dying shot must have severed the hydraulic brake line. I saw Grace, still inside, sitting up and looking dazed.

"Grace!," I shouted. "Jump! Jump out!" But the wind was against me. It carried my words away, unheard.

Then, suddenly, Turk shot past me like a large mutant greyhound. He ran after the car, opening the door on the driver's side, and jumped inside. He hit the brakes hard. The huge tires skidded in the loose gravel. For a moment the silver spokes stopped. Then they moved again. Slowly at first, and then faster. The large car picked up speed, leaving an ever-larger trail of the viscous black fluid. I could see Grace straining to push the heavy chest. The old Marmon scarcely slowed as it hit the folding table, crushing it under the large tires and throwing the picnic basket, the wine bottles, and the blue-checkered tablecloth high into the air. The old car then crashed through the feeble wooden barrier and bucked and pitched down the precipice. Several hundred feet down it hit a large boulder and burst into flames. The explosion echoed and rumbled across the vast valley.

And then, after a long series of echoes that I thought would never end, silence. Sickening, awful silence. The sound of the grave itself.

Holding my head in my hands, I turned away, trying to block out the sight, the sounds. And then the silence.

Roguin was cradling Coindet's lifeless body, his own body racked by violent but silent sobs. Two gunmen lay dead in the parking area, and another on the rise above. Two of the three had been beaten to death, torn limb from limb by a vicious but virtuous human guard-dog. Who was himself now dead or dying in the inferno below. Along with my beloved Grace.

I took the hard sharp object out of my pocket. Lucky arrowhead, my ass, I thought. Drawing back, I threw it as hard as I could. The black slice of stone sailed through the air, glinting darkly as it disappeared over the precipice and into the valley below.

◄ 41 ►

"Jack?" I heard a voice calling my name on the wind and from so far away that I thought I was imagining it. "Jack, would you help me, please? I'm stuck. I can't move." I ran, or rather limped, toward the edge. Far below I could see the orange flames and swirling black smoke of the burning Marmon. But I still couldn't see Grace. All I could hear was a voice. I'm delirious, I thought. In shock. From my shoulder wound. Hearing what I want to hear. I started to turn away.

"Jack! Are you there? Are you all right? Jack, please, answer me."

"Grace! Grace, where are you?," I shouted downward, at the top of my lungs and against the updraft.

"Down here," the voice answered.

"Wait. Don't move. I'm coming," I shouted as I scrambled and stumbled down the slippery sixty-degree slope. But I didn't get very far. Less than a hundred feet down, a sharp rocky ledge stopped my descent. I wish Ted were here, I thought. With his climbing ropes and harnesses and 8-rings and carabiners this descent would be a piece of cake. We'd rappel down in no time.

From far away, and then ever closer, I heard the rising and falling sound of sirens. Suddenly the ear-splitting sound stopped. Lots of commotion above. Someone shouted down to me, "*On veut de l'aide?*"

"I don't speak French," I shouted up. "Do you speak English?"

"A little, yes," came the heavily accented reply.

"I need ropes," I said. "And a couple of harnesses and 8-rings to rappel down this slope. My . . . my wife is trapped somewhere below me. I can't see her."

Almost as soon as I had spoken a coil of brightly colored climbing rope came whipping and whirling past me. Then a young man came rappeling down, his bouncing blond locks looking like an extension of his bright yellow helmet. He took one look at me, shook his head, called up to his mates in French, and said something about a wounded man. Then, extra harness in hand, he made his way past me and disappeared over the ledge. Two more men, guiding a stretcher suspended by parallel ropes, came down to me and motioned to me to climb in.

"Not until she—not until my wife, *ma femme*—comes up," I shouted, shaking my head defiantly. They looked at each other and shrugged, apparently not knowing whether to throttle or to humor me. They let me be, for the moment, while their mate made his way down the rope. The stress and the loss of blood was beginning to take its toll. I was starting to go into shock. Feeling faint and cold, and trying hard not to vomit, I dropped to my hands and knees on that hard rocky ledge. My right hand felt a familiar object. Picking it up, I looked down into my dark distorted reflection. The sharp shiny arrowhead seemed almost to mock me. I smiled a weak and twisted angular smile, and, surrendering, slipped it into my pocket.

Then, from far below, a full-throated shout. "Je l'ai trouvée!" Suddenly, the slack rope to my left began to writhe like a long lithe multicolored snake before becoming taut and straight. It seemed to take forever, but Grace finally came into view. Her face was swollen, she was bleeding from her head and nose, she had cuts and scratches everywhere, and her once elegant clothes were in tatters.

"I'm sorry, Jack," she said as she was pulled closer, "I tried. Really tried. I just couldn't . . . My God, you're a mess!"

Before I could protest, she was pulled past me and continued upward. Finally, utterly exhausted with pain and relief, I lay down on the stretcher and felt myself being hoisted heavenward.

Four months later

After nearly a week in the hospital in Geneva, Grace and I were released. While there we saw each other every day. We were both messes. She had jumped from the Marmon only moments before it crashed and burned. That jump saved her life but left her with a broken collarbone, two fractured ribs, a mild concussion, and multiple contusions and lacerations, several of which required stitches. I had buckshot in my left shoulder and upper arm. Swiss surgeons removed most of the pellets; others are still there, and while I live will remain as none too subtle reminders of that terrible day. Grace, who used to sleep like a baby, now has nightmares from which she awakens shaking and sweating. She feels the fire's heat, hears explosions, sees a burning box. Always the burning box, which seems to shimmer and glow with a kind of toxic intensity.

It's not imagination or fantasy that produces these nocturnal terrors. The beautiful old Marmon did indeed crash and burn, with Turk at the wheel. Inside with him was the chest containing Mme. Levasseur's diary, several letters to and from the original Roguin, and Rousseau's *Institutions politiques*, finally reduced to ashes, as he had commanded nearly two and a half centuries ago.

And Roguin? He is dead in every sense except the physical. For a time he wept for his beautiful ones. For Danielle, the ostensible traitor. For Coindet, the real traitor. For his beloved Master's burned manuscript. Even for his beautiful Marmon. But most of all, and perhaps most surprising to him, this self-described lover of beauty mourns most pitifully the passing of his ugliest but most faithful friend and companion, with all his rough canine virtues.

I come, finally, to my dear dead friend. In the will that I drew up for him nearly two years ago, Ted stipulates that "I, Theodore John Milton Porter, do hereby instruct my executor"—that is, his daughter Jessica—"to personally destroy by fire any articles or books that were unfinished or otherwise incomplete at the time of my death."

Jessica objects that this is too extreme a step—that *Rousseau's Ghost* is sufficiently complete and polished to merit publication. I'm half inclined to agree.

But only half. I also want to respect Ted's wishes, which, in this instance, seem clear enough ("even for a lawyer to understand," Grace tells me to add). Nearly three months ago, shortly after resigning from Anderson Davis to become chief counsel for FAIR (Free Access to Information Resources), I began seeking outside opinions on the merits of Ted's manuscript. Unfortunately, the experts disagreed at great and learned length, as only academic authorities can.

Frustrated and confused, I finally sought the views of the only experts I know personally. Sir Jeremiah Altmann calls Ted's unfinished manuscript "a magnificent fragment . . . Teddy's fireworks light up the darker recesses of Rousseau scholarship . . ." And Martin Thompson writes that "Although very good indeed, *Rousseau's Ghost*—at least in its present unfinished, and unfortunately final, state—is not Teddy at his very best." He goes on to say that "in matters scholarly, as in matters sartorial, Teddy never liked to be anything but his *very* best. It is with a heavy heart that I recommend that his final wish be carried out." And Sir Jeremiah, "with great reluctance," concurs. "*Rousseau's Ghost*," he writes, "should share the fate of Rousseau's *Institutions politiques*."

Rationally, at least, Jessica acknowledges the force of these friendly arguments. But still her heart resists. And so does her head. She reminds me of the final footnote in the long insert to Ted's manuscript, where Ted approves of the actions of Marcus Aurelius' lieutenant and Kafka's literary executor, both of whom disobeyed orders to destroy unpublished manuscripts. Her father's manuscript is in her hands, in both meanings of that phrase. Just yesterday she rather reluctantly accepted Grace's and my invitation to bring Ted's manuscript to the old Long Island farmhouse that we bought last month and are now restoring. Our plan, Grace told her, is to celebrate what would have been Ted's forty-ninth birthday by going into the back garden and carrying out his final wish.

I'm able to put the finishing touches on these recollections only because Jessica is running even later than usual.

Afterword

In the course of my research and writing I have received invaluable help from many friends and several strangers. For kindly answering several specific queries, I am grateful to F. M. G. Willson, Setsuo Miyazawa, Alan Ryan, Robert Hammarberg, and John Zumbrunnen. For reading and commenting critically and helpfully on various drafts of my manuscript, I thank Stephen, Jonathan and Judith Ball, Sally Brown, Richard Dagger, Abigail Davis, Mary Dietz, Peter Euben, Denise Guilloud, Sister Eva Hooker, Doug and Bobbie Long, Jean and Glenn Willson, and Renée Wilson. I am deeply indebted to the three anonymous reviewers for the Press, whose critical comments and suggestions were most helpful. Although authors are supposed to avoid clichés, I nevertheless persist in maintaining that Clay Morgan is a prince among editors. I am also grateful to Diane Ganeles and her staff at SUNY Press.

My greatest debts are to the scholars whose labors have given us an ever clearer and more accurate account of the life and political philosophy of Jean-Jacques Rousseau. I should like, in particular, to single out the work of Robert Derathé, Maurizio Viroli, Roger Masters, James Miller, Patrick Riley, the late Judith Shklar, Jean Starobinski, Joan McDonald, Robert Wokler, the late Ralph Leigh for his magnificent edition of Rousseau's *Correspondance Complète* (50 vols.), and the late Maurice Cranston for his splendid biography of Rousseau, the third and final volume of which was published posthumously in 1997. All translations are my own.

Finally, for their very warm hospitality—and help they didn't know they were giving—I am grateful to the Warden and Fellows of Nuffield College, Oxford; the Dean and Students at Christ Church, Oxford; and the President and Fellows of Corpus Christi College, Oxford.

This is of course a work of fiction. Any resemblance to actual events or to persons, living or dead, is purely coincidental.

T. B.
Madeline Island
in Lake Superior

About the Author

Terence Ball holds a Ph.D. in Political Science from the University of California at Berkeley. After a long career at the University of Minnesota he moved in 1998 to Arizona State University where he now teaches political theory. He has thrice been a visiting professor at Oxford University (most recently as the Fowler Hamilton Fellow at Christ Church in 1993 and Visiting Fellow at Corpus Christi College in 1995). He has been the recipient of fellowships from the National Endowment for the Humanities, The Woodrow Wilson International Center for Scholars in Washington, D.C., The Center for Advanced Study in the Behavioral Sciences at Stanford, the Ford Foundation, the Bush Foundation, and the McKnight Foundation. His most recent book, *Reappraising Political Theory* (Oxford University Press), was named "Outstanding Academic Book for 1995" by *Choice*. *Rousseau's Ghost* is his first foray into fiction.